THE DRAGON'S GAME

L. E. Green

Published by: L. E. Green

For Sheldon and Grandpa.

PROLOGUE

The end of shift alarm rang out over the HempaTex Fiber hemp textile mill in Cummington, Massachusetts early Friday morning as the sun burned the dew into a misty fog. Massachusetts was the fourth state to legalize hemp farming after being banned more than 60 years earlier. The cool October morning air welcomed the exodus of 75 tradesmen that had just completed the night shift. The dense fog welcomed their feet through the exit gates. HempaTex was a newly built and operated, state of the art mill in the middle of Hampshire County, less known for its agricultural productivity but more for narrow unlit roads, hillsides peppered with trailer homes or drawing in spectators for what used to be miles of the fall foliage. In recent years, twenty percent of the forests were cut down to open up land for hemp and solar farming.

Today was the mill's 5th year of operation and, as its employees left, they were each given an ivory hemp fiber handkerchief with the company name embroidered in emerald green in the bottom right corner. The cloth was wrapped in a small green fiber case, made of their patented faux leather material HempaHide. A gold scripted "Thank You" was screen printed across the button snapped flap of the case.

Clapping at the gate were shift supervisors and top management, applauding its employees for their hard work in making HempaTex the region's top hemp textile producer for the second consecutive year. Thanks to HempaHide, production went through the roof.

As Dennis Emerson walked to the gate, he grabbed his little green package with pride. He and his shift supervisor, Jean Bird, exchanged an arm bump with their forearms as a gesture of gratitude and smiled as they passed. Dennis said, "Thanks Jean!"

"No Doubt Denny," Jean replied. "See you Monday."

"Bright and early!" Dennis happily responded.

Dennis waited by the gate for his friend Samuel Lockstone. The guys at work called him Lock. Denny called him Sam most of the time. Samuel jogged from behind to catch up, meeting him at the gate. Samuel snatched his prize and tipped his hat to the supervisor on his way out. Samuel pushed Dennis on the shoulder to welcome his comrade, "Denny... I guess now I can wipe my ass in style."

Dennis replied, "It's not only for the shit coming outta your ass, Sam, but the bullshit that spews out of your mouth."

They laugh.

Dennis continued, "A flowing fountain of poop."

The two friends continued laughing as they quickly advanced to Sam's SUV, a silver hybrid Toyota Rav4. Sam was one of the few workers with a car. Most of the commuters lived in the city where personal vehicles were not allowed for transport, so they took the bus to the commuter rail. Sam and Denny lived 20 minutes outside of city limits, known as the Green Zone, where public transport was more difficult.

"Whatever, Denny. I'm just glad it's the weekend." Sam responded. "It's Charity's third birthday party. You're more than welcome to bring Amy and the baby."

"Thanks, Sam but I promised Amy I would tile the basement bathroom," Denny says as he opens his back door and takes off his work shirt. Samuel does the same.

Sam was not happy with the answer and said, "Dude, we're having a roast," he said with a lowered voice.

"A roast. A real one?" Denny questioned.

"Four pounds. We've been saving up credits for it."

Denny paused and admitted, "That is hard to pass up, but, sorry, friend, I can't. I do *not* want to hear another complaint from that woman. Her mother's moving in in two weeks and it's best we get that bathroom finished."

Sam remembered, "That's right. I won't be

getting in the way of that. I understand, but if you find time. You're always welcome."

Denny tossed his bag onto the back floor, grabbed a hoodie off the back seat and closed the door. With Sam as the driver, they both entered the car, shut the doors, and drove off down the smoothly paved blacktop. As Sam turned left onto the main road, he stuffed a mini chocolate bar in his mouth that he found in the cup holder. His SUV made its way down the town road, as splashing through potholes and bouncing over bumps and cracks formed during the unforgivable winter months.

The sun barely shone through the dense trees of the reigning forest. There was a little light and a blanket of thick fog smothering the narrow road that wound through towering pine, oak, hemlock, and ash trees. Sam and Denny quietly listened to the New England Media Outlet for the morning news. Sam's eyes were low. After a long double shift, it became increasingly difficult to stay focused on the lonely road and Dennis drifted in and out of sleep from the moment they hit the pavement. Third shift work never grew on Sam. He took the shift because HempaTex offered $5.25 more per hour for the third shift and took the previous shift to earn a little extra money.

All was quiet on the road. There were not many cars passing, but that was typical for this time of day. Sam wanted a distraction to keep himself awake, so he reached behind himself grabbing towards a small white box on the back seat in hopes for a cigarette. Sam's fingertips barely touched the box. He peaked back to the road to make sure he was on track and reached again to get a better chance at grabbing that box. He got a little more of the box the second time but missed again. Sam quickly looked back at the road for reassurance. *I got this,* he thought. He looked at Denny who was fast asleep with his mouth hanging wide open.

Sam would not be defeated by this box. He wanted that cigarette. Sam reached back again, stretching his arm farther, *Little fucker!* He cursed the box in his head. He pressed his left foot against the floor of the car to get a longer reach. Sam looked back to the road and reached again, a little longer he reached. *Got it!* He looked back at the road and swerved a little to accommodate for the turn of the road. He straightened out the car, and checked on the copilot who was fast asleep, unaware of Sam's victory.

Sam smirked as he relished in the sharpness of his daredevil skills. He pulled a lighter from the dashboard, raised the lighter and met the cigarette with a small flame. Sam cracked his window. He took a puff and turned his head to blow out the smoke. When he looked back, something ran into the road. He jammed his foot on the brake, but it was too late. BOOM!

Dennis was frightened out of this sleep. Sam grabbed the wheel with both hands, dropping the cigarette between his legs. The car slid to the side about 15 feet after impact. Sam's SUV came to a screeching halt. Sam grabbed the cigarette and put it out against the glass of the window.

"Jesus Christ, Sam! What the fuck?" Denny yelled.

"I hit something. I didn't see it!" Sam yelled back.

Denny looked back through the rear window and unhitched his seatbelt. He asked, "What was it? Was that a person?"

Sam replied, "I don't know." Sam's heart pounded through his chest. He was shaken up, completely afraid and distraught.

Dennis opened the door and got out of the SUV. He squinted his eyes to get a better look. Sam turned and looked through the rear-view mirror. Denny said, "We have to check it out, Sam."

Sam got out of the car. He inspected the front of the car which was now dented with blood on it. The headlamp on the driver side was broken. His heart dropped. The two friends walked over to the immobile creature laying in a mound on the edge of the road. The two men inched closer until the view of the creature was clear. It was a male deer lying in a pool of blood. Its last breath rose from its snout. Its eyes were glassy and black like obsidian stone reflecting what was left of the rolling fog. They knelt over the body. Dennis pointed to the bruises caused by the car and a small hole in its side. He lightly touched it and asks, "What the fuck, Lock? How'd you do all that?"

Sam concluded, "Probably glass from the

headlamp."

Perplexed, they looked at each other unsure of what to do. Suddenly Sam stood up and ran back to the car. He jumped into the car and backed up until he was a few steps away from Denny and the deer. Denny is confused. "What are you doing?" he asked while gesturing with his hands. "We have to call this in!"

Sam opened the hatch of the SUV and jumps out. He took off his shirt and tossed it onto the back seat. Sam spoke quickly and softly, "Denny, grab the legs. Help me get it in the trunk. Hurry up!"

Dennis walked over to Sam and pushed his hand into Sam's chest. "Sam, are you out of your damn mind? We have to report this or..."

Sam pushed Denny's hand away, "Or what? It is fucking dead already, Denny. Look around. No one is out here! We call it in and it's a waste! They'll throw it away. Now, help me get it in the car before someone comes around that bend."

Dennis was reluctant. He was more afraid of taking the deer than the fact they had hit it. Sam tried pulling the deer by himself. He managed to get a few inches at a time with each tug. He was tiring out. Denny stood with one hand on his hip and the other scratching his head. He shrugged his shoulders and decided to help Sam. *Fuck it!*

Dennis and Sam heaved the dead deer into the trunk of the SUV. Dennis quickly kicked dirt over most of the blood on the ground, while Sam wiped blood off the front bumper. They jumped into the car and sped off down the road into the morning sun.

As they sped off, a female hiker emerged from the tree line and called her dog over, "Muzzy, come here!" Muzzy ran over and was immediately drawn into the scent of blood. He sniffed over to the small pool left uncovered with dirt and began licking. The woman grabbed Muzzy by the collar and pulled him away from the blood. She put on his leash, took out her phone and made a call.

"Good morning, I would like to report an incident," she said. Muzzy pulled away. "Sure, I can hold," she said as she waited. Muzzy continued to pull away from her, licking at the small blood droplets he found on the muddy grass.

CHAPTER 1

Kennedy Avenue in E-City 103 was a bustling street with double yellow lines, one lane on each side and double bike lanes at the edges. The morning commute buzzed with electric public vehicles that moved steadily, but no faster than 20 miles per hour. The morning air was chillier than expected as a few early risers made their way to the morning bodegas and shops for coffee, breakfast and morning chats with their old retired friends. A string of cheese stretched from a frail old man's teeth back to the English muffin that housed his fried egg sandwich as he sat at a small, round, cast iron table at the Pitchfork— a small cafe and sandwich shop on the corner of Kennedy and Chaplain Street.

A slender, dark young woman, with black locks wrapped into a messy bun, exchanged a scan of her bracelet for a plant-based bacon and egg wrap. The server plopped the paper wrapped sandwich into a small paper bag with "K-A-Y-O" written on the side. "Order up for Kayo." He pronounced her name incorrectly. The woman nodded and hurried over to the counter. The server handed her a brown napkin on the side made of recycled paper along with a receipt. "Kayo?"

"No. No. Kayo, rhymes with bio. Thank you," she said with a forced smile. Kayo Brooks nodded to the clerk as she took her sandwich, in the crinkled bag, out of the shop. She checked her watch and began her trek to the bus stop. The 27 year old was easily distracted by the tiniest sounds that anyone else would have blocked out as insignificant noise pollution. She jerked her head at the sound of an old woman dropping her keys into her purse. The woman was 40 feet behind Kayo. She noticed the sound of a crow, calling from the top of a billboard across the street.

Kayo often wore headphones and listened to music to help her from being distracted by the random sounds of day to day life. Kayo suffered from hyperacusis. Most of the day she wore hearing aids or ear plugs as her ears were sensitive to loud noises. She could smell the distinct scents of coffee, tea and cocoa coming from the various cafes that littered the busy commute on Kennedy. Every insignificant vibration, aroma, whistle and squeak called her attention. She opened up her purse and reached for a pill bottle. *Breathe*, she thought to herself. Her hand clutched the bottle, but then she dropped it back into the bottomless pit of her purse. She hated taking them and like today, skipped her daily dosage.

As she walked, electric cars zipped across the asphalt, the rubber treads met the road with a subtle squish. These were reserved for city officials and those who could afford the congestion tax. Most major metropolitan areas banned the use of gas powered vehicles within city limits, and the Clean Car Act of 2034 required car companies to cut production of gas vehicles to 15% and raise production of electric vehicles to 85%. Only delivery trucks were allowed to approach the city and drop deliveries at drop points where manless Delivery Bots would then use solar powered vans to complete deliveries. Oversized deliveries, too large for vans, were only allowed in the city from 1:00 am to 4:00 am to ensure less traffic on the roads, allowing trucks to move swiftly in and out to minimize idling.

Construction of the Sub-City Delivery Tunnels were set to be completed in three years. The city's plan for an electrically run, underground freight system would completely replace the trucking and shipping industry within the city and surrounding towns. Next month, November of 2047, the country will celebrate its fourth consecutive year of its climate change reversal initiative. Kayo walked past the political propaganda ads that covered the bus stops and billboards overhead. Looking up, surveillance drones swarmed like mosquitos photographing and scanning the streets.

The morning bus had just arrived when Kayo reached the stop. She waved her hand at a van driver who was gracious enough to let her pass as she lightly jogged her way across the street to grab the last bus that would get her to work by 8:00. As she ascended the slippery metal stairs, she clutched her bag and waved her badge past the scanner on the console. The driver nodded. She smirked as she passed him and plopped in the front row of seats. Her breathing and heart rate were a bit above normal as she sat back in the seat. She anxiously tapped her fingers on her leg praying her anxiety would cease in a few minutes.

Kayo was tired and jittery. She took out her phone and looked at the time. 7:15 am. As she gathered herself, she flipped through a few headlines that popped up in her feed. She reached past her half inch gauges to put on her headphones and relax. *Breathe.* She took a quick glance at the chipped red paint on her stubby nails and rubbed together her rough fingertips. She rolled her eyes and huffed. She adjusted the black paracord bracelet on her right wrist that had slid up her wrist and became stuck under her sleeve. It was equipped with a compass, whistle and LED light. As she moved it down her wrist, closer to her hand, the compass wobbled around in its plastic bubble housing. They were heading east, which was obvious due to the early morning sun beaming directly into the front window, from beyond the buildings ahead. The bus driver squinted as he tried to check the traffic lights.

"What's that?" some kid asked from the row behind her. He squatted with his feet in the chair and leaned over her seat. Kayo couldn't hear him, but he made his presence known by bumping her shoulder.

Kayo turned around and removed her headphones. "Excuse me?"

He asked again, "What's that?" and pointed at her wrist.

"Sit down, Nick!" said a frustrated mother as she yanked him back into his seat. "Sorry, he's all over the place today."

Kayo smiled and said, "It's ok. Well, this bracelet has got a lot going on. This is a whistle. This is a signal light. This part right here is my favorite. It's a compass." She wiggled her wrist around and the compass bobbled and spun around.

Nick was even more interested and asked, "A compass?

"Yes. It's old science. The original GPS. This little arrow helps you know which way we are facing, so we know which direction we need to go," Kayo said with a friendly face. "It was given to me as a gift.

"Why do you need a compass? Do you always get lost?" he asked

"Nick, that's enough," Nick's mother said with a hint of embarrassment. "Leave the lady alone.

"I'm fine ma'am. He's no bother to me." Kayo smiled again at the curious young boy and said, "My aunt gave it to me when I moved into the city. She told me to always wear it and maybe one day I'll find my way back home." Kayo shrugged and turned around.

Kayo's aunt Nahla Brooks lived out in the countryside. After refusing to sell her 50 acre property, the town raised her taxes for the past 6 years consecutively even though property values had fallen for four years straight. Even if the town lowered the valuation, they could raise the rates and the payments would still go up. They even created a new zone and rezoned the property as a Private Homestead, which required yearly safety inspections which cost $1000 per inspection. Since the property also had chickens and a small river running through it, she was banned from building any structures or growing any crops within 50 feet of the bank and had to secure a license to fish it, since there were "fears" the water would become polluted. This decade-long battle was ongoing and Nahla always found a way to fight the town. She and a few other landowners banded together to fight for their property rights, but most of the town had been convinced that no one needed this much land. No one needed their own chickens or crops. They were convinced that supermarket food was safer for consumption and safer for the environment.

Kayo used to live with her aunt but left 6 years earlier after a few years returning home from college. She quickly thought about how much her aunt was a menace to society. Nahla was Kayo's father's youngest sister who took her in after he and her mother were simultaneously deployed by the National Guard. They went to the Canadian border and never returned.

The young boy sat back in his seat on the bus amazed by the wobbly compass. He looked at his mother in awe.

"NO!" she said, anticipating the request for one. "Don't even think about asking."

Kayo winked at Nick and turned forward in her seat just in time for a new headline which popped up on her phone screen. *CARNAGE: Meat Processing Center Raided and Destroyed by Anarchists.*

She opened the article on her phone and quickly scrolled through and went on to the next article. *POACHING: Investigation Underway.* "Shit," Kayo whispered under her breath. *This is the third one this quarter*, she thought to herself. Hunting had been banned for the past seven years. It started with a two year moratorium that was extended for another two years and was finally made permanent in the fifth year. The following year, private farming was banned due to a mysterious outbreak of the bird flu. *Fishing will be next,* she thought.

Suddenly the bus stopped. It was Kayo's stop — just across the street from the post office. She threw the strap over her shoulder and grabbed the side of her paper bag. She stood and exited the bus as she waved goodbye to her new friend, Nick. Her left heel wedged into a crack in the asphalt causing her to lose her balance for a moment, but Kayo barely flinched at the idea of embarrassment. Kayo turned the corner where a line of people emerged. As she walked past the line, firm glares tracked her movements. Unaffected, Kayo marched her way to the front of the line where it began— the Department of Civilian Welfare Services where two security officers stood firm at the front door with M16s. Their faces were covered with dark tinted shields. They wore black suits, with kevlar body armor over the top of their shirts.

"Good morning. Excuse me," Kayo said to a client as he stood at the front of the line. Kayo pulled her badge out and waved it past a sensor. A red LED light turned from red to green followed by a soft click. The closer security guard opened the door for her, putting his hand up to make sure none of the clients followed. "Thank you," she said.

He nodded.

Kayo walked into the office, past the waiting room and walked towards her desk. Her eyes scanned the empty chairs and low lit space that would soon be a madhouse. She approached the maze of cubicles where hers was tucked half way on the left side. She approached cautiously. Her name tag KAYO BROOKS sat proudly at the front edge of her small white desk. The elements on her desk were very neat and organized. Papers were packed into labeled folders which she adjusted to ensure the folders aligned with the 90-degree angle of the desk corner. She pulled her laptop out of her bag and attached it to the secondary monitor placed in the corner. In front of her desk were two chairs reserved for clients. In a rush, she hung her coat on a hook attached near the corner of the cubicle wall. "Hurry up," she whispered to her computer as it booted up. Kayo kept her eyes on the screen as she tucked her bag away. She typed in her password and her face turned blue as the computer screen came to life.

"Hey Brooksie! Good morning," Monty Clark interrupted.

Kayo smiled, "Hey... Monty. Good morning," she said as she pointed to the clock overhead. 8:00 am was seconds away. "Early again I see."

"Trying to be like you. I'm starting to understand why you come in so early."

"Because I like my mornings quiet and peaceful. I like to read and not be interrupted," Kayo said sarcastically. Slightly annoyed with Monty she asked, "What happened to the days when you would come in a minute before nine? I used to have the whole place to myself," she said as she turned and faced her computer. "I miss those days," Kayo said as she removed her sandwich from her purse.

"Me too. Coming in early is tough. They don't pay us for being timely, but I realized how much I like my peace too," he giggled as he plopped his coat over the back of his chair in the adjacent cubicle. "I like to sit back and listen to harmonic tones that will elevate my frequency."

Kayo nodded and said, "Well, go take your frequency back to your cubicle, Monty. I have to review some paperwork. I'm already later than I'd like to be."

"Don't let your OCD get the best of you, Kayo. Live on the edge! Come in tomorrow with 30 seconds left on the clock," Monty joked as he walked away.

She laughed, "You know that will never happen,

Monty." Kayo, turned back to the article about a poaching incident and swiping through it. She shook her head as she absorbed every word of the article. *Cummington, Massachusetts,* she thought to herself.

By 8:45 am, the morning office quiet began to fade into a hustle and bustle of social workers slowly settling in for their 9 - 4pm shift. Precisely at 9:00 am, the last few counselors scurried in and clients began pouring into the front door, taking numbers by scanning their phones past a sensor as they walked in. Each client took the first available seat they could find. Around the room were 15 monitors playing only three channels. National News House displayed the daily news streamed directly from the White House. This station was on five of the screens in the waiting room. One of the screens was discolored with the image tinted red with fuzzy white lines running through the images. Another five of the televisions played the Wild World Station, which consistently played documentaries about the animal kingdom. Today, the focus was a bear family in Yellowstone National Park. Every other commercial was sponsored by ARPA, the Animal Rights and Protection Agency. The last five televisions projected a variety of fitness and healthy lifestyle habits by Your United Health Channel or YUHC which protesters referred to as "Yuck"!

Monty walked back over to Kayo and said, "I can't believe they get here so early, just to be first in line. I still make them wait 10 minutes," he joked, referring to the long line of clients standing outside. "Gotta teach them boundaries, ya know?"

Kayo shook her head, "You're horrible."

Monty added, "Well, since I know you think it's mean to make them wait, I'll do something nice for you! I'll get your morning tea for you so you can take your first client."

She sarcastically replied, "Black!"

"Two Splendas."

"Make it three. I'm feeling spicy today." She winked at him and called her first client to the desk.

From an overhead beam in Sam's garage, hung the remains of a butchered deer carcass. Blood was all over the garage floor. Even though Sam put a large basin and a tarp underneath to collect the blood, much of the blood found its way to the porous, gray cement floor. The blood and water bubbled as it was absorbed into the concrete slab and slipped into a diagonal crack that stretched from one corner of the garage to the other. The two men stuffed the meat in Ziploc bags, labeling the bags with their names "SAM" and "DENNY". They stuffed Sam's portion of meat into a freezer in the corner of the garage.

They had already filled a cooler with most of Denny's portion, layering the container with meat, then ice, more meat, then more ice, until the small cooler was full. Denny helped Sam cover his share of the freshly cut morsels of muscle with the items they had removed from the bottom of the freezer. Their arms were covered in wet and dried blood up to the elbows. They were not butchering experts by any means. They had no experience besides cutting chicken breast into smaller portions or separating the chicken leg from the thigh. But as beef rations had dwindled over the last few years, chicken increased in demand. They got smaller in size and more expensive. These newly initiated surgeons spent hours scraping as much meat from the bones as possible. Even the smallest shavings were perfect for a stew or hamburger. They even salvaged the offals with the intent to waste as little of the animal as possible. The more they saved, the less evidence left behind.

Dennis was uneasy. His stomach had done 1000 flips and he jumped at every sound he heard outside the garage. He jumped again which startled Sam every time. Dennis looked through the small window and said, "Sorry. False alarm. I thought I heard something."

"Again?" Sam said with a whisper. Sam was frustrated, "Calm down, bro, you're making me nervous! We're almost done."

"Sorry, man. This is just making me crazy! I'm nervous, anxious, excited...woo! My emotions are all over the place." Dennis walked over to his cooler and opened it. "Look at this shit! I've never had so much meat in one place at the same time," he said as he shuffled around the ice in the cooler to get a tighter close of the lid.

Sam replied, "You probably won't ever again," he replied as he covered the loins with frozen broccoli.

Dennis was shocked. "I can't believe people used to do this regularly."

"Steal roadkill?" Sam asked. "Happens all the time. I know a few guys that make a great roadkill stew with squirrels and rabbits. I was thinking about taking the course to get my salvaging permit. We drive through those woods every day. Might get us a kill and with the permits we can keep it."

Denny giggled, "No, no. I mean actual hunting. Real hunting for meat. Not an accidental kill. I'm talking about stalking an unsuspecting turkey or deer, hiding in a bush in the frigid cold. It all seems pretty badass."

"Yeah well, that was banned about 8... 9 years ago. Unless you have surplus meat vouchers, you get your 6 pounds a month and that's that," Sam added. "You know how much this is worth on the black market?"

"Man, I don't care. I'm eating my entire share," Dennis said with excitement. "I wouldn't suggest trying to sell it. You might get caught that way. Just, keep it to yourself and your family. Enjoy it."

Sam smirked as they closed the top of the freezer, "Shit. I'm eating all of mine. I dunno If I'm gonna share with my bad ass kids. They don't deserve it!"

The two men laughed.

"Either way, I don't trust selling it, Denny. It's

not worth the risk," Sam added.

"Agreed!" Denny said as he watched Sam close the freezer door.

All that remained was a headless skeleton hanging by what was left of the hind legs and inedible parts which they packed tightly in an old roll of drafting paper Sam had saved from a tag sale. They packed the hide and remaining carcass into a box and made their way with two shovels to a back corner of Sam's yard.

Sam said, "We can't burn it. It will smell like a Barbeque out here."

"Let's drive it to another part of town at least," Denny insisted.

Sam paused to think and said, "Okay. Next ride, on the way to work. Let's bag and bury it. I'll put it in the hatch, pick you up and we will dump it on the way to HempTex. Someone will think a bear got it."

The day continued as the two men dug a shallow hole. Sam rolled the carcass into the dark cold pit of dirt. Dennis covered the top with ashes from the firepit before they tossed the remaining dirt back into the hole. They were tired and dirty. The unsuspecting world was warming up to a new day and these two were in the yard already covered in blood.

Dennis suggested, "Let's bleach down the garage and get out of these clothes. I gotta get home. My wife is gonna start bugging out if I don't get home soon. And if I show up covered in blood I'll never hear the end of it."

"Don't worry about it. I got some sweats for you," Sam reassured Denny. "I'll throw your clothes in the wash with mine and get you home before all hell breaks loose."

The Department of Civilian Welfare Services (DCWS) had been busy all morning. The disinfectant scented room buzzed with elevated conversations between social workers and embittered clients. Complaints and hissing whines filled the artificially purified air. The clients who patiently waited for their numbers to be called were not permitted to speak in the waiting room. As eager as they were, they knew that even minor elevations in the volume of their voices could result in an arrest. There was a line that extended from the front door to the mini mart around the corner. For their leisure, they were free to listen to the preprogrammed channels through the DCWS app, where they also made their appointments and tracked their voucher levels. The anonymous security guards covered the corners and entry points of the main room.

Behind the cubicles, on the perimeter of the room were the executive offices where Executive Director Beckwith's office sat in the middle. Beckwith wasn't much of a speaker. He walked past every desk in the morning and would not formally greet anyone. He'd hear the "hellos" from the workers and simply reply, "Hmm."

Kayo sat at her desk. The name KAYO BROOKS shined in a brushed gold finish, displayed on the nameplate sitting at the front of her desk. It was so outdated. Most others had digital name displays, but she liked the classic look. Kayo looked at her calendar and read the name *Jasper Holliday* in her head. She opened the appointment on her computer. His face popped up. She clicked his image with her finger on the touch screen surface. His name turned green.

Jasper Holliday sat quietly in a seat by the door. He nervously played with his hat, running his fingers across the stiff brim. He looked at his watch. 9:05 am. His glazed eyes were laden with fatigue and worry. His hands were coarse and dry bearing the marks of many years of hard labor in the tunnels. Last October was the end of his 33-year career working in construction. His navy blue duffle coat laid open against his tired limbs.

Mr. Holliday received a text, "LOVE U PAWPAW," accompanied by a silly faced picture of his eight year old granddaughter, Gracie.

"LOVE YOU MORE, GRACIE!" He took a silly picture with his tongue hanging out and sent it in a text to Gracie. He checked to see if anyone noticed and tucked the phone back into his pocket. Immediately it began to buzz.

He took it out of his pocket. "PLEASE PROCEED TO CUBICLE 7. YOUR COUNSELOR IS READY FOR YOUR APPOINTMENT. PRESS 1 to ACCEPT. PRESS 3 TO CANCEL." Holliday pressed 1. It was time to see

Kayo Brooks.

Mr. Holliday, a 65 year old, solid, six foot, white man with gray hair, stood up and straightened his coat on the sides. He vigorously brushed the lint off his sleeves. He didn't know what to do with his hat. Fold it, tuck it into his pocket... Inclined to make a good impression, he tightened his tie and patted his pockets flat.

"Move to your appointment," one of the guards said. The guards had learned to be cautious of anxious clients. Five years earlier there had been an attack on one of the counselors by a woman who felt slighted at her previous appointment. She threw a stapler and attempted to hit the counselor a few times before being subdued. The woman was sentenced to 6 years or 3 million watts in The Cycles — whichever came first.

The Cycles was a jail facility where low level offenders could earn their release based on the number of watts they generated on power generating bikes. Cycle sentences were becoming a favorite of the state. The idea of generating electricity through cycling was such a hit, consumers bought them for personal use to supplement the cost of electricity in their homes.

Mr. Holliday nodded and made his way to the back of the room. He walked like he had a bad back, but his stature was that of a man who had been very strong once before. He still had a little left in him. He proceeded to the cubicles. Click, click, click. The counselors typed away sharing inaudible exchanges with their clientele. Jasper reached Kayo's desk.

Kayo waved her hand and said, "Come in Mr. Holliday."

Holliday confidently walked into the cubicle.

Kayo pointed him to the chair in front of her desk. "How can I help you today?"

Mr. Holliday looked at Kayo with resentment, *You know why I'm here*, he thought to himself. "Ms. Brooks, I left a summary in my request and we have talked about this before. I'm really trying here. My allocation is just not enough. I ran out last month, I'm on my last pound and there are two weeks left in the month. If you can just increase my credits..."

Kayo interrupted, "Mr. Holliday. You're right. We have discussed this. You turned 65 two months ago and your allocations have been lowered due to your age. Theoretically, you don't need as much animal protein as you used to. We made a plan for you, sir. The cut off was gradual. It wasn't abrupt."

"It wasn't that easy either. My body feels weak. You guys lied about the amounts we were supposed to get when all these changes were made," he said with a stern voice. He gripped the arm rests on the chair and continued, "This was supposed to be a temporary compromise and it turned into permanent treason!" He realized his voice level was too high and took notice of a guard. He lowered his voice and said, "They docked me two pounds for jaywalking. The light was unclear. I couldn't... the sun..."

"I know, Jasper. Listen, the structured plan was

clear that allowances may adjust based on supply, demand, delays, fines, policy changes, etc. I'm sure you heard about the meat processing center in Upstate New York that was just burnt down. That will probably limit supply as well." Kayo looked at Jasper's face. He was enraged. "Okay, if you're in need of more protein volume, you're more than welcome to trade your beef credits for double the weight in our gluten or soy replacements."

Monty was just in time to pass a pamphlet to Kayo advertising government issued soy products. She handed the paper to Mr. Holliday, who was slowly turning red. On the cover was a juicy soy burger with lettuce, tomato and ketchup. On the back was a family barbeque photo with soy hotdogs as the focal point. The slogan, "Enjoy the Soy" ran across the back. Mr. Holliday was livid.

"No!" he pushed the paper away and stood up. "I have supplemented all I can, Ms. Brooks. This is ridiculous. That stuff gives me gas and my wife can barely take the smell, she's gonna divorce me. There isn't enough liquid smoke to fix it. It's all processed, full of sodium and I'm not eating anymore of that shit. I have had my share. My blood pressure..."

"Which is why a part of your plan is to incorporate more leafy green vegetables into your diet," Kayo said as she typed into Holliday's file. "Have a seat Mr. Holliday. It's not worth it." Kayo pointed to the guard who had taken notice of Mr. Holliday's voice and started to approach the cubicle. She pointed to her screen that showed the security cameras pointed toward the main waiting room. The guard got closer, but stopped when he realized the raised voice had lowered. Kayo added, "I'm going to add a vegetable increase recommendation to your file."

Jasper Holliday was a God fearing man but almost more than God he feared the government, the guards and the Cycles. "This is a violation of my human rights! Do you people really think this is fair?"

"What I think has no bearing here, but I do know it is necessary that you follow the plan as prescribed," Kayo replied as she typed. Eye contact with Mr. Holliday hadn't occurred in two minutes. She refused to acknowledge his complaints. "Holliday, you have been my client for 3 years. I have always taken care of you."

"I want to file another appeal," he said. "This is cruelty."

Kayo maintained a straight emotionless face as she spoke to Mr. Holliday. "Sir, you just filed an appeal last month. It's still being processed with 1000 others. Now, as a part of your session, I am going to mandate a referral to a dietician."

Mr. Holliday was completely frustrated. He asked, "Are you serious? Oh you're fucking insane." He pointed at her with his hat.

Again Kayo ignored him and continued, "You will meet with the dietitian biweekly. His name is Mr. Cal Sonji. He'll help you plot out your consumption for the next two months. He'll also set you up for some tests. You will come back in two months and we will reevaluate."

Gritting his teeth he insisted, "I don't need a fucking dietician." Mr. Holliday choked on his own anger. He began coughing and breathing intensely. Monty, right on queue passed Mr. Holliday a small cup of water. Mr. Holliday grabbed the cup and took a sip. He wiped the cool beads of sweat from his brow.

"Mr. Holliday. You need to calm down," Kayo said with a sincere voice.

Mr. Holliday nodded and gasped for air.

Kayo continued, "I'm here to assist, but ultimately it's your job to stay on budget and my job to help you figure out how to make those little adjustments in your life to make this work. However, if you want anyone to reconsider your appeal, do not miss our appointments or the recommended appointments with the dietitian. If Sonji decides that you need an increase, then he will let me know and I will make the adjustment, and no more jaywalking. Is that clear?"

Mr. Holliday nodded his head. "I hear what you're saying, but..."

Kayo looked at Mr. Holliday, watching his ego slip away from his exasperated body. Mr. Holliday was defeated. Again.

She continued, "Jasper, they want to see you trying. *I* want to see you trying."

Mr. Holliday huffed and rolled his eyes and said under his breath, "Trying... Ms. Brooks, my whole life, I've done more than try. I built these streets you walk on and those tunnels that deliver you your nick nacks from that... What's that online thingy? Shipshop."

"Mr. Holliday..."

"The comfort you enjoy is because of people like me who bruised their backs and ripped their skin, fractured bones, hands and skulls for *you*. Then, here you come with your utopian ideals and ruin our lives forcing us to comply with your vision."

"It's the majority that rules, sir. We live in a democracy."

"Tell that to a sheep in a room full of wolves when the vote is on what to have for dinner."

"Point taken." Kayo looked at the time on her computer screen as Mr. Holliday stood firm and ready for a debate. However, Kayo would not entertain his posture. "Following through on this will help you with the appeal. That's all I can do. Make your appointments. Don't miss any and I'll put in a word for you. You screw up, it's over. Nothing I can do. Let's check back in a month."

Mr. Holliday gathered himself. In the midst of his emotional instability, he gathered himself enough to make one final point to Kayo. He looked deeply into Kayo's eyes. "You are so disconnected from reality, others and yourself. You don't even recognize a room full of rage." He pointed to the security screen showing the people in the lobby. "These people are up to their necks in frustration. It's right in front of you and you don't see it. You must have no soul or are you so despicable that you wouldn't feel it if it punched you in the face?"

Kayo's emotionless facade broke. She pushed her index finger into the woodgrain of the desk and said, "You know nothing about what I feel, Mr. Holliday. You know nothing about me."

"I've been your client for three years and you know nothing about *me!* Young lady, I feel sorry for you. "

Kayo was empathetic and said, "Don't feel sorry for me. I'm doing just fine. I can't do favors for everyone that begs and pleads for one more pound of flesh. I'm doing my job. Nothing more. Nothing less. I can live with that."

"I bet you can!"

"Have a good day, Holliday before you get yourself into trouble," Kayo said with a red face.

Monty's head slowly rose over the top of the cubicle. He stopped rising when his eyes could form a clear view of the scene.

Holliday stood tall and said, "We may be nothing to you and your guards, but when people are angry enough they will rise. You can't shoot us all Ms. Brooks. Now, if you'll excuse me. Have a good day" Mr. Holliday turned his back to walk away.

"You're not nothing to me, Mr. Holiday."

Mr. Holiday waved his hat and continued hobbling away.

Kayo blurted out, "246 Weatherville Street, apartment 704. Wife named Cheryl, Cherry for short. You met and eventually married her at St. Thomas Cathedral over on Parker Road.

Sons... Adam and Michael. Daughter Chamilla. One granddaughter, Grace."

Holiday stopped. Keeping his back turned he said, "Not impressed. All in my file."

Kayo smirked and said "Maybe. But, I also know before your appointments you walk 26 minutes from your home, stop at the Russian deli on Kennedy and have turkey bacon and black coffee for breakfast. You wear Ocean Spice cologne *every fucking time* I see you. It's always too much and you stepped on something on your way here. Your phone has been vibrating in your pocket since you sat in that seat and you wash your hands with seabreeze scented Dial soap. And you paint. Is it artwork or handy work? Doesn't matter. I can see it under your fingernails and you drink too much. You attend mass every Sunday at 8:15 am because that gets you home in time for baseball. Thursdays you meet with your friends at an old bar on Jasper Street. I can't remember the name but..."

"Kipplings. Kipplings Kup." Mr. Holliday was awestruck. He looked up at Kayo and shook where he stood. He asked, "They're watching me. Are you watching me?!"

Kayo's frustration softened when she realized how much she frightened her client. She didn't mean to let him get to her this way. She exhaled and returned a soft look to lessen the intimidation she showered upon Holliday. "No... Mr. Holliday. I *do* know you. I listen to everything you tell me. Sometimes you go on and on and I listen. I know all my clients. That... That's the only point I was trying to make. You aren't just a name on a screen to me."

"Well, how'd you know about the turkey bacon?"

She smiled and said, "My e-bike has been in the shop the past two weeks but, I usually zip on my e-bike past you in the mornings on my way to work. I also have a keen sense of smell."

Holliday put his hand over his nose and took a whiff of his fingers. He said "I guess I do smell like food."

"And whiskey and Ocean Spice," she said with a full sarcastic smile on her face.

"Is it that bad?" Mr. Holliday was slightly embarrassed.

"Eh. Not exactly my personal favorite but..."

"I get it!" he said. Mr. Holliday lowered his head and fiddled with his hat. "I'm not mad at you Ms. Brooks. I'm just..."

"I know. But, even if you were mad at me, it's not going to change the course of action so, please, just do what I asked. I promise if there's anything I can do, I got you. Okay?" Kayo looked at her calendar and stood up. "Now if you'll excuse me, I have another client. Thank you for stopping by. We'll notify you just before your next visit."

After Mr. Holliday disappeared around the corner, Monty entered Kayo's cubicle. Kayo huffed and sat down in her chair. Monty placed a strawberry drop candy on her desk. Kayo crossed her eyes and stuck out her tongue. They both giggled.

Kayo appreciated Monty for consistently making her smile.

"You know what I'm gonna say, Brooksie," Monty taunted. He took a sip of water and continued, "This is your fault because you gave him extra protein credits last month. He feels entitled."

Kayo flipped through her calendar on her computer screen as she replied, "Monty, a little empathy goes a long way. And I need a caffeine boost." Kayo gets up from her desk. "Shall we?"

Monty nods and gestures for her to go first. Kayo grabs her mug off the shelf in the corner and walks out of the cubicle. He follows.

CHAPTER 2

The day passed at the DCWS with clients in and out the cubicles, complaining, pleading or storming out. They were never pleased and incidents were increasing. Every client left unhappy, feeling slighted and frustrated. By the end of the day, Kayo had met with eight clients and completed an equal number of reports. She set up her schedule for the next day and headed out of the DCWS door with her bag flung over her shoulder. The air was clean and fresh. Breathe. She took a deep breath. Before heading off, she adjusted her locks. The sun was setting and the windchill made her shiver a little. Monty and another colleague Beth James walked swiftly out of the front door.

Monty sported a Bruins cap, a black goose down jacket and a leather satchel which carried a few notebooks, a tablet and a handful of comic books he intended to trade in at the comic shop on his way home. He swung it over his shoulder as he led the way. Beth donned a feminine look with pink heels, a gray wool peacoat with a belt wrapped tightly around her waist. Her neck was stiff, choked up in a pink fluffy scarf around her narrow neck. Her red curly locks were pinned into a messy bun at the top of her head.

"Ready?" Monty asked.

Kayo took a deep breath and exhaled through her nose, making it clear to Monty that this was a lot for her. Hanging out after work was a rare occasion. She rarely went to Christmas parties, birthday gatherings or anything social. She only stopped for a drink on Monty's birthday and once she showed up to Beth's dog's funeral. She didn't like social gatherings. She loathed crowds. Monty wasn't sure if Kayo liked people in general.

The two women followed Monty's lead. Beth's heels clicked against the pavement like tap shoes on a stage. As they walked down the road, pedestrians on either side of them passed forcefully, making their way to get out of the chilly air. Kayo liked the cold air. It felt familiar. She took a few deep breaths as the short walk ensued. Surveillance drones zipped by overhead and electric bikes whizzed past them on the edge of the road. All she could think about was how much she missed her bike. She called it Busy Buzzy. It was an all black e-bike with dark green handles that matched the hunter green seat. Monty regularly made fun of the basket she kept attached to the front. She didn't care. She found it useful.

The time was 4:45pm. Kayo, Monty and Beth, found their way into a local pub not far from the office called Chatterbox. Full of chatter of sports talk, flirtatious banter and laughter, the Chatterbox was a popular hang out spot amongst Generation Alpha. Occasionally the lights flickered but this was usual.

Kayo immediately grabbed her hearing aids from her purse. She fought the temptation of jamming them in her ears permanently after the third squeal unleashed from the red headed woman in the corner. Before long, Beth was on her second beer. "Will you look at this shit," Beth said as she pointed to a TV screen on the opposite wall. Protestors stood outside of the federal building, some were dressed as cows— others as chickens and pigs. "Sometimes I leave the office and feel like I have to watch my back. Know what I mean?"

Monty reassured her, "Beth, they can protest all they want. Nothing is going to change." He took a huge gulp of beer, swallowing all that was left in the glass. "It's their generation that caused this."

"Right. Not many people eat that shit anymore. Warning after warning and they didn't change their behavior. Then the fires came, the tornados and hurricanes... They had 10 years in a row of record heat and yet not one alarm went off in their heads? Shit, the cholesterol levels in their bodies should have been enough. They just refused to change." She pointed at her glass, signaling the bartender for another round. "Their addiction to food and fossil fuels... ridiculous!"

Monty pushed back and said, "You're not gonna like what I have to say but moving completely away from fossil fuels is why the electric bills are so high and the blackouts are happening more often now. I think we could diversify."

Kayo nodded and said, "Monty has a point."

"Rubbish! I can deal with blackouts here and there over ocean water boiling. They pushed the planet to the point of no return. Now they've lost all privileges and want to cry about it. Something had to be done. Someone had to step in. They didn't get it."

"Welp," Monty added, "hopefully they do now." He took a sip of a glass of water he had ordered. "I need another drink." He sipped again. "I do feel bad for them though. Maybe since the climate has gotten better the government will let up."

"I doubt that, Monty," Kayo insisted. "They're an aging minority. The government is basically waiting for them to die off."

"And good riddance!" Beth insisted.

"RUDE, Beth. Rude!," Monty scoffed.

Beth shrugged, "Will NOT be missed!" Using her phone as a mirror she fixed her hair.

"It's kind of fucked up though," he added. "They grew up eating whenever they wanted, you know? Can you imagine how many memories are jarred just by the smell of the fat sizzling on the flames. McDonalds, Burger King, family cookouts... Shit, I'd take an extra meat credit if offered just to toss that baby on a grill. Red meat is pretty damn good."

"It is good but not that serious," Kayo added.

Beth gagged, "Can you imagine family cookouts? Thank God grills are illegal. And, since when did you like red meat, Kayo?"

"Good question," Monty added. "You give away your meat credits to the clients, which is why they harass you," Monty insisted.

"It's a great bartering tool. How do you think I got Busy Buzzy fixed?" Kayo said as she stuck her finger in her ear and squinted when the crowd cheered. The Bruins scored.

Beth interrupted, "Well, I've never been a fan of it. I don't feel it's moral to eat animals."

"WE KNOW!" Kayo and Monty blurted out at the same time.

"Well, damn. Got anything else to say?" Beth said in a slightly embarrassed tone.

Monty and Kayo laughed.

Monty added, "Listen. Beef is good, no doubt, but I'll stick to my budget and be done with it. The government is all over the black market and they are not playing. I'm not dying or going to jail over it."

"They're gonna end credit transfers at the end of the year. People have been selling them. I can only see protests getting worse before it gets better," Beth said before taking another sip of beer.

Monty quickly looked at his phone before speaking and said, "I have six clients on suspension now for taking bribes from undercover ARPA agents. Now they're whining about appeals and second chances."

"Rookie numbers. I have 13 on suspension," Beth commented. "All begging for help with appeals. Nope!"

Kayo whispers, "You know the appeal process is a farce. By the time they get a court date, they're arguing about rations from months ago if not a year. And to be fair, even though we grew up without some of the restrictions, the rations have become normal to us. Someone Mr. Holliday's age didn't have them until the latter parts of their lives. It's gotta be hard."

Monty responded, "I get that it's difficult, but we can't say that to him."

Beth intercepted, "We can't go back to the way things were. We can empathize but they need to adjust and make due with alternatives. I have noticed those protest crowds getting younger. That's not just Millenials and Gen Z out there." She raised her fist and took a huge gulp of beer.

Monty gave Beth a look and said, "Very true. Maybe we will witness a revolution," Monty jokes. "Anyway, the alternative is soy burgers and everyone is complaining of bloating. Not good for old stomachs. I do feel bad, but there's nothing we can do. They're really going to be pissed when the cricket burgers are fully scaled in and let's stop talking about work before these people realize what we do for a living and attack us."

"That's a felony," Beth said. New laws made it a felony to attack government workers.

"True!" Monty agreed. "Anyway, any plans for this weekend?" Monty smirked because he already knew what Kayo was up to but wanted her to admit it.

"I'll probably hang out and smoke with a friend," Beth stated. "Either of you are free to join me."

"Say less! I'm there."

"What about you, Kayo?" Beth asked.

Kayo smiled and said, "Oh, I don't..."

Monty smirked and said, "Kayo smoke? Please. Anyway, she has plans."

Right when Kayo was ready to speak she recognized a shift in Monty's posture as he took notice of a man who walked into the room. The man was coming in from behind Kayo. She didn't want to turn around because given Monty's comment she knew who it was which would make sense as to why he asked the question about this weekend. Kayo looked forward towards the bar which had a mirror on the wall and in the reflection of the mirror behind the bar she saw him.

"Oh. How interesting is that?" Monty said with a sarcastic whisper. "How does Patterson always find his way to where you are, Brooksie?"

Kayo quickly looked back, brushing her loose locks over her shoulder and pulling them back into the bun that they have continuously escaped today.

"I think you have made an interesting point, Monty. And... Han-Zelllll is coming this way," Beth said with a giggle. "Han-Zelllll. I need a shot!" Beth got up from the table and walked away.

Hanzel Patterson was a fit man with red toned skin. His dark black hair was straight with a few gray strands highlighting the wispy hair above his left eyebrow. Patterson seemed to brighten the room even though everything about him was dark. He entered the room with two comrades, shaking hands, intensely smiling and greeting familiar faces. Patterson worked as the Executive Director of the DCWS for six years— four years before Kayo and Monty arrived and left two years later to take on a position at ARPA. He and Kayo caught each other's eyes and he smiled. She smiled back. It was a subtle flirtatious yet awkward smile. *God why did I come here?* she thought to herself.

Beth returned with three shots of Jack Daniels. She passed them out.

"We need answers about this weekend, Brooksie!" Monty demanded.

"Monty, stop trying to make a big deal of it," Kayo insisted. "I don't even know if I'm going."

"Going where?" Beth asked, trying to catch up on what she missed.

Kayo reluctantly confessed and said, "I got invited to that stupid Gala tomorrow night."

"BOOM! There it is. Patterson invited her," Monty yelled. "And you are going!"

"You mean Han-Zelllll? As in the former ED of our DCWS branch coming this way right now Han-Zelllll?" Beth smiled.

"Beth, stop. It's not a big deal," Kayo said as she anxiously played with her bracelet.

"That's big. The ACPP Awards Gala. Everyone who's anyone will be there. Better you than me though," Monty said. "I can't wear a face all night and neither can you. You're gonna look like

Wednesday Addams."

"Patterson emailed me about it asking if I or anyone else from the office was going. Then he asked me to go."

"What did you say?" Beth asked.

"I told him I would think about it."

"And he emailed her back insisting that she meet him there. It's a date! Let it go." Monty giggled.

"It's not a date," Kayo insisted.

"How is it not a date, Kayo?" Monty added. "You two have been seeing each other for the past three months."

"Oh really?" Beth inquired.

Kayo was annoyed, "Thank you, Monty." Kayo hadn't told Beth about her and Patterson hanging out. "We hung out a few times, but that's it."

"At least once a week," Monty added for context.

"3 months? Oh this is a borderline relationship at this point," Beth added.

"Umm, no," Kayo insisted. She took the shot of whiskey that Beth brought to the table.

Beth's eyes grew. "Well, whatever you two are doing, can you put on some damn makeup and do something with those eyebrows for God sake?"

"It's not a date," Kayo insisted as she refused to look in Patterson's direction. "The managers are always invited to go, but they always send in the flunkies as a representative from their offices and I am the designated flunky since no one else wants to go!"

"Kayo, the man is trying to present you to the

public," Monty held up a shot. He threw it back. "That's a bit much for a flunky. However, you do make a good one."

They laughed and Kayo stuck up her middle finger.

Monty continued, "An invitation from Patterson is pretty sweet, so you should go. He likes you, I think you like him and in the worst case scenario, the food will be great."

"Yeah. The food was great right before they sent Katniss into the Hunger Games," Beth said.

"Exactly," Kayo added. "And I like no one." Lie! "The ACPP are out looking for sponsors and donations for A Vegan Planet." She spreads her hands as if she read it off a banner somewhere. "But... anyway, are you sure you don't want to suffer with me? You could be my date, Monty."

Monty laughed, "Oh, no. Don't try that one on me Ms. Brooks. This is all you. I'll be in a onesie, with a beer, playing Polyworld all night. You go have a blast. Unless you wanna join me, Beth. Cuddle a bit... you know..."

"Eww!" Beth blurted.

Kayo laughed and said, "I gotta get outta here. I'll text you." She grabbed her coat from the back of the chair. "I'm calling it a night. I have a lot to do," she said as she put on her jacket and tied the belt around her waist.

"Me too," Beth added. "I have to pick up my niece tonight. She's staying over so my sister and her husband can have some alone time. Oh, that reminds me. Will you guys be around for Thanksgiving? I wanted to check out that new restaurant, Trappers."

Kayo replied, "No. Sorry. I'll be visiting family Up Rural. I'm actually heading up there Thursday or Friday next weekend. I'll be gone for a few days. Maybe a week. Depends. We have some business to take care of before I head back." "Up Rural" was what the new generations called the more rural areas of the state. Most of the rural areas were taken over by government agriculture farms, solar farms, government run cycles facilities and cricket farms.

"Eww. Why do they still live out there? Anyway, I'll be around," Monty said happily.

As the trio walked out of the bar, Kayo caught Patterson's eye. Kayo's face and heart softened at the same time. Monty smirked as he watched the two connecting from across the room.

"Kayo. Hey!" Patterson said in a gentle voice as Kayo passed.

"Hey, Patterson." Kayo responded quickly. She turned to leave, but Patterson gently grabbed her hand. Kayo froze.

"So, you're not going to speak to me?" Patterson asked.

Kayo smiled and said, "I don't want to interrupt you. You're here with your colleagues."

"Kayo, they're my friends and they know about you. It's okay."

Kayo shyly smiled.

Patterson looked at her for a second before

continuing. "Can I text you later?" He asked. "I'd like to talk to you now but you seem in a hurry to leave."

Kayo nervously responded, "Kinda but, sure. Please before nine."

Patterson grinned and said, "Yes ma'am."

She smirked awkwardly and took her hand back before turning away and exiting the door.

The night was cold and quiet. Dennis's head pressed heavily against his pillow as he snored loudly with his mouth open in his warm bed in his room on the second floor. Amy laid next to him seemingly unbothered by the grunting in her ear. Dennis had been up all morning moving meat around and cleaning blood from around Sam's yard. He was exhausted. His body was half covered with a sheet and one of his legs dangled off the edge. Through the window, the soft moonlight shined against his face but suddenly began flickering blue and white. Moments later a loud bang occurred and the front door was forced open. Dennis was startled out of his sleep confused. He sat up straight and jumped out of bed. His head turned left, right then left again. He noticed the lights flashing and looked out the window. A drone shone a light inside making Dennis pull his head back quickly.

Amy woke up and asked, "What is going on?"

"I don't know!" he said, equally as confused as his wife.

Suddenly with a loud bang, USDA agents rushed into the house with their flashlights on and guns pointed at the various dark corners of the house. They split up, strategically circling the perimeter and seeping into the rooms of the house and eventually up the stairs.

Dennis could see the house was surrounded. "Amy, get the baby!"

Amy ran out the door just as the agents made it to the top of the steps. An agent shoved her to the ground. Dennis ran out of the room where he was met with a shout, "On the ground now!"

The black cyclops eye of the rifle barrel stared back at Dennis burrowing into his soul. Dennis immediately dropped to his knees, instinctively placing his hands in the air. An agent shoved his head to the ground and twisted his arms behind his back. One agent drove his knee into the center of Dennis's back sending a shooting pain through his body.

"What's going on?" Amy yelled, but Dennis knew. Deep down he knew exactly why they were there. Amy crawled on all fours to her knees and put her hands in the air. "Let me get my baby!"

I'm such an idiot, he thought. His heart pounded against the carpeted landing. Sweat slowly seeped from his brow. His shoulders were straining with the stretch of his arms which were sore from the day's work and now from contortion. In the background, he heard the agent repeating a muffled version of his Miranda rights which faded into an indistinguishable mumble of nothingness. His mind was too busy racing with ideas, questions, lies, thoughts and excuses. *What do they know?* He wondered. *How did they find out? Was it Sam?* Under duress, his imagination put pieces together to try and make sense of the situation, but he had no starting point.

"Get off him!" Amy yelled to no avail.

The agents ignored her demands and made their own. "Hands behind your back!"

"What's happening," Amy asked. "Get off him! We didn't do anything!"

The agents cuffed Dennis. Amy ran over and grabbed the agent's arm. "Back off!" One of them yelled as he pushed her away.

"Amy, Amy! Relax! I'm cooperating, sir. Amy, please just get the baby," Dennis pleaded to his wife.

The arresting agents pulled Dennis up by his arms and got him to his feet. His legs wobbled underneath his torso. "Do you understand your rights Mr. Emerson?" The agent asked as he lifted Dennis higher so he could plant his feet on the ground. "Do you understand?" he asked again.

"I do," Dennis replied. He didn't have a choice. He was caught. All he could think about was Sam and his family— the baby. He felt terrible, but there was nothing he could do to change what was happening at the moment. He was led down the steps. One step at a time, one foot in front of the other, Dennis watched as the men searched every inch of his house. Finally an agent dragged a cooler through the kitchen door. Denny shook his head and put his head down.

His house, his job, his freedom were all at stake over... steak. "I need to call my lawyer."

The precinct smelled like a wet mop and armpits. The cell was cold and dank. The floor had traces of blood, urine and all remnants of human excrements imaginable. The bars were rusty with chipping black paint curling off of the metal rods. As the gate opened, Sam looked up to see Dennis pushed into the cell across from him. Dennis sat down quietly with nothing to say. Sam stood up, grabbed the bars expecting his friend to do the same, but Dennis wouldn't budge. *Maybe he doesn't see me,* Sam thought. *But he can hear me.*

"Psst. Denny! You ok?" Sam whispered with his mouth sticking through the bars. "Denny. Is Amy ok? My girls are fine. Denny! Denny!" Sam tried to get his attention.

Eventually Dennis looked up with tears in his eyes. He shook his head.

Sam squatted down and leaned his forehead against the bars. He was completely crushed. "I'm going to fix this, Denny. I promise."

Just then, a loud buzz, red light and a guard entered the block. He opened the gate with a wave of his watch against a keypad. He pulled out a tablet and scrolled with his middle finger. "Lockstone.

Samuel Lockstone," he said with a scratchy voice.

Sam stood up and said "That's me."

The guard demanded, "Let's go." He turned Sam around to cuff him for the escort.

Sam stepped into the corridor between the cells. He looked at Dennis and said, "Get a lawyer and don't say anything. I'll take care of it. You have my word."

The gate closed with a soft electric buzz but the lock locked with an authoritarian clank! The guard escorted Sam out of the block.

The interrogation room smelled no better than the cells. It was cold and hard. The table was hard. The metal chairs were hard and freezing to the touch. It was a deliberate act by the police force to make the interrogated uncomfortable and restless. Sam was placed in a chair. He immediately shoved his arms into his t-shirt to get warm. They watched him from the cameras for five minutes before entering the room.

Detective Germain Gaynor walked in and plopped into the chair with a folder full of papers. He chewed his gum like a horse chewed cud. Every burst of saliva and pop between the teeth was a spectacle for all to experience. He sat there chewing, shuffling through the papers, occasionally lifting his eyes to glance at Sam. "Hmm," he said as he flipped through the paperwork. The cinnamon scent from the gun finally reached Sam's nose. "Hmm," he said again. Finally he stopped shuffling and looked up. Sam could see his light brown eyes staring curiously back. "Samuel Lockstone, right?"

Sam said, "Yes, sir," as he shivered from the cold air. "May I have my hoodie or can someone grab me a blanket?"

Gaynor ignored the question and said, "I'm Detective Germain Gaynor from the Controlled Substance Enforcement Agency. Do you understand your rights as they were read to you earlier?"

Sam nodded his head.

"I need you to say 'Yes' or 'No'," Gaynor said with a commanding voice.

"Yes I understand, but can you tell me why I am here?" Sam asked.

Detective Gaynor scratched the side of his face. Another agent opened the door, placed coffee on the table and stood in the corner of the room. "Thank you, O'Brien." Keeping the gum in his mouth, Gaynor took a loud sip. He added, "Samuel, I don't intend to be here long and I think you would appreciate getting back to your family as quickly as possible. So, I'm going to cut to the chase. You're going to cooperate and we're going to go home. Understood?"

Sam leaned his head to the side and said, "I would love to go home, but I would appreciate it if you told me exactly what I am being charged with."

"Do not play with me, Mister Lockstone." Gaynor opened the file and pulled out pictures of various chunks of deer meat Sam hid in the garage. He continued, "I want to remind you, there's a hefty price to pay for poaching and smuggling..."

"Wait, poaching!? Smugg.. What?" Sam said with frustration.

"*With* the intent to distribute," Gaynor continued. Gaynor grabbed one photo of the Toyota SUV. He shoved it in Sam's direction. "Is this your vehicle?"

"Yes."

"Dennis... your friends call him Denny, right? Listen up, we know you and Denny poached a deer. You know it. I know it. I just want to know the details. We found a few pounds in a cooler at Denny's house. We also found pieces of the carcass at your home as well. We know *you* were driving and transported it."

"Poached? Why do you keep saying..." Sam shouted confused.

Gaynor was unaffected and continued, "We recovered approximately 50 pounds from your garage. So... you're going to tell me where the rest of the deer carcass is located. We have men waiting at both you and Dennis's house and do not waste my time or theirs, I have things to do."

"What do you mean the rest? I want my lawyer, before I say anything else. I want him now!" Sam said angrily.

Smirking, Gaynor stood upright and walked away. His gum moved to his front teeth then back to the molars. He said, "You're insisting on wasting my time tonight. Hmm." Gaynor reached into his pocket and pulled out a plastic bag and threw it on the table. Inside the bag was the end of a broken arrow with about an inch of the shaft left. The bloody fletching was yellow and white with black stripes and a broken notch."

"What the fuck is this?" Sam asked.

Gaynor responded, "Why don't you ask your lawyer when he gets here?" Gaynor folded his hands behind his back and walked out of the interrogation room.

At 4:15am, Kayo's alarm went off. She had already been awake and laid in the bed lifelessly, but the ringing alarm screamed in her ear like a drill sergeant, "GET UP!" She looked at her phone and shut it off. She rolled to her back and checked her phone for messages. She had two texts from Patterson. One was delivered at 8:58pm.

I STAYED OUT LONGER THAN EXPECTED, OTHERWISE I WOULD HAVE CALLED. I HOPE YOU COME TOMORROW. I WOULD LOVE TO SEE YOU.

The second text was received at 8:59.

I'M WEARING A DARK GREEN BOW TIE AND HANDKERCHIEF IN CASE YOU WANT TO MATCH. ;) LOL. NO PRESSURE. GOODNIGHT.

"Green. Of all colors, I don't have anything green," she whispered to herself. Kayo smiled and closed her eyes and for a few moments she was lost in the futile idea of companionship with Patterson. The thought of him made her feel warm inside and lighthearted. She didn't understand it. Patterson gave her all the feels but her fear of commitment, their differences, and her secrets just wouldn't allow her to fully open up the way she wanted. As much as she wanted to be normal, Kayo was not. She was quiet and awkward with an aversion to loud noises. Patterson was a socialite, he was outgoing and friendly. He'd make a great politician. He always lit up the room and he knew everyone. Kayo imagined herself being the weird girlfriend in the corner with hearing aids, lost in a book during one of his events or sitting in the car waiting for him to stop talking so they could leave.

She thought about the Gala. As much as she didn't want to attend, she wanted to see Patterson and couldn't resist the idea of making a good impression on management. Kayo had ambitions to move into a supervisory role, which meant she needed to be more social and she needed to be liked. She could stop dealing directly with clients and oversee operations, schedules, contracts and funding. The people she needed to impress would be there. She hadn't quite told Monty or Beth her real reason for going because they would never believe her and she didn't want to tell them about her plan to leave them behind as case workers.

Seeing Patterson would be a plus. He had always been a gentleman and Kayo couldn't resist the mellow tone in his voice. When he said her name...

Kayo... The way he said it just made her question her purpose in life, all her responsibilities and aims. The first time they met, they connected eyes and it was as if they knew something more was beyond the look. Kayo knew she had to steer clear and it was easy to avoid him since he was already in a supervisory position and was in a different area of the office. It would be inappropriate and Kayo was very serious about her profession. She barely gave him eye contact whenever they passed in the corridor. They always spoke to each other but it was as if they both knew not to test it with a glance longer than a second.

One morning, Kayo showed up to the office early. On her way to make her morning tea she accidentally bumped into Patterson who was rushing through the aisle heading to his office. She didn't even hear him coming, which was unusual. He bumped her tea cup out of her hand. As she lost her balance, Patterson grabbed her and held her closely to his body. He didn't ask her if she was ok. He didn't say anything. He kept a firm grip on both of her arms. She slowly backed up allowing his hands to slide down her arms to her fingertips. She stepped away slowly looking into his eyes. She stepped back until her hands were free. The two of them had passed each other 50 times. With all the tension in the air the only logical next step was to kiss or fight. Kayo wasn't sure which way it was going to go.

Patterson reached down and picked up the cup.

He finally spoke. "What's your favorite color?" he asked.

The question was not what Kayo expected. She was nervous. She answered, "Green," and stood there. The silence was awkward. "May I have my cup back? I need to remake my tea."

Patterson shuffled his things and said, "Yes. Of course. I... Have a good day today."

"You as well," Kayo responded.

Kayo swiftly walked away into the lounge and grabbed her chest. *What's my favorite color? What kind of question is that?* She wondered. *How did he sneak up on me?* she thought to herself. Then she cracked a little smile and leaned her head back against the wall. She took a few deep breaths to calm her nerves. Whatever happened, she knew the ice between them was broken forever.

Patterson and Kayo ran into each other again three months ago. He finally got the nerve to ask her to meet him for coffee. She agreed. Next they met at the butterfly museum. They met again at the park. She refused any request for an actual date, but didn't mind spending an hour or two here and there with him in quiet spaces.

After a few moments toiling with the ideas of Patterson in her head, Kayo snapped out of her nonsensical daydream and turned cold again. *Focus.* She jumped out of the bed and went to the bathroom. She brushed her teeth, washed her face and rummaged through her drawers pulling out a sports bra and gym pants. Before leaving, she grabbed a few items from her refrigerator, put them into her backpack and secured the straps around her chest and waist. She slapped on a headband and hoodie and headed out of her condo.

Kayo stepped out into the city street; it was tranquil and frosty outside. At 4:30am, Kayo put on her headphones, looked at her watch and turned on the fitness tracker. She began to run. Her feet tapped against the pavement, pulling her forward as the crisp morning chill pressed against her cheeks. Soft and rhythmically panting, she ran through the city past very few signs of life as her breath left a small puff that quickly vaporized behind her. She could smell fresh sweet bread and pastries in the oven at the bakery. A few drones whizzed overhead but she could only see the little red light of the infrared camera. She ignored them and ran forward. 30 minutes into her run she arrived at an industrial park.

The brick collection of edifices were surrounded by a worn wrought iron fence and a sign at the guard post that read: SOLEMN OAK MANUFACTURING. It was located on the edge of the city where most didn't travel due to the lack of transport. Half of the buildings were empty and many had been abandoned after the zone was deemed contaminated. Only a few buildings were usable as personal storage space.

Kayo jogged her way to the back corner. She took off her backpack and threw it over the fence. She then scaled the fence, pulling herself up and over.

She landed softly on her toes only to be surprised by a light that suddenly shone in her face. It was the guard holding a flashlight in his left hand and a leash in the other. At the end of the leash was a muscular growling rottweiler. The badge on his chest read "BAKER."

"You know you can come through the front gate. I've told you this 100 times," said Baker as he tugged on the leash.

Kayo picked up her backpack and unzipped it. She pulled out a frozen roast and handed it to the man. He tucked it under his armpit. Then she pulled out a bone and tossed it to the dog. She walked over and petted the beast.

"Diggy don't like *nobody* but you, Kayo. Nobody!"

Kayo smiled, "Let's keep it that way. No one else feeds him but me and you."

"You got it boss," Baker agreed. "He's yours. Whatever you want you got it."

"Anyone been here?" She asked as they started walking towards the buildings. Diggy gnawed and drooled on the bone in his mouth.

Baker smirked, "Building A had just the regular clientele checking in on their storage units. Building B, had a truck pick up some used pallets last week. That building is all cleared out. I got a call from Juno. He said he got business Up Rural, so he should be picking up his car next week, Thursday or Friday."

She nodded and looked at her watch. She said, "I'll call him. He needs to make an appointment for the pick up. When he comes, have the car ready by the gate. I don't want him back in here. Our business is just about done and he was supposed to pick up that car six months ago."

Baker nodded in full compliance to Kayo's commands. When his nose started to run, he sniffed and rubbed his sleeve across his face.

Kayo bent over and gave Diggy one more pat on the head and said, "I gotta run. I'll have something for you next time I see you." Kayo took off with a light jog and disappeared around Building C.

CHAPTER 3

It was 6:26 pm when Kayo Brooks arrived at the Ringgold Museum of Fine Arts. The building was a remodeled library that now hosted a media center, three small art galleries and a modest sized movie theater for 50 viewers. The escalators and elevators led to the lower level, which housed a thrust stage theater with seating for 200 guests. Towards the back of the building was a 10,000 square foot banquet hall, with an upper level. It was the former main library space, which was used regularly for gala's, weddings and political fundraisers.

Wrapped around the walls in the upper level were display cases reminiscent of old book shelves, full of vintage books from the library, encased by glass. Libraries had become obsolete, thus most books were digitized and destroyed, but since the Ringgold was technically a museum, they were able to retain banned books such as *1984* by Orwell and *Anthem* by Ayn Rand. Many vintage book enthusiasts would visit just to see the covers and bindings but were never allowed to touch nor read the books. The city had an ongoing "Banned Book

Buyback" program that would exchange banned books for protein or digital cash credits. Whenever an old house was demolished, dumper divers would rummage through and find old gems to turn in. Kayo grabbed the lower half of her dark green gown and stepped out of the Hitch — a private transport vehicle which allowed city residents up to 3 private paid rides or 6 shared rides per month. The service was always booked a month in advance. Kayo called in a last minute favor to secure the ride to the museum and back home which counted as two rides. Public transportation and electric cars or bikes were the only transportation allowed within city limits. In this gown, Busy Buzzy wasn't feasible and no way Kayo wanted to fight with this dress on a bus.

As Kayo's second foot hit the pavement, she looked up at the building. Her face was flawless. Her makeup was subtle but immaculately placed against her skin. The QuikFlix tutorial that Beth sent came to her rescue. Her dark skin radiated from the beams of the strobe lights that danced around the pillared front entrance. The bronzer on her face sparkled like glitter as she looked around. The dress had one strap over the right shoulder displaying her muscular neckline and shoulders. The top half of the dress remained snug to her upper body and relaxed a little at the waist. The dress flowed to the floor. As she stepped her strappy sparkling silver shoes peeked under the hem. She had a matching silver evening bag and a black shawl tossed over her left arm. Her locs were twisted together into a design gathered up into a high bun.

There was so much noise it was all chaotic and unclear but no one else seemed to be bothered by the pomp and circumstance going on about the premises. The media surrounded the main entrance. Shortly Kayo could see security patrolling with sniffing dogs and wands checking for weapons and regulated substances.

Kayo hadn't been in the museum in years. It never looked so grand and important and she never felt so miniscule and insignificant. *I don't belong here.*

Each step closer to the building gave Kayo a clearer picture of what was happening ahead. The red carpet was within 20 yards. Then the cacophony surrounding her head started to break into distinguishable and recognizable banter and music. The protesters' chants became more clear as she walked closer and closer to the building. Protesters were roped off on both sides of the red carpet mixed with paparazzi, security and familiar political faces. The rebels carried signs. Some read, "BURGERS WITH A SIDE OF LIES", "HAVE COMPASSION, INCREASE MEAT RATIONS" and "NAZI ACPP".

Kayo huffed in frustration as she walked past them. She prayed none of them were clients or people she would ever run into on the bus or at the Pitchfork.

The crowd began to chant, "NO MEAT! NO PEACE! YOUR TIME IS UP A-C-P-P! NO MEAT! NO

PEACE! YOUR TIME IS UP A-C-P-P!"

The Alliance of Climate and Planet Protection was the larger arm of the DCWS and it was run by its president Vernell Bailey. Vernell was a graduate of Amherst College in Amherst, MA. He started working at the ACPP when it was a grassroots organization protesting on college campuses for animal rights and pet liberation. As veganism became more popular, the government passed its climate change initiative and scooped up the ACPP as a leg of the EPA. The ACPP caught the attention of the EPA Director when it linked the climate crisis to meat consumption mainly through farming of cattle for commercial use. Through their research, they calculated the amount of meat wasted on average by Americans, determined the approximate number of cattle that were needlessly slaughtered just to be discarded into the trash and used that number to develop a meat budget for everyday Americans. They also convinced the government that this budget would drastically point the climate in a positive direction in 20 years if everyone agreed to comply.

They promised that this would be a temporary measure to give the planet a break. The next phase, they determined that beef was an unnecessary source of protein and they cut back the rations. A black market developed after the second year. Beef was being sold and traded in back alleys or restaurants and supermarkets. The ACPP was losing its grip on the situation and recommended government takeover of all cattle farms. It was approved.

Vernell hadn't stopped there. His engineer buddies from MIT developed an application and monitoring system for cattle on the farms and rations for citizens. Within 4 years, all cattle farms were consumed by the government and red meat could not be purchased privately or commercially with cash. The production and consumption of beef was strictly monitored. The DCWS was developed 15 years later to help citizens cope with the changes and to oversee operations, monitor rations and ensure adherence. For Vernell it was a success. The ACPP was given authorization to create and adjust consumption, sales and beef farming regulations. The ACPP was also given reign over violations. They linked public behavior to ration allocations and docked rations for poor behavior. Any violation regarding the environment, meat consumption and allocation was given to the ACPP. Only they could determine the impact of such violations and were put in charge of sanctions removing the burden of these infractions from the traditional legal process.

Vernell was obsessed with the output levels at the DCWS when Patterson was the Executive Director. They met quite often and Patterson was often flown to other sites in the US to tighten up operations. After a three week visit to DCWS Nashville Unit 4, Patterson came home to an offer to work as an Operations Manager at ARPA. He accepted without hesitation and Beckwith took over as ED. Since then, upper management eyed Patterson for a senior position at the ACPP.

Vernell was a short stocky caucasian male with sandy blonde hair, standing by the front entrance wearing black framed glasses, a black tuxedo and a multicolored bowtie. His socks matched. His belly pressed firmly against the inside of the tux putting pressure on the buttons which were holding on for dear life. Vernell smiled as he schmoozed over the media with his girlish cackle and large toothed smile. His wife stood by his side. She was taller than him and way too pretty for him, but he had money.

As Kayo approached the carpet flashing lights flickered like sunbeams through a tree canopy causing her to squint. She saw a sign: MEAT CONSUMPTION IS A HUMAN RIGHT!

"What an exciting night," a familiar voice exploded onto the carpet. Isabella Gerena glided swiftly as if she was on a skateboard hidden under her gown. "We're here at the Ringgold Museum of Fine Arts for the 8th Annual ACPP Awards Gala and Fundraising event. "The who's who of New England are all gathered tonight to honor and celebrate the various agencies, trailblazers and figureheads who have led the charge on reversing climate change. The event certainly has been met with protests at the gate. There are at least 100 radicals with signs displaying discontent with recent policies, spewing hate speech... Let's talk to one now." Isabella walked over to the crowd of protesters and stuck her microphone in one man's face. She put her finger in her ear to hear better and said, "Good evening, sir. Tell us about your gripes with the ACPP."

The man yelled, "You can read can't you? Meat consumption is a human right! The ACPP is not an elected government entity. It makes laws as if it is. It's an organization of elitists, with their heads up their asses, passing down unconstitutional laws that violate our personal freedoms. Since the dawn of time humans have eaten meat. They have no right to regulate that!"

The reporter pushed back and said, "Well, wouldn't you say the 'dawn of time' would include when we were cavemen and didn't know any better?"

"We have personal freedoms to do as we choose, regardless of the outcome, you don't get..." he shouted.

"What about the personal freedoms of the animals? Don't they have rights? Don't you think it's cruel to kill an animal when you could just eat something else?" she interrupted.

"Eating meat is not animal cruelty! We have..."

She interrupted again, "What about the climate? Don't you think that shutting down the commercial beef industry is for the greater good?"

He responded, "To solve one issue, you've created another. The obesity rates of children have quadrupled. And it doesn't matter. It's been 25 years. No government agency nor the ACPP has produced any evidence that there has been a positive impact on the climate."

Isabella was not there to listen. She said, "There are plenty of studies that show that the climate crisis is stabilizing."

Another protester interjected, pointing his finger into the camera. He said, "Ten years ago they also said we had hit a point of no return. It's all bullshit. They're forcing us to be vegans. Commercially produced beef is one thing, but the anti beef agenda has spilled over to meat in general. The price of poultry and pork have gone through the roof and there are shortages due to routine cullings! They won't let us keep our own chickens, barely let us fish and totally banned hunting. Then they force us to buy expensive soy products. Fuck the ACPP! NO MEAT, NO PEACE!"

The cameraman panned across the crowd as they screamed in unison, "NO MEAT! NO PEACE! YOUR TIME IS UP ACPP!" The chanting ended the interview and Isabella turned back to the event focusing her attention on pointing out local officials and celebrities arriving on the scene.

Luckily for Kayo, everyone's attention was on the interviewer and most of the radical protesters were acting out for the cameras. Kayo's walk down the main carpet to the lobby was mostly uninterrupted until a thunderous boom took over the night sky and heavy rain fell upon the media and protesters. The crowd quickly dispersed. Most of the drones retreated back to their charging stations since this level of rain was too heavy for them to stabilize in the air.

She arrived at the lobby opening and walked through the main entrance. The domed ceiling came together at a center point. In the lobby a violinist and cellist played a tune that caught her ear— Il Dolce Suono, a song she remembered from the movie *The Fifth Element*. It was a nostalgic memory from her Aunt Nahla's DVD collection back home. They must've watched *The Fifth Element* 100 times.

Saturday nights were for movies. Sundays were called Freedom Day. Nahla allowed Kayo to do whatever she wanted. She would always say, "Freedom of choice doesn't mean freedom of responsibility or consequence. You have to live with your decisions. Use your time wisely." Nahla would disappear for the day, leaving Kayo to do whatever she pleased, and would return late in the night or early Monday in time to start the chores.

RESERVATION TABLE 17

Kayo found her table. No one looked familiar, but she could tell they were B list dignitaries based on the location of the table. She slowly approached, walking suspiciously to her seat. *I do not belong here.* There were six people already seated and four empty seats at the table. Kayo looked around for the closest exits. She finally locked eyes with a man who was seated at the table with what she assumed to be his wife. It was too late to retreat. Kayo uncomfortably smirked as she approached. She had no idea where she should sit. Then a hand gently grabbed hers.

She heard his voice, "Come with me," he said. Hanzel Patterson lightly grabbed the tips of her fingers and escorted her safely to the table. Relieved, she couldn't help but smile as he smiled back. She suddenly felt a sense of protection and calmness. He leaned over and whispered in her ear, "You look stunning," and kissed her on the cheek. He pulled out a seat for her. The men at the table stood up. "Kayo Brooks, this is Cranston Asher-Smith the president of the board of directors at the ACPP.

"Pleasure to meet you Ms. Brooks," Cranston said.

"The pleasure is mine, thank you." Kayo sat down and Patterson sat next to her.

The other guests said hello and they settled in.

Patterson whispered, "Thank you for coming. You really look amazing."

"Thank you. You look debonair yourself. You've got me dolled up in green today."

He smiled and whispered, "I like it. I don't know if I can leave you here at the table to give this speech."

She jokingly asked, "Why not?"

"I can't have someone snatch my date away while I'm busy."

She grinned, "I didn't say it was a date."

"You wore green. Let it go. It's a date," he insisted.

They both laughed.

Kayo said, "Well, don't worry about anyone snatching me. I can take care of myself."

Patterson looked Kayo in the eyes and said, "I know you can, but I at least want to make sure no one tries. Just be here for me when I get back. Okay?" Kayo nodded, "How could I say no to you?" *Kayo, shut up!* was all she could think to herself. She couldn't help but flirt back. Patterson was handsome and his eyes were hypnotizing her into submission.

They almost forgot someone was speaking and they were in a room full of spectators. Patterson gently grabbed her hand under the table and rubbed it with his thumb. 100 hearts were broken that night. Patterson was the most eligible bachelor in the city and a random no name social worker with big hair, big teeth and holes in her ears had taken up his attention indefinitely. For the two of them, the romance was long overdue but was slowly taking shape.

Patterson leaned over and said, "Before the end of Vernell's speech, I have to head backstage."

Kayo nodded.

Thirty minutes after her arrival, there was a 15 minute cocktail break. Vernell Bailey was setting up to give a speech. Patterson whispered to Kayo, "Let's check out the books on the upper level." She took his arm and he led the way. She also made sure to lift her dress as they walked towards the steps.

When they reached the top, Kayo was amazed by the collection. She let go of Patterson's arm and marched over to the first display case. "*Mutiny on the Bounty*," she read out loud.

"Familiar?" he asked.

"I read that book. I..." she stopped herself. "Well, not the book but, there were some think pieces... articles disputing the tone and speech..." *Mutiny on the Bounty* had been banned for longer than she was able to read.

Patterson smiled and said, "I used to see you reading all the time on lunch breaks. Where do you find the time to read and stay so fit? How do you find the time?"

With her eyes still scanning the collection she replied, "I don't watch TV. I have one, but it's rarely on. We weren't allowed to have one growing up, so I'm used to it. Everything I need to know is in a book, on my phone or computer. Oh my God, *Charlie and the Chocolate*... Why is this banned?"

Patterson smiled and said, "The depiction of the Oompa Loompas was considered to be politically incorrect and demeaning to little people and... people of color," he smiled. "I think this was banned about 2 years ago." He watched her closely as she was glued to the display. "I'm feeling like I've lost your attention. I'm kind of jealous."

Kayo turned around and said, "I'm sorry. I just..."

"It's totally fine," he said as he stared into her eyes. "I can't stop looking at you, Kayo. You're beautiful." He grabbed both of her hands with his and stepped closer. "I want more of this. More of us."

"Hanzel, I'm not good at this," Kayo said.

Patterson stepped closer and said, "I'm not either. I've fucked up so many times. I want to work on this, but with you." He stepped closer. "We've hung out a few times, flirted and teased each other with looks and... I want to be more serious about us. I'm not trying to rush anything with you. I like you. I think you're beautiful and I think you like me a little bit," he said with a smile. "Give me a shot."

Kayo looked away for a moment. She looked back at Patterson and said, "Oh... I'm so complicated. I..."

"Just let me get to know you exclusively. Let me spend more time with you. It won't hurt," he begged.

Kayo pulled her hands away and said, "It's not that simple, Hanzel. I have... things like... unresolved... things going on. I wouldn't want to put that on you. Commitment is like... a lot."

"Are you seeing someone? Is there..." Patterson nodded his head and stepped back. He put his hands in his pants pockets and said, "Okay. I get it. I uh..." He cleared his throat. "Vernell is about to go on so..." he began to back away.

She grabbed his hand and said, "No. Please listen." Kayo looked him in the eyes. Her face was glowing. His face was perfect but she could see his disappointment and didn't want the night to start or end this way. She continued, "This is hard for me to say." Her eyes were locked into his. "You wouldn't know this." Kayo took a deep breath and slowly exhaled through her nose. "I've always had feelings for you and regardless of how difficult saying this may be, I would never let you walk away from me thinking otherwise. I can't. I *want* to get closer to you. I *want* to spend more time with you. I want to do all those things when I'm 100% ready to focus on you. Otherwise, it won't work. I want to be ready for you and I can be."

"Just not right now," Hanzel said disappointingly.

Kayo replied, "How about this? I'm down to hang out more frequently. No expectations and I will make it a priority to resolve these things swiftly. If I can't, I promise I won't waste your time."

Patterson smiled. He said, "You just friend zoned me."

"It's a temporary solution to a pressing matter," she joked. "'Friend zone' is a harsh way to put it. I don't go on dates with men in the friend zone."

He laughed, "So now it's a date?"

They both giggle.

"Well, since tonight counts as a date, you can't let anyone snatch you away from me," Patterson demanded.

"I promise," she reassured him.

Patterson grabbed her face and kissed her on the forehead. Then he lightly pecked her on the lips.

Kayo closed her eyes and placed her hands on his waist to receive it. She smiled.

"I put my mark on you so that should keep them away," he laughed.

Kayo used her thumb to lightly brush the remnants of her lipstick from his lips. They walked away from the displays and he escorted her back to the table.

In a side room, to the right of the podium, Patterson paced back and forth. He mumbled words from his award acceptance speech and pulled flashcards from his pocket. He glanced, mumbled a few words and glanced again. He could hear Vernell's speech coming to a close where Vernell planned on presenting Patterson with the ACPP's Activist of the Year Award.

Vernell Bailey stood at the podium with his name and picture displayed on a screen behind him. The lights in the hall were dim and his body was highlighted with a spotlight as he spoke. His voice bellowed over the room like a trombone, vibrating the water in the glasses on the table and tickling Kayo's inner ear. She looked around for the sound engineer wishing he or she would adjust the levels, but no one else seemed to be bothered besides her. She quickly pulled earplugs out of her purse and snuck them into her ears. *Much better.*

Dinner was being served. Waiters zipped across the hall floor carrying plates of soy steak, rice and string beans. They placed a plate in front of Kayo. She softly grabbed the waiter's wrist and said, "My date is about to speak, but he's coming back here. He will need to be served."

The waiter nodded and said, "Thank you. All speakers will be served once they return to their seats."

Kayo nodded as he walked away. She looked around and waited for everyone at the table to get her plate before she ate. Vernell continued his speech.

"The Alliance for Climate and Planet Protection has made great strides in stabilizing the climate crisis. We have received countless donations and we thank you all for your continued financial support, but we have a new threat that we believe will hinder our efforts if it is not contained immediately. Poaching." He pointed to the screen. "POACHING!" he said. The audience gasped. "Yes. Meat Murder we call it. There is a black market for wild meat eaters and we are putting millions of dollars into shutting it down." A cheesy reenactment of a poacher hunting played on the screen where a man jumped out of a tree and stabbed a deer to death with an arrow. Kayo laughed but no one else was laughing. She immediately stopped. She realized she was the only person that knew that this was not how an arrow was used.

As she looked around, she could see many audience members flabbergasted, taking out their phones, scanning the donation QR code and sending money. This was quite the emergency. Photos of slaughtered animals were posted in the slideshow. The gasps continued. One woman hid her head in her husband's chest. The ignorant audience didn't know the difference between a hunted animal and roadkill that was wrongfully categorized as poaching as if someone killed it intentionally.

"There are hundreds of these people hiding in the woods torturing animals. Some of them live in your backyard. They venture out to the forest lands Up Rural, murder living creatures and come back here and then sell the meat for profit. Just the other night, authorities caught two poachers who live just on the outskirts of the city. We are struggling to contain our efforts in these areas and are currently in negotiations to expand city limits so that these massacres will finally stop." Suddenly on display was the same bloody broken fletching from the incident with Sammy and Dennis. The photo was in black and white but Kayo could see black stripes on the sides.

Kayo was shocked, "Impressive work." The guests at the table agreed with her sentiments. However, she wasn't referring to the fact that they caught the suspects, but the craftsmanship involved in the making of this weapon.

"Yes. Insane isn't it? And we are doing everything we can to make sure these meat murders are a thing of the past. This leads me to our award winner. He started his career at the Department of Civilian Welfare Services as a case worker and swiftly moved up to Executive Director, his..." BOOM... BOOM, BOOM!

The room shook and turned pitch black when a series of explosions went off in the room. All the lights were out. Covering her ears, Kayo quickly ducked down beside her table. Suddenly gunfire rang out. People started screaming from all directions. She scooted deeper under the table and lifted the table cloth. After a quick glance, she counted five red beams from red dot scopes and noticed men in tactical gear carrying rifles, wearing gas masks, slowly walking from the far side of the room shooting everything moving. BOOM! Another explosion went off. Kayo turned around under the table and covered her ears with her hands again. She peeked under the table cloth and saw one of the exit signs. It was next to the kitchen. She looked around and made a run for it. Shots rang out behind her head and she hit the floor crawling on her hands and knees. Instead of going out of the exit she ran into the kitchen. *Fuck! Wrong door!*

Kayo realized she entered the wrong room so she slipped into a back corner where she found an apron and a broom. Quickly, she rolled up the long dress and tied it into a knot at her thighs. She walked over to the apron, ripped it into smaller strips and twisted the head off the broom. *Breathe.* She peeked back into the kitchen. The coast was clear. She looked around and grabbed a carving knife then ducked down behind the counter. She began wrapping the knife to one end of the broomstick using the apron she tore. As she sat on the floor, she heard the door open. One of the gunmen opened it with his gun drawn. He slowly looked around with his gun pointing from corner to corner. *He knows I'm here.* Kayo could hear him stepping closer to her left. She grabbed another small knife from the floor and put the tip of the blade in her fingers. He was coming her way. Kayo sprung up and quickly threw the knife and hit him square in the neck. He grabbed his throat and dropped to his knees. Blood spewed in every direction. *That's one.* She ducked back down and finished making her weapon. Breathing heavily, she reached up and grabbed another knife. Kayo crawled on the floor over to the man she had just slain. She took his gun and strapped it to her back. The smoke in the room made it difficult to see, but she could hear their slow footsteps looking for victims who were now playing dead or hiding. *Where is Patterson?* she thought.

Kayo stood up and quietly stepped back into the smoky room. She removed her earplugs and listened carefully. Every so often she heard a shot. *They must've found a live one.* She listened. One was behind her. She took the homemade spear and whipped it around slicing the man in the neck then stabbing him in the belly. He grunted and hit the floor. *That's two.* This alerted the other assailants to head in her direction. She listened and walked softly while crouching low. She found a table and crouched low behind it. *Where are the police?* she thought. She heard a sound. *He's behind me.* She used the end of the broom handle to trip him. He fell. She took the gun and shot him twice. The third squeeze of the trigger proved the gun was now empty. She ditched it and speared him one more time in the chest. *Three.*

Two more. She went back under a table where she saw a red headed woman hiding. *Shhh,* she directed the woman with her finger to her mouth.

The two men walked around kicking the other bodies on the floor. They pulled tablecloths from the tables, finding a few people and shooting them. As she hid there, one man's boot appeared from under the table cloth. She took the knife off the stick and stabbed him in the foot.

He screamed, "Arrgh!"

Kayo grabbed the woman in her arms and rolled her from under the table as the man fired shots at the table. He missed. His partner ran towards the chaos with his gun drawn. Kayo ran toward him, threw her knife at him and hit him in the stomach. He grabbed his belly where the blood gushed out. She reached the man she had stabbed in the foot, dropped to the floor, and using her legs she swept him to the ground. She quickly stood up. As she stepped closer, he used his foot and kicked her in the leg tripping her. She fell on top of him, but started punching him repeatedly in the face. She then pulled out another knife and stabbed him multiple times in the chest. He punched her in the eye and she lost sight for about five seconds. Her head rang. The man was losing blood and slowing down. He used his last bits of energy to shoot his gun and shot the woman Kayo tried to protect in the leg before he died. She quickly used the knife to cut a piece of the table cloth and wrapped it around the woman's thigh. "Shhh. Hold it here. Someone will come," she whispered. She pushed herself up and the other man grabbed her by the hair. He caught her off guard.

The man dragged her backwards across the

floor. She grabbed his wrists, to take away some of the pressure. She had no weapons however as he dragged her past the tables she saw a fork. She picked up the fork and stabbed the man in his forearm, lodging the fork into his flesh. The man growled and let her go to remove the fork. When he looked back up, she had disappeared under another table. He walked swiftly in her direction. She was getting herself ready to pounce on it in a surprise attack. She listened carefully to the sound of his footsteps when *Bang* he was shot in the back and fell face first directly in front of Kayo. She jumped up to see a shadowy figure in all black standing with a gun drawn pointing directly at her. The figure stood there holding the gun with the laser on her chest. They looked at each other for a moment. Then suddenly the figure ran away into the smoke and disappeared. Kayo ducked down and scurried back under the table.

Moments later the room went quiet and the alarms went off. Police crept into the room from the far end of the hall pouring in like black ants marching into a pile of spilled sugar. As the police slowly progressed towards Kayo surveying the area with their weapons drawn, Kayo used the low light and smoke to slip away while it was still hard to see. She snuck back into the kitchen and used the pilot light on the stove and oil to set fire to a cloth and tossed it back into the room right outside of the kitchen door. The rug fire spread quickly. Everyone ran frantically screaming and suddenly the sprinklers and emergency lights were on. Police grabbed the survivors and escorted them to the nearest exit. Kayo removed the knot from her dress and snuck out the back door, disappearing just before the location was swarmed.

In the rain, Kayo walked two blocks before arriving at the bus stop. Her phone buzzed in her purse. It was Patterson. He left 4 voice messages and 5 text messages. Kayo grabbed the side of her head. Her right eye was swollen and her top lip was busted. Thankfully the rain made the dress wet and washed most of the blood away. A few moments later the bus arrived. She was happy to see a human behind the wheel at this time of night. Kayo got on the bus.

"I'd prefer not to use credits, but can I give you something for the ride? I have to get out of here."

"Just come on." The bus driver asked, "Ma'am are you okay?"

With bloody teeth and a raging headache Kayo said, "You should see the other guy," and smiled. In her rain soaked dress, she sat down and put on a pair of shades and began reading Patterson's texts:

ARE YOU OKAY?

WHERE ARE YOU?

THEY TOOK ME AWAY AND WOULDN'T LET ME RE-ENTER THE BALLROOM.

I'M SO SORRY. PLEASE RESPOND.

NO ONE CAN FIND YOU. WE ARE LOOKING.

JUST NEED TO KNOW UR SAFE.

Kayo's throbbing head caused her to squint as she read the messages. Her bloody hand shook uncontrollably yet she managed to write back, "I'M OK. HEADING HOME. I WILL CALL YOU IN THE MORNING."

Patterson immediately called her phone and asked, "Hey where are you? Are you okay?"

Kayo hesitated to answer but finally responded, "I'm fine. I'm heading home now. I'll be there in a few minutes. I'm on the bus."

"I'm outside your house."

"Patterson... no... please, I..." Kayo did not want Patterson to see her this way. Her swollen and bruised face was only part of her worries. She was also afraid that he or someone would know that she was the one who killed those men. "Patterson. I promise I will call you in the morning."

"I'm not leaving until I see you," he insisted. "I want to know what happened."

Kayo huffed. She knew that his intent was noble, but her face was so badly bruised she didn't want him to see her like this. "Patterson. I look crazy." She wanted to add, *And I killed four men. I'm bloody and tired!*

"Kayo, I don't care. I'll be here."

Kayo huffed again and hung up the phone. *Is this what a relationship will be like?* She didn't want to answer to anyone right now, especially not Patterson. A few minutes later her bus arrived at the stop at the north corner of her street. She descended the bus to see Patterson swiftly walking in her direction. When he reached her he grabbed her and hugged her tightly. She was sore and grunted. He reached for her shades and pulled them off. He could already see her lip was busted and swollen. She jerked her head away and pushed back.

"Kayo, what happened?" Patterson inquired. He tried to touch her face. "You need to see a doctor."

Kayo put her hand on her head. "Please Patterson. Don't. I'm okay." She took the shades from him and put them back on.

"This doesn't look 'okay'. You need to be checked out," he insisted. "What happened?"

"I don't even remember what happened. I could barely see. Something or someone hit me. I must've passed out for a bit. When I woke up I saw the exit door and crawled through the door and snuck out the back."

Patterson acquiesced and raised his hands up, "Let me walk you up to your condo if you don't mind."

Kayo led the way to the elevator. They got in and went up to the 5th floor. Hand in hand, they walked down the hall to her door. The corridor was dark and felt a mile long. Kayo arrived at her condo and leaned her back against the door. She said, "I know I keep pushing you away, but thank you for being a gentleman. I'm not used to that."

Patterson leaned forward and kissed her on her forehead. He said, "Anything for you." He saw her wince from the pain in her head and said, "You should put some ice on that eye." Patterson stepped back and said, "I'm sorry I wasn't there for you. I know I can't fix that, but you've gotta let me try."

"Patterson, there's nothing anyone could have done differently. This is why I didn't want you to see me like this. I don't want you blaming yourself. I know that's hard for a person to do, but please do not do that. You showed up when you could. That means everything to me."

"Does it mean enough for you to give us a try?" he winked.

They both laughed.

"I had to slip that in there," he said giggling. "Okay. Okay. Last attempt for the night. I was hoping you changed your mind."

She smiled and said, "Maybe I have."

Patterson was shocked. His smile slowly grew larger across his face and he stepped closer to her. He asked, "Are you sure?"

Kayo stepped closer to him and grabbed the lapel of his jacket. She said, "Let's take it slowly."

"I can do that," Patterson reassured her.

"Okay." Kayo exhaled a sigh of relief, then grabbed her head. "I need to go inside."

Patterson agreed, "Of course. Sorry."

Kayo used her shaky hands to find the key. Patterson stood behind her taking in his last glimpse of Kayo. She opened the door and stepped half way in. Patterson kissed her again on the forehead. She leaned in and kissed him on the face right next to his lips. She closed her eyes and held it there for a while. His face was so smooth, warm and soft she could have leaned against it and fell asleep. She pulled her head away and smiled. "Goodnight, Hanzel."

"I'm bringing you breakfast in the morning. Goodnight," he said.

She nodded, shut the door and leaned against it taking in the moment. She again felt her phone buzzing. It was Beth and Monty in a group chat. She barely read the text, but knew they were concerned about the breaking news regarding the happenings at the Ringgold. She responded, "I'M HOME. I'M OK. CATCH UP TOMORROW."

Kayo needed a shower. She immediately stripped naked, leaving everything on the livingroom floor. She stepped into the bathroom and shut the door.

The water was warm. She let it run over her face and bruised limbs. She washed the grime and blood off her body along with every sin she had ever committed in her life. She assumed the police would be looking for her, but the plan was to say over and over, "I don't remember." She doubted anyone could make her out in the dark smoky room, but she wasn't sure about cameras or drone footage. She could barely see six feet in front of herself, so she was sure no one could make her out. Her mind raced considering all the possibilities and lies she could fabricate. She just had to wait.

Kayo turned off the water and dried herself off. She rubbed shea butter across her achy body and back. Her hand rubbed over a large scar, four large scrapes that went from the middle of her back down to her right side. She could barely reach it. Once she was finished, she walked out of the bathroom. She took her phone and turned on a Billie Eilish playlist. The music played as she walked across the living room, she picked her clothes up off the floor. The rush of blood to her head from bending over made it throb. She put the clothes in the hamper in her bedroom and got dressed in her usual home attire — black tank top and black shorts. She wiped up the bloody water left behind from her dress then went back into the kitchen island that separated the kitchen from the living room and took a deep breath.

Kayo stood still for a moment trying to relax. Suddenly she reached under the island. Hidden on top of a small wooden lip was a metal staff attached by a magnet. Kayo took the staff and ran it through her hands as if she missed it. It was slick and cold. She rubbed her fingertips across the cold smooth surface looking back at her shined a warped reflection of her beaten face. She held it up to her cheek and closed her eyes. *Old friend*, she thought.

Suddenly, Kayo whipped the staff around her body, spinning it, tossing and catching it and spinning again around her neck then her waist and her hands again. It spun swiftly in a circle as she passed it back and forth from hand to hand. She then stopped the spinning by quickly catching it in her hand and said, "Hmm. Rusty," as she looked at it. Kayo took the staff and put it back under the quartz top. It clicked into place.

Knock, knock, knock!

Kayo was startled by the unannounced company. She hated that. Barefooted, she tiptoed over to the door and grabbed a machete she hid between the wall and a bookcase. She looked out the peephole and sighed, accompanied with an intense rolling of the eyes. She opened the door and walked away. "Close it behind you."

"New boyfriend?" Juno asked as he closed the door. Juno was a tall brown skinned male with with a strong build. He had freckles and a tribal tattoo on his neck. His hair was curly and black. He had a full beard.

"You know I don't do boyfriends. How's Gira?" she inquired.

"Getting big. You look like shit," Juno responded.

"And you're high. What do you want, Juno?" Kayo asked with her arms folded.

"Who's the guy?" he asked. He folded his arms in return.

Kayo was frustrated, "I don't have time for this. It's not your business."

Juno walked over to the couch and plopped down. "Kayo, everything you do is my business because it affects *my* business."

Kayo grabbed the side of her head, "Juno, our business is mostly settled. Next week it will be done and then I'm done. I've been quiet, staying low... I've tolerated your dumb ass car in my lot, which you need to move by the end of the week or I'm selling it."

"You had a big night tonight didn't you? And

yes I'm watching you," Juno said as he picked his finger nails. "I don't care if we have business or not. You will always be an asset to me and I'm going to always make sure you're good. Just in case I need you or... you need me." He reached into his inner jacket pocket and pulled out an envelope that had something in it. "I'm trying to figure out why you went to that gala. You fucked up, you know."

Kayo walked into the kitchen and pulled two glasses out of the cabinet. She poured a shot of bourbon in each one and passed one to Juno. They tapped glasses. She walked over to the kitchen island and leaned against it as he continued to talk.

"You haven't changed much. Cheers." He took a sip. "This is for Nahla." He placed the envelope on the couch. "It's from Marly. Someone left it in a lockbox here and she asked me to grab it and get it to you to give to Nahla."

"Marly?!" Kayo shook her head and rolled her eyes. "What the hell this about?" she asked as she inspected the envelope.

"That's all I know. Make sure Nahla gets it! Do not open it please. 'It's a favor she didn't know she needed,' Marly said," he said as he smirked before downing the shot. Juno had on the same bracelet Kayo had with the compass on his wrist.

"There's no such thing as a favor from Marly," Kayo insisted. She walked over to refill his glass. "It always comes at a price," she said as she shook her head. The bourbon flowed smoothly into the glass. Kayo walked away.

Juno stood up and walked over to Kayo. He took the second shot and put his glass in her face for a refill. She poured him another and took down her second shot. He leaned into her and whispered into her ear, "Now... who is the guy?"

Kayo moved her head away from him.

"You like him?" Juno reached over and grabbed her chin, inspecting every inch of Kayo's face. "My God, what a mess. They got you good." He let her face go and asked again, "Do you like him?"

Kayo looked into the bottom of her glass. She swirled around what was left of bourbon and watched the legs flow slowly down the edges. Her loose locs dangled down over her braless breasts. Kayo looked directly in Juno's eyes and said, "I do. I really do." She drank her second glass and placed it on the counter behind her.

"Oh? Hmm." He turned his head and scratched his neck. "So what are you gonna do, Kay? Huh? Make him fall for you then look for an excuse to run away again like you did the last one?" said Juno in a snide fashion. Juno turned and walked away. "You're fucking good at that. A God damned pro!"

"Oh here we go. You can't help but to start shit with me tonight. That is *not* what happened, Juno," Kayo replied. She felt a sudden buzz from the alcohol. "You know that's not true. I did not run away from you." The volume of her voice was rising.

"Yes you did."

She slammed her hand on the island. "You had a baby, Juno! Right after I lost ours!" Kayo yelled.

"Fuck!" Her hand was already hurting from fighting earlier. This only made it worse.

"I didn't know she was coming. What did you want me to do?" Juno responded. "I was with Christa. You were..."

"I know. I was a thing on the side. I get it. Doesn't mean I wasn't hurt."

"I would have left her for you!" Juno yelled.

Kayo calmed down and took a deep breath. "I couldn't let you do that, Juno. We have been in and out of each other's lives since we've known each other. It's too much! I wanted you to go be a father without the guilt of us losing our child. Gira needed you and I needed to be out of the way so you could focus on that. Plus, we were still wrapped up in Marly's mess. There wasn't any space for us to be a family. We weren't living a life conducive to that. You know that," she said passionately. "The child wasn't meant to be. Neither were we."

"Oh you're a fuckin' gem. Who talks about a child like that?"

"I'm just saying it wasn't meant to be. And I'm admitting what you don't want to admit. A baby was too much. We were all over the place. We still are."

"You sound like you didn't want it and would have gotten rid of it anyway," Juno said angrily.

Kayo pointed in his face and said, "Don't you dare, Juno. I would have had that baby for you. You have no idea what losing the baby did to me and when I found out you had another on the way... I cried everyday for weeks. I was emotionally unwell."

She took a sip and said, "I wanted to kill myself."

"I didn't know that. How the fuck would I know unless you told me, Kay?"

"I wasn't gonna put all that on you! It wasn't your fault, Juno. I didn't tell you because *you* needed to be there for Gira, so I hid that from you. Everything I did was for you."

Juno spoke in a calmer voice and said, "Everything but talk to me."

"Ugh! All we do is fucking argue. I'm really sick of this shit. Juno, I'm tired. I'm so damn tired. I don't wanna fight anymore."

Juno turned around and said, "Kayo, sometimes I hate you so much. I could just..." He pretended to choke someone. "You have no idea." He started making choking sounds and laughed.

Kayo threw a pillow at him.

Juno continued, "But, I'm also your best friend. Shit, I'm your only friend, and don't tell me about Beth and Monty, they are not your friends. Monty could never be me and Beth will never be India."

Kayo's face turned red. She walked up to Juno and pointed in his face and said, "Juno, unless you want me to slit your throat, do not speak her name. You hear me?"

"You still can't say her name? That's *your* problem. I will say her name anytime I want! India!"

"You're an ass!"

"India! She was my friend too, Kayo. Deep down you know it's true. You cannot replace us. They are friends with who they think you are— the person you pretend to be. Around them you're reserved, quiet and introverted. You're such a fraud! I could die watching you interact with them."

"Fuck off, Juno!"

"That's my potty mouth, Kayo. You'd never talk like that in front of them. They don't know you! You keep them around to feel 'normal', but you're not, no matter how much you try and 'Clark Kent' yourself, you can't make it work. 'The life' always finds you. Look at you. During the attack, did you lay under a table and hide like everyone else? I doubt that very much. I can see you were fighting. Look at your hands." He grabbed her hand and she snatched it back. "How many did you kill, Kay?" He smiled a sinister smile and said, "I know everything about you so I'm going to tell you the truth. It doesn't matter what that man tries to do, you're going to sabotage everything. You're going to make excuses and fuck it up."

"I have shit going on, Juno."

"Are you still saying that shit?" Juno giggled and continued, "Grow the fuck up." He marched over to the bottle and poured a heavy shot. He pulled a tin container out of his coat pocket. In it were a few joints. He took one out, put the tin back and lit it. He took a deep hit. He signaled Kayo to come to him. As if she was hypnotized, having no other choice but to comply, she walked over. They leaned in towards each other. Gently holding her face, with his thumb gently pressed against the corner of her lips, he passed the smoke from his mouth into hers.

She closed her eyes and slowly inhaled the ghostly fumes. His lips barely touched hers for the exchange. She held it in and blew it out over their heads.

"Why do you care?" She pressed her forehead against his while he held her face and asked, "Why do we hate each other? How did we get like this?" She ran her fingertips across the edge of his pants. The bourbon she drank, the stress and the THC had reached her bloodstream and her decision making ability was compromised.

He smiled and said, "We are so fuckin toxic, Kay. Since you left me this is what it's become." Juno gulped down the heavy shot of bourbon. Some of it spilled over the edges of his mouth. Kayo wiped the corners of his mouth with her thumb. He softly grabbed her hand and pressed it against his face. With his other hand he dropped the empty glass on the coffee table. He pulled his hand away and walked over to the door and opened it and said, "We hate each other because we still love each other but we can't have each other. And we resent each other for that shit. Trust me I wanna be over you, but I'm not. Not yet."

The word "yet" punched Kayo in the stomach. She couldn't imagine a life where Juno emotionally let her go.

Juno looked at Kayo, waiting for her to contest his point but she didn't. "Give that envelope to Nahla when you see her. Maybe you can help her figure out what Marly wants."

"Juno, I'm done," she said. "I mean it!"

"Me too," he replied and quietly shut the door. Then he opened it again and said, "I have a grudge against you. I'm never letting it go. Just so we're clear. 'Til the sun meets the sea." He slammed the door shut.

"And the moon leaves the sky..." She whispered.

KAYO BROOKS - JUNIPER CHARLES - INDIA ALEXANDER

Juno and Kayo met when Kayo was 11. Juno was 10. They met India a year later when she was 13. Nahla had a group of rebellious homesteader friends which included Marly and Chopp. They called themselves The Citizens Cooperative. Juno was the eldest son of seven siblings. India lived with her mother on a small alpaca farm about five miles away from Kayo. She met Kayo while randomly fishing in the creek one early morning. They'd been friends ever since.

India had curly brown hair and usually kept her hair in box twists pulled back into a ponytail or braided. She had one dimple on the right side, a big smile and a septum piercing in her nose that her mother hated. Under her bushy eyebrows were somewhat slanted brown eyes with a small mole under the left one. India was a year older than Kayo but always looked up to her.

There were 7 families in the cooperative that would meet once a month to talk politics, trade goods, learn new skills and physically train and bring their children around to learn basic skills. They were Gen Z doomsday preppers that moved Up Rural prior to the climate change restrictions that had more recently been imposed. They all agreed to homeschool their children and train them to be self-sufficient. They learned farming, hunting, fishing, basic crafts, construction and self defense.

Juno, India and Kayo clicked and became best friends right away. They were mostly interested in hunting, fishing and fighting. They would spar and tell each other what they needed to fix to do better. As they got older Juno and Kayo's friendship budded into an attraction and by the time Kayo was 16, they were in love. India was always the third wheel but the trio was inseparable. She had a knack for getting raven's to bring her lost items found in the woods or directing her to find prey. She would always leave them the spoils as a reward. "I dunno how you do that shit," Kayo would say.

India would smile and say, "They don't trust you, Kay. You have to be nice to it, just because, not because you want something in return. Once you connect with one, like an endless tie, he's yours for life." Occasionally Kayo could get the raven's to eat from her hand but only if India held it underneath. One in particular would return frequently. India called him Shadow. Shadow would sometimes follow them in the woods or show up while India was in the stand and give India a heads up on the direction the prey was coming from. She knew it was him because one of his talons and the upper part of the digit was missing on his right foot where he had been injured from a fight.

Together Juno, Kayo and India taught the younger kids in the cooperative families various skills but Juno and Kayo would slip away and spend many evenings alone together. It seemed they were both fully committed to the homesteading lifestyle. Juno often discussed his dream of them having their own homestead and even planned out the layout of the land and discussed having children. India met and started dating a young man named Paul from Putney, Vermont who frequented the market for produce and trading. She visited him just about every weekend except during hunting seasons, he would travel to see her.

As the restrictions became more prevalent in the city, and shortages increased, there was an influx of city dwellers lurking outside the city limits looking for fresh produce and wild game to supplement their red meat cravings. Marly and Nahla had an idea for the co-op to start a market and they did well. At the time, the restrictions did not include wild game. The kids were tasked with fishing and hunting, gathering eggs and produce from the gardens at the various properties. ARPA was not fond of this loophole and came up with data to support the idea that the lead bullets used in hunting were bad for the environment. They were forced to use copper bullets and casings, which cost double the price. Marly convinced the group to make their own bullets using melted pennies. ARPA and ACPP began targeting more loopholes by adding additional restrictions to hunting like decreasing hunting hours and eventually came the gun bans, which made hunting harder. The cooperative always complied, but it was getting more difficult. Some rules had to be broken.

Nahla eventually taught Kayo and India how to hunt with bows using saddle harnesses Chopp found at a flea market. She taught them sign language to communicate during the hunts. The girls started a class, set up a field course and started teaching the other kids how to shoot. Bows weren't as easy to carry as the rifles but they were lighter, quiet and effective. Marly was very excited when business was booming again. It got so demanding, they began taking orders before the seasons started and the farmers market became busier than ever. Marly gave Juno a loan to purchase his own homestead across the river. Kayo cosigned. They planned to start their own homestead with a school. The land was 24 acres of raw land for $50,000. They agreed to 10 years of service to Marly and 5000 lbs of game meat as a part of the repayment plan. Marly made many loans and many of the homesteaders were indebted to her for various reasons. Marly held all the cards.

Soon enough, the government began cracking

down on farmers markets until they eventually banned them for "safety concerns". This, along with increased property taxes and regulatory fees imposed by the government specifically on homesteads, caused a financial burden on the group. This is when Marly came up with another plan. She became the leader of the collective and started an underground market for wild fish and game to help homesteaders keep up with the fees and make a living. The demand was overwhelming. Every class of people came to the homestead for meat: turkey, rabbit, quail, bear, duck, and mainly deer. Venison was the bread and butter of the operation and most demanded meat of them all paying up to $30 a pound depending on the cut. Bear wasn't as prevalent but when available would sell out almost immediately at a premium of $50 a pound. The group still followed the old hunting seasons and bag limits to make sure the population stayed under control. They also decided it would keep demand high which would keep prices in check.

The black market also made homesteading more dangerous. The entire group was participating in illegal activities which often brought them negative attention. Besides dealing with the government, gangs would try and attack, bribe or extort the group. They'd often catch trespassers on their properties and get into altercations removing people from their land. Sometimes they would find slaughtered animals that were not processed appropriately nor discarded in a respectful manner.

Marly began politicking with police, judges and policy makers to keep business up running. She paid them bribes, gave them meat for favors; she did everything she could to keep the underground market open.

One late afternoon Juno, Kayo and India went hunting. They split up to cover more ground. Getting closer to sunset, India sent Kayo and Juno her location in the chat and a text, "FIND ME. I NEED HELP!" She was excited about her kill and sent them a selfie with her tongue hanging out to match the deer's tongue hanging from his mouth. As India began field dressing the deer, three trespassers caught up to her. She heard something coming but thought it was just another deer passing by since the rut was in full swing. They put a gun to her head. She put her arms up, but they kicked her in the back and pressed her face into the mud. Two men held her down while the other focused on the deer.

One man said, "Scream and you die!"

They stuffed her mouth with a rag and wrapped a handkerchief around it to keep it in. They tied her hands in front of her. Next they ripped her pants down to her ankles and dragged her across the ground by her hair. She twisted and turned her body as much as she could but the men had full control. Kayo had no idea what she was walking into but saw what was happening and quickly ducked down. She drew her bow striking one man directly in the heart. His body immediately dropped. The man who had his back to her turned around and fired his gun but it was too late. Kayo was already there. She spun and kicked the gun from his hand, and pulled a knife from her waist. She jumped onto him, bearhugged him with one arm around the back of his neck, she repeatedly jabbed him in the throat until they both fell. She tossed the knife to India then approached the last man who had been working on the deer. He stood up with a knife in his hand ready and waiting. India quickly pulled up her pants and used the knife to cut the rope around her wrists.

Kayo and the last man stood about 10 feet away from each other. They were both covered in blood but for different reasons. India stood by Kayo's side with the knife in hand. Suddenly, the man sprung forth towards India. He got a hold of her wrist and made her drop the knife. He tried to stab India, but Kayo was there and grabbed his arm. The two women wrestled the man until Kayo was able to get his knife wielding arm into an armbar. She snapped his elbow and he dropped the knife. The man bellowed and Juno realized he was only a few yards away. He came running to see the man laying in the dirt with Kayo's foot on his neck.

Juno arrived in awe. Juno was proud of them. Juno didn't hesitate when he saw the third man. He took his large hand, covered the man's mouth and stabbed him in the stomach, driving the knife as deeply into the man's belly as possible. India immediately grabbed Kayo, hugging her tightly. Juno hugged them both, "You okay?" he asked them.

Through the heavy breathing, they could only

find the energy to nod.

Once there was no life left in the man, the trio took the clothes off the men and buried the bodies. They took the deer to the butcher and burned the mens clothes afterwards in a fire pit. Kayo isolated herself for two weeks after that. She wouldn't talk to Juno nor India. She took a break from hunting and would only fish the lake alone.

Kayo needed to get away. Against her initial plan with Juno, Kayo went to university at 18. Juno was crushed at news of the idea but waited for her. He wrote her letters once a week. She wrote back. She came home every weekend her first year but as time went on the visits became more scarce. The world was changing and so wasn't Kayo.

By the time Kayo finished University, she came home finding her room had been taken by her cousin Ayrah, since everyone assumed the plan was for her to move in with Juno. She also didn't know how to tell Juno that she was seeing someone... sort of. She went to the house he built on the property and a woman opened the door when she knocked. Juno wasn't expecting this but it was clear that Juno had moved on. Rightfully so, but seeing it in person was gut wrenching. Juno had no idea Kayo was coming home, but when he saw her he couldn't speak. She couldn't speak. Kayo got back into her car and left. Kayo found a spot to sleep at India's cabin and was immediately back to work for Marly. She was indebted to Marly over a property where she was no longer welcome.

Kayo spent many days in the trees hunting. Her hearing was very keen and her sense of smell grew stronger as she got older. She was a master bowman, bringing home turkey, rabbit, foxes and quail regularly. She and Juno refused to speak and would zip past each other on their e-bikes without one acknowledgement exchanged until the day Kayo shot a bear. She texted India, but India had left town to visit her boyfriend in Vermont. "CONGRATS, BABE, BUT YOU MAY NEED TO SUCK IT UP AND TEXT JUNO FOR ASSISTANCE," India responded.

Even though Kayo hadn't texted him for a long time she sent the message, "JUNO, FIND ME. I NEED HELP." She dropped him a location pin and within 30 minutes Juno found her. She knew he would show up without hesitation. Juno could not believe the size of the bear.

Kayo broke the ice and said, "I didn't want to bother you but I need help. India's out of town, and I don't trust anyone else."

"What about Oree?" he asked, referencing her cousin Orion.

"If I call him, someone else may come. I've heard stories about how things work out here. Anyone else helps, they get a piece. It only makes sense if you help."

Juno tried to act normal, "Yeah. I got robbed once asking for help. Everyone owes Marly one way or another."

"Well, I figured getting this bear for her would be good for both of us. It goes toward the same debt."

"You know you don't have to stay with India," Juno said. "The property is half yours."

"I don't think so, Juno."

"It's just me at the homestead. No one else lives there."

She said, "I know. We can sort the property out later. I have things I want to do and this is in my way."

He changed the subject. "How much do you think it weighs?" he wondered.

"Not sure," she replied, "but we better process this ASAP. It spoils fast. We can field dress it, salvage the offals and use our bikes to drag it back."

After 40 minutes of work, with bloody hands, the two former lovers dragged the bear down the trail and managed to get it into the back of Juno's truck. Marly got the call and was extremely excited and even more excited to see her two best hunters working together again.

"How appropriate is this celebration? 417 pounds dressed out!" she said as she circled the carcass. "We haven't gotten a bear in a year. Are we partnering back up or..."

"Just business," Juno said.

"What's left on the tab?" Kayo wondered.

Marly smirked and said, "I'll review my receipts and let you know."

"I'll check ours as well. Have a good day." Kayo marched out of the butcher shop with her chin high. She got to her bike and waited for Juno to get closer. She asked, "When did she start walking around with bodyguards?"

Juno spoke quietly and said, "A lot has happened since you left. No worries, I have every receipt in my safe. I think we owe about 2000 lbs. We should be able to knock that out in a few seasons."

"I've given them about 60 pounds of fowl this week alone. Between us, I heard there was a bear family sighting in Monroe on the Danby property and there's a male frequenting that property that is enormous they say. I'm going to see if he will let me hunt the land for a deer, but I keep whatever else I get and I want that bear. If there's a family we may be able to get two if you're down," Kayo said. "I plan to ask India too. Nahla was talking about how Pat Danby is getting old. He can't really hunt like he used to and the place is overgrown."

"The Danby's aren't a part of the co-op."

"That's why I'm interested. I don't want Marly feeling entitled to everything I get," Kayo said.

"Let me know." Juno said with a straight face. "I'll ride out with you."

Kayo added, "There's a cabin on the property. We can stay there if he agrees."

Kayo and Juno eventually secured the property. They spent a lot of time on the property in the off seasons preparing for upcoming hunting seasons, cutting back grass, adding stands and clearing out shooting lanes. India was happy to help. It felt like old times again. Cleaning and clearing out the dusty cabin was a great bonding tool. They rearranged the books, cleaned out the closets and shook years of dust from the space rugs. Kayo and India added new bedding and covered the old couches with afghan blankets. Juno patched holes and sprayed foam in some of the holes where mice found their way in. There was an old grandfather clock that didn't work but India was in love with the craftsmanship. It was rare to see an analogue clock these days. Not many could read it so they called it the Old Man. This one was stuck at 3:27. "He's such a liar," India would say at least once each visit referring to the fact that the time was always wrong. It was an ongoing joke in the cabin.

The first two seasons they spent in the cabin at the Danby property repaired their friendship and by the third season, rekindled an old flame within them. Kayo and Juno started going to the cabin just to get away. They made repairs, watched old movies, drank bourbon and made love. It was the life they imagined sharing on the homestead when they were young. They figured once the hunting debt was paid, Kayo would make a deal with the Danby's to continue hunting the property and made a plan to sell game on her own but knew if she got caught undercutting Marly by selling the meat in her territory, there would be trouble.

Kayo moved into the city and took a job as a social worker at the DCWS four years after returning home.

She returned home on weekends to hunt and would take extended time off during the hunting seasons to meet Juno and India at the Danby's to stock up on meat. She and Juno smuggled their meat into the city and sold it there, sometimes through Chopp. Other times, Baker. Juno and India continued to work for Marly.

Kayo picked up some photos from the trail cam showing that the massive male black bear had been back around. The locals called him The Tank. So, one weekend Kayo and India went up to the Danby's to look for the bear. She and India decided to try and track the bear to hunt him down when the unspeakable happened. India never returned from that hunt. A week later Kayo got into a fight with Nahla and left the homestead and quit hunting for good.

Even though Juno would visit, their on again off again relationship continued until Kayo found out that Juno had gotten his girlfriend Christa pregnant. She didn't care how it happened, but it did. It would not have hurt so badly if she wasn't also pregnant. Kayo lost her baby 8 weeks in. Four months later, Gira was born. Their friendship and relationship was never again the same.

CHAPTER 4

Sunday morning around 9:40 am, while Kayo was putting birdseed on her windowsill, she heard a knock on the door. She closed the window, looked out the peephole and saw Patterson. She grabbed her hearing aids from the bookcase and popped them into her ears. Patterson had arrived at Kayo's place with breakfast in a brown paper bag. He had two cups of hot water for tea in a cup holder. He scrunched the bag in his hand and knocked on the door. A few moments later, Kayo opened the door with a big smile, "Good morning," she said as she grabbed the hot water cups from him. Her hair was up in a wrap. She was wearing a long sweater and leggings with flip flops. She stood in the doorway. She wasn't ready to let him in the condo.

"I know you don't drink coffee so, I got hot water to make tea and I wasn't sure which kind you liked so I grabbed a few."

"Black. Black is fine. Thank you. You didn't have to," she said to him as she grabbed the bag from his hand.

"I promised to bring you breakfast last night. You don't seem like a sunny side up type of person so I had them fry the egg hard. Hope that's ok." He realized he was still in the hallway. "You're not going to let me in?" Patterson asked politely.

Kayo smiled and said, "We're not there yet." She looked back into the condo and then said, "Hold this." Kayo handed him back the bag and walked over to the kitchen island. She grabbed a stool and then walked back and grabbed a place mat and two cloth napkins. She placed them on top of the stool for a makeshift table and shut the door.

"You don't have to make it fancy now," Patterson said. He smiled and placed the food on the stool.

"I always set the table." She didn't care that it was not comfortable. He could not come in. Not yet. Kayo grinned and said, "How'd you sleep?" She put sweetener in her tea and swirled it with the little wooden stirrer.

Patterson let off a sigh and said, "Not very well. I kept hearing people screaming. My head was throbbing, and I got a visit from the police this morning. If they haven't been here, expect them today. They know we were on a date so, they know you were there."

"I don't really remember much to be honest, Patterson. Did they find anything? Did they figure out the motive?" she asked, but she really wondered if anyone said anything about her fighting.

"They didn't say but my lawyer said whoever attacked the Ringgold scrambled all the drones and cams in the building and the area. They can't see anything for about 55 minutes. They also boobytrapped the entrances so police couldn't get inside until the signal was dead."

"Well that's not good," she said as she handed a napkin to Patterson. *That's not good. It's GREAT!* she thought.

He tore his sandwich in half and asked, "How'd you sleep?"

"Like a log," she giggled. "My head hurt so badly. I took something for the pain..." she had a flashback of herself inhaling smoke from Juno's mouth, "and that did a pretty good job putting me to sleep."

"Good. Looks like the swelling of your lip went down a little. How's your head feeling this morning?" Patterson wondered.

Kayo shrugged her shoulders and said, "Eh. About the same as yesterday, but I'm ok. Thanks."

"Oh shit I forgot!" Patterson reached into his jacket and pulled a small four leaf clover from the inside pocket. "This is for you. I saw it on the way here and I knew I was a lucky man."

Kayo took it from him with a smile and said, "Thank you. I'm a lucky lady. Probably a little dog poop on it."

"Wow. Dog poop. Maybe I should've gone with flowers."

"It's perfect. It's the best gift ever," she said sarcastically.

Patterson turned his head away and said, "Nope! Feelings crushed."

"Please! I promise I love it," she said as she pressed it against her heart. "I hope you don't mind if I squeeze it into one of my favorite books."

"Of course not," Patterson said. He bit into his sandwich. Kayo used a napkin to wipe a few crumbs off his face. "I have to take you on a proper date, this... this just isn't it!"

"You don't like the Brooks Cafe?" she asked jokingly.

Patterson had a mouth full of food and put his finger up as if to say, "Wait a minute," so he could swallow his food. "I love the Brooks Cafe. Elegant, exquisite, fine dining. But... I want to take you somewhere I like to go. But I do think the cafe is fine... for now. I'm just enjoying your company."

"Well, again, thank you for breakfast," she reassured him. "I'm enjoying your company too. It doesn't take much to please me. I'm a simple girl, so I've been told." She took a bite from her sandwich. After she chewed and swallowed the bite she said, "This is really good. I don't know if I can top this." She took a sip of the tea.

"You have plenty of time to try," he said.

Kayo smirked and pretended to think for a moment. She leaned into him and softly said, "I want to try right now." She gently touched his face, leaned in closer and kissed him on the lips. He returned the kiss and for a few moments they were lost in it. Kayo pulled back and said, "How'd I do?"

"Topped! Completely topped!" Patterson said with a big smile. He leaned in and kissed her again.

He smells so good. Kayo stared into his eyes and smiled with a little giggle. She focused back on her sandwich. They each took another bite of their sandwiches when they heard the elevator door open.

Please do not be Juno, Kayo thought to herself. Into the low lit hallway, two figures emerged from the elevator. They stepped closer and it became more clear who they were. They were investigators.

"Good Morning. Sorry to disturb your picnic," the female agent said, "I'm looking for Kayo Brooks. Is that you?"

Kayo nodded. Patterson and Kayo put their sandwiches and tea on the top of the stool.

"May we come in and ask you a few questions?" the agent asked.

"Here is fine," Kayo replied. Patterson put his arm around her as they stood all four of them in the hallway outside of the door.

"We figured we would talk to you with a little more privacy but the hallway will do if that's what you prefer. Kayo, my name is Detective Juan Ortega and this is Detective Brenna Cain of the FBI. We wanted to ask you a few questions about last night if you don't mind."

Kayo immediately tapped into her first lie, "I wish I could help you but I don't remember much."

Patterson immediately butted in and said, "She took a pretty good blow to the head. I tried to get her to go to the hospital but she refused. She told me the same thing when I asked last night. She's having trouble remembering what happened and frankly, I don't think she should be answering any questions right now."

"I'd prefer to have a lawyer present," Kayo added.

Detective Cain asked, "I want you to know you're not in any trouble. You're not being investigated. We just want as many details as we can gather while it's still fresh in your head." Detective Cain inspected Kayo's face and said, "I can see you've been injured. You should have that looked at immediately. It would also make sense to take pictures of your injuries."

Kayo did not want to be involved in the slightest way. "It's just a bump. Not a big deal."

"Big enough for you not to remember anything," Detective Cain said with contempt.

"We also want to make sure you're okay," said Detective Ortega. He sensed things were getting tense between the two. "The night must have been pretty traumatic so we can understand your reluctance to speak with us."

"Thank you, detective, but I really don't have too much here. If it helps I can write down what I remember, talk to my lawyer and get a statement to you at another time."

"That would be helpful. Here's my number when you're ready to talk. Your lawyer can reach me here okay?" Cain held out her card.

"Thank you," Patterson said. He took the card from Detective Cain. "Have a good day."

Detective Cain and Detective Ortega slowly walked away, down the stairs. Kayo and Patterson stayed silent until they could no longer hear the steps. Kayo listened until she heard the front door slam behind them. *I'm so fucked*, she thought.

As soon as he knew the coast was clear he said, "I'm gonna make some calls. They won't be back." Patterson looked at his watch and said, "I have golf with the mayor in an hour. Another fundraiser thing I have to attend. I'm sorry, I have to head out."

Kayo went over and gave him a hug, "Go. You've done enough for me the past two days. I really appreciate everything."

"Why don't you take a couple days and rest? Are you open for dinner Tuesday?" he asked. "There's this restaurant I really like. I'd love to take you there."

"Sure. Just let me know the time. Oh also, I'm heading Up Rural to see the family Friday. I'll be there for a few days, maybe a week. I haven't decided. Depends on how crazy things are."

"Anything I can help you with?" he asked.

"Thank you but, no. I have to help settle some family affairs," she told him.

"Ahh ok. I will leave you to that but I want to see you before you leave."

"You got it," she said with a smile.

Patterson took his large hand and moved her hair away from her face. He grabbed her on both sides of her face and kissed her on the forehead. He said, "I'll call you later." He left jogging away down the stairs.

Kayo went back into her condo, latched the lock across the door. She went over to the window where she saw Patterson swiftly walking down the street. She began cleaning up the kitchen. She put away the shot glasses from the previous night that she and Juno left on the counter. She grabbed a book off the shelf, opened it midway and put the four leaf clover inside. The Hunger Games, also banned three months ago.

Her phone rang. Juno. Kayo picked up the phone. "What?!"

"Don't sabotage," he said.

"Goodbye!" Kayo hung up and smiled. "So fucking annoying." She continued putting things away and said, "Oh my god. I gotta call Monty and Beth. Totally forgot."

Kayo, Monty and Beth agreed to meet for a late lunch around 1pm at the Pitchfork Saturday Afternoon. Beth and Monty had already been waiting. When Kayo arrived, Beth and Monty jumped up and hugged her together. "Oww oww!" she said as they squeezed the life out of her. Her body was still sore from the fiasco. They gave her a quick inspection, flipping back her hair and looking closely at the bruise on her eye which was still visible even though she tried to cover it with makeup.

"Guys. I'm fine," Kayo insisted.

"Are you okay?" Monty inquired. "Where's Patterson?"

"What happened?" Beth asked. "Have you been shot?" Beth saw Kayo's hands were scratched up. She pulled at Kayo's hand but Kayo shamefully snatched her hand away.

Kayo's head was spinning from her ongoing headache and now the interrogation from her friends. "Slow down, I can't keep up. One question at a time and I'm starving."

"We put in the orders already." Monty guided Kayo to her seat. "So tell us, what the fuck happened?" Monty asked. "We've been freaking out all night."

Kayo looked around at the small crowd before speaking. She said, "Everything happened so fast. Vernell Bailey was speaking. Then a bunch of booms, like explosions went off and I don't even know what happened after that. I felt this massive pain in my head and I'm pretty sure I passed out. Next thing I knew, I was on the ground and started crawling to the first door I could find." *This is my story and I'm sticking to it,* she thought to herself. Less was more. She remembered Juno telling her she fucked up by attending that event and he was right. She had no business there and now the police would be all over her. How ironic that the DCWS had employed a hunter. She was sure she would need to testify at some point. *How the fuck do I get out of that?* Kayo sipped the water they had waiting for her. "I really don't remember much. Sorry I don't have anything more to say."

Beth's hand was over her mouth, "Oh my goodness. I can't even imagine. You're totally going to have PTSD. Has anyone offered therapy?"

"No. I'm fine. Just tired. The police... FBI... whatever they were came by today but I don't really have much to say. Patterson basically told them to go away until I get my lawyer."

"Wait," Beth said, "Patterson spent the night?" Beth put her hand over her chest. "Do tell!"

Kayo shook her head and said, "No no. He left last night then came back."

"So you kicked him out after and he still came back? Savage!" Monty smiled.

Kayo shook her head. "What's wrong with you?"

"What?" Monty held his hands up. "I'm just trying to understand. Did he come over last night or what?"

"Yes, but not like that. Get your mind out of the gutter. He just made sure I got home okay, left and came back in the morning to check on me."

"Well, that's not exciting," Beth said.

Kayo rolled her eyes and said, "I guess neither is surviving a terrorist attack. How'd you guys hear about it?"

Monty said, "X. That's where all the juicy stuff is."

Beth was nervous, "I told you to stay off that site, Monty. Nothing but Chinese bots and radicals. I'll give you a pass this one time because in this case it was important. It never showed up on the major news networks until this morning. I thought Monty was lying at first. Then we tried to call you and your phone wasn't even going to voicemail."

Monty added, "Yeah. All we got was a busy signal."

"Wow. Patterson said they scrambled all signals in and around the premises. The drones weren't even working. All cameras were shut down too. Everything for an hour. Anyway, I'm glad he's okay."

"We're glad *you're* okay too. I heard a lot of people didn't make it," Beth added.

The waiter arrived with their orders and placed them accordingly.

"Are you coming into work Monday?" Monty asked.

"I don't see why not. I have too much work to do and I'm going to be gone Friday and the following week. I have to finish up my work."

Beth wondered, "What happened with Patterson?"

"We talked. We decided to be a little more serious but take things slowly and see how it goes." Kayo cut her soy burger in half and picked up one of the halves.

Monty clapped his hands and said, "Well congratulations to you. Finally."

"So what about you, Monty? You're so worried about me, who's the lucky lady in your life?" Kayo joked as she bit into her burger.

Monty grabbed a few fries and said, "I'm waiting on Beth to come around," and then he smashed the fries into his mouth.

Beth rolled her eyes and said, "I'd rather have my eyes gouged out."

"This can be arranged," Kayo said.

The three friends continued laughing as they enjoyed their lunch.

"Monday, the office is going to be crazy. Everyone is going to ask questions. It's going to be insane. I'm gonna have to tell people to back off," Monty said.

Beth agreed, "He's right. Maybe you should stay home. Take a sick day. I think people will understand."

Kayo took a few fries in her hands and ate them. Her mouth was still sore but she ate anyway. She said, "If I didn't have so much going on at work, I would stay home. Don't forget I'm off next week so I don't want to come back with a pile of work waiting on my desk."

"You really need to take a break, Brooksie," Monty reminded her.

"Seriously, Kayo. Are you okay?" Beth said as her eyes began tearing up. She stared at Kayo demanding an answer with her eyes, but Kayo said nothing. "You're not okay, Kayo. I'm going to walk you home after lunch," Beth said.

"I'm coming too," Monty added.

This was too much for Kayo. *I gotta get outta here*, she thought. "I uh.. I have to get Busy Buzzy in a little bit, so I'm gonna head out and I probably should take that trip alone." Kayo said and she stood up. "I appreciate the two of you checking in on me." She played with her phone and said, "I just transferred you some credits for the meal. I have to go." Kayo turned away.

Beth called out, "Hey!" Stopping Kayo in her tracks. "No! Kayo, stop. I know a lot happened but it's not normal to just go on with your day like it didn't. You don't have to be alone. We're here to process this with you. It's okay to be vulnerable with us. We got you." Beth embraced Kayo from behind like she hadn't seen her in years. "Stay with us. You don't have to leave."

Kayo held onto Beth's arms and squeezed tightly. She didn't worry that her body was aching from the previous night. She only remembered that Juno said they weren't her real friends. *Was he right?* she thought. They've never met her family nor she theirs. They've never been inside her home. She didn't work out with them or have anything in common with them besides a cubicle wall. Beth wore pink every day, did her nails and clicked around in heels. Monty was annoying and metro. She couldn't tell if he was into men or women even though he flirted with Beth regularly. *I don't even know them.* She barely communicated with them on weekends. They've been to a bar a couple of times on a few Fridays in all the years she's known them. She blew them off every chance she could, declined invites repeatedly, and made excuses about being busy when she was just sitting home on the couch reading. The truth was they were great friends to

Kayo, but every effort they made to get closer to her, she ruined. *Sabotage.*

Beth's embrace was beyond comforting. It was reassuring, affectionate and felt like home. She remembered this feeling when she found Ayrah stranded in the woods one summer. The way Ayrah embraced her when they found her. It was reminiscent of the time Nahla hugged her when she returned home after her first year at University. Kayo couldn't let go. Then she remembered India. The warm embrace was overdue and what she needed the most in that moment. Her eyes watered. Monty noticed and joined in on the hug. *I'm going to be a better friend,* Kayo promised them in her head. It wasn't them. It was Kayo who was the lousy companion. *Focus.* Kayo had things to do. "I have to go," Kayo said and she swiftly marched out of the cafe and disappeared down the street leaving Monty and Beth alone... again.

Kayo walked quickly down the street making her way to the closest bus stop. She paced, listening to her mind ramble about everything that was said to her in the past 24 hours. She heard Beth saying, "You don't have to leave." It relentlessly repeated in her mind along with all the other judgements and criticisms that Juno threw at her at one of the neediest moments of her life.

I'm a piece of shit and they know it. She didn't realize her introvertedness was this noticeable and obvious that it was weird and off putting. Maybe they were getting tired of it. That would be fair.

Beth had never been so emotional with Kayo. Maybe this was their final attempt at connecting, but Kayo couldn't prioritize their feelings. She needed to remain a quiet member of society and friends are a messy liability. Juno was all the mess she could tolerate.

The driverless bus arrived. Kayo got on and exchanged credits for a ride. She sat in the middle on the street side of the bus so she could watch the sidewalk. There were about six people already on the bus, spread out from the front to the back. She assumed everyone's personality by the location of their seat and temperament. The woman in the front row was confused. She was watching the street signs as if she didn't know where she was. The man in the back was paranoid. He was sitting at the edge of his seat tapping his foot, looking at his watch. The kid by the back door is up to something. He's watching the sidewalk as if someone may be waiting for him when he gets off. The other girl behind her, she assumed, was hiding from someone. She watched the street as if she wanted to make sure no one was following. *What would they assume about me?* she thought. *Maybe they'd assume I escaped a terrorist attack by killing four men and the police want to speak to me about that.*

A few moments later, she received a text. It was from Patterson. "GOLF IS BLAH! THINKING ABOUT YOU. HOPE YOU'RE STAYING OUT OF TROUBLE," he wrote. She suddenly felt a sense of ease and smiled. She couldn't get her mind off Patterson. She quickly fell into a daydream about him but snapped out of it when she realized her stop was approaching.

She quickly replied, "OF COURSE. THINKING ABOUT YOU TOO :)"

She pressed the button on the side of the window. When the bus came to a full stop, she disembarked and hopped onto the sidewalk. This wasn't a side of town that she entered very often, but she was familiar since she brought her bike here twice a year for maintenance. She strolled a couple blocks down the street passing a few shops and cafes. She was still sore but managing. She rubbed the back of her neck as she stepped in front of the bike shop called Cycledelics.

Cycledelics's showroom was full of bikes of all different styles, new and used, traditional and hybrid electric. Most of the inventory was in the basement. There was a woman at the counter taking calls on the phone and another young man talking to a customer about a bike. The lights flickered. Kayo looked up at the lights then walked to the back where a middle aged, thin, man was bent over working on a bicycle. He had a thick salt and pepper beard and a tapered salt and pepper blow out with twists at the end. His skin was smooth and brown. Veins popped out of his arms and neck. He was thin but strong. He heard her approach and said, "My girl, Kay." He stood up and fist bumped her hand. His hands were covered in grease. He took a cloth from the counter and wiped his hands.

"Hey Chopp. I see you're working. Did I come at

a bad time?" she asked as she smiled at his familiar face.

"No, no. Never that. You'll never catch me at a time when I'm not busy, my love. I got bills to pay, but I'm never too busy for you, baby girl." Chopp winced at Kayo. "What happened to your face, Kay?" Kayo shrugged. "Still fuckin' around with Juno? Y'all ever work that out?"

"Eh, you know how it goes." Kayo wasn't up for answering questions. "It's complicated and messy at times but we're cool. Just a lot of unresolved feelings I guess."

"Hmm." Chopp started walking through the store and Kayo followed. He said, "Your girl is over here. She needed a tune up and her frame was bent a little. What the hell were you doing?" He walked her over to the bike. It was clean and shiny. He oiled her green leather seat bringing back the finish.

"You know I take care of her. A delivery truck hit her when I parked her outside the grocery store. He took off too." Kayo inspected the bike. "She looks good. What do I owe you?" she asked.

"Come to my office for a minute. Let's chat about something."

Kayo and Chopp walked into the back office. The walls had a vintage Lauryn Hill poster and framed t-shirts on the wall. Jeremiah Thomas aka Chopp was a soccer player in his early years. He sat at his desk and pulled out a flask from the drawer. He offered a sip to Kayo. She shook her head. There was an old picture of Chopp and Nahla on the wall. They were younger.

Chopp and Nahla had an open relationship. Kayo remembered that Chopp would visit on weekends and the two would disappear on Freedom Day. He was very helpful on the homestead. He taught Kayo how to start a fire and fish. He used to cook chicken stew for them and fried fish for breakfast. Then he would disappear for a month and stay another few weekends in a row. Sometimes Nahla would disappear. Kayo wouldn't even see Chopp but she was pretty sure he and Nahla were together. Nahla was happy on those days. Kayo remembered the first time she heard about the city and understood why Nahla hated it so much. Chopp decided to stay in the city to be closer to his children. Instead of moving onto his own homestead, he opened the bike shop. Nahla, Kayo, Orion and Ayrah all had e-bikes on the homestead which they charged on a solar generator. Nahla would occasionally call Chopp to come fix the bikes. The two of them would disappear for a few hours, then Chopp would return and fix the bikes. He'd usually stay for dinner and then leave late in the evening or slip out of the cabin early the next morning.

"How's Nahla?" He took a sip from the flask. "When's the last time you spoke to her or seen her? Is she okay?"

Kayo shook her head and said, "I don't really talk to her like that anymore. Don't you? Are you still seeing her?"

"Eh, you know your auntie. We could never get

too serious. Between the co-op, the farmers market and Marly always finding a way to come between us; your aunt can't settle down. Like water in a river. No shore can contain it, nor man can claim it. She owns my heart but no one owns Nahla's. That spitfire woman won't have it. You're the same way. She's probably a little worse, though. I haven't talked to her in maybe four months."

"So go see her," she said as the lights flickered.

"It's never worked like that, Kay. Nahla calls me and without hesitation I go. She don't call, I don't go. That's how it's always been. I can't seem to shake her. I just keep going back. That's how endless ties work. You should know." He could barely look at Kayo as he spoke about her aunt. She reminded him so much of Nahla it made him uncomfortable. "Anyway, I need a favor and I will trade you the favor for services rendered on your bike," he said with a smirk. He took another sip from the flask.

"What do you need?" she asked curiously. He has never asked Kayo for anything.

"I have about four motorbikes I need to get out of the city. They're obviously gas powered. Nothing you want to get caught with in city limits. I fixed them and I have a buyer who will transfer me the credits upon delivery. Word has it you're heading Up Rural. I can arrange for someone to pick them up from you."

"Can you get them to Solemn Oak by tomorrow or do you need a pick up?" she asked.

"I need a pick up from here."

Kayo thought for a moment and said, "Okay. Baker knows some people who work the delivery tunnels. They owe us a favor. I'll get them picked up by Tuesday night. I'll have to use the pick up truck to get them Up Rural. That's fine. What else?"

Chopp reached into a safe under his desk. Kayo could hear the dials turning. He pulled up an envelope and handed it to her. "Give this to Nahla. Tell her I need a package. Whatever this can get me."

"No, Chopp. I don't get into that anymore. I told you I'm out."

Sarcastically he asked, "Which is why I'm soliciting business from Nahla, not you. Listen, I don't expect you to bring anything back. Just get her the money. Juno can get things back to me. I don't need you to deliver anything more than the cash. I would bring it myself but she hasn't called me for a visit and I don't want to intrude."

Kayo pursed her lips and snatched the package. "Everyone's got something for Nahla. First Marly, now you."

"Marly? Why are you talking to Marly, Kay?"

"I'm not. She sent Juno with a package for me to give to Nahla. And no I don't know what it is. I didn't look. I don't want to be involved in whatever my aunt is doing. I'm only going to settle some business, then I'm coming back. I'm not involved..."

"No ma'am. Once you've touched that envelope, you're on Marly's payroll. You're involved. You lose it and it won't be forgiven. Get that shit to your aunt ASAP! Something is up. I'll try and figure out what's going on."

Kayo snatched the envelope and placed it in her bag. "I'm not worried about Marly."

"You should be. If she can't get at you... You've gotta think of Oree and Ayrah."

Kayo hadn't considered that. "You're right. Thanks, Chopp. 'Til the sun meets sea."

"And the moon leaves the sky," Chopp responded. Kayo left the office and reentered the showroom floor. She grabbed her bike and rolled it out of the store.

Sam and Dennis were escorted into the interrogation room one by one. Since they were sharing a lawyer, they were allowed to be in the same room at the same time. The room was low lit, cold and musty. The two of them sat there and didn't say a word. They were denied bail and family visits weren't allowed due to the nature of the crime. They were considered safety risks to themselves and others. Their hands were cuffed in front of them. A guard stood in the corner of the room with a rifle pressed up against his chest. They waited for the lawyer to arrive. Denny faced the small window and could see it was a cloudy day.

Dennis looked Sam in the eyes. Just when Dennis opened his mouth to speak, Dennis shook his head signaling Sam to wait. There was nothing to be said and now wasn't the time. Everything they say is going to be used to incriminate them, even the smallest thing was questionable. They hadn't had much time to get their stories straight, but there really wasn't much of a lie to tell or a reason to lie.

Suddenly the door swung open with a squealing creak. A thick bodied woman walked in with a black briefcase. She had a pretty round face with a skirt and black blazer. Her hair was straight and black. Her cheeks and nose were rosy from the chilly air outside. She sat down in between the two men on the far side of the table. "Excuse me," she said to the guard. "Lawyer/client privilege. I'm going to ask you to leave now. Thank you." She waved him away with her hand. The guard turned and exited the door. She glared at him until he left and then looked at the two men and smiled.

"Which one of you is Dennis Emerson?" she asked.

Dennis looked up and said, "That would be me."

"So you must be Samuel Lockstone." she said.

Sam looked up and nodded. He was completely lost about what was happening. *Who is she and where did she come from?* Things that had been moving slowly suddenly felt like they were moving too fast. "I'm Sam."

As she spoke, she flipped through her files. "Grrrreat. Okay. So, I know you're probably wondering who I am and where I've come from. I was made aware that you didn't have a lawyer and was assigned your case so here I am." She smiled. "Anyway, I'm Attorney Jessica Humphries, Yale Law blah blah blah. I don't think you care so let's get on with it. As you know, ACPP and ARPA have been given authorization to try these cases. They still have to follow the law, and use judges but they tend to be heavy handed when it comes to charges and sentencing. First, I want you to know that I have read the witness statements. These will include statements from the police who entered your home. There's a statement from a witness to the meat murder..."

"Why are they calling it a murder?" Sam asked. "It was not a murder, the damn thing ran in front of the car!"

"Well, that's good to know and that's why I'm here. I intend to get a formal statement from you both in a moment. But I want to tell you what's at stake and what's on the table before you tell me anything. There is a witness who saw you leave the scene. The cops found animal carcasses and blood in both your residences and in your car, Sam. There's enough suspicion to convict. We need to convince the judge exactly what you are guilty of. Let me read off the charges. We're looking at a felony charge of poaching, a felony charge of animal cruelty, possession of murder paraphernalia, distribution of controlled substances, conspiracy to commit a crime and a litany of misdemeanors..." she said as she pointed at the paper bearing the charges.

"What!?" Dennis yelled. "That is insane!"

"I know. That's how this goes. All of these charges won't stick, but enough will. We have to play this correctly and minimize your sentences as much as possible. Best case, you were in possession of a federally protected animal and didn't report it. Worst case you poached and they will have a field day with the other charges," Attorney Humphries informed them.

"Why are they saying we poached this animal?" Sam asked. "I already told you it ran in front of the car."

"That's a good question, because something isn't right about that. In order to prove poaching, you would either have to admit it, which you haven't or they would have to have a weapon. According to my files, I only have a picture. I've asked to see the actual weapon but prosecution is stalling. I want my expert to review it. The stalling is telling me something is off.

Sam's eyes opened wide. "Wait. A Weapon. Is that the thing they showed me?"

Humphries asked, "What thing?"

"It was like a broken stick with, these feathers, and..."

"A fletching? Was it a fletching, because that's what they said they had?" she asked.

Sam shook his head and said, "I have no idea what that is."

Jessica Humphries dropped the file on the table and took out her phone. She got onto the internet and looked up "FLETCHING IMAGES". The cellular connection was bad, but good enough to pull up an example of an arrow with the fletching intact.

"This is what it is." She reads from the search but skims its purpose, "It goes at the end of an arrow to stabilize the arrow when it's shot. I guess making it spin in the air to maintain accuracy."

Denny said, "Wouldn't we need a bow to shoot that with?"

"Do either of you have one?" she asked.

"NO!" they both said in unison.

"Hmm." Attorney Humphries sat for a moment. She crossed her arms. It was apparent she was thinking. "Is it possible... What time was it when you were driving home?"

"We got off at 7am. Probably hit the road about 7:15ish," Sam remembered. "It was foggy outside."

Humphries slapped her hand on the paperwork in front of her and said, "You guys may be some unlucky bastards."

Denny and Sam looked perplexed. They didn't understand her point. Obviously they were unlucky. Denny was frustrated and said, "We know! We hit the deer and took the meat but..."

"No. I get that. But, I think someone was hunting. The deer ran and you two hit the thing as it ran away. You didn't even have much time to leave work, pull over, hide and hunt, then drag the deer into the car. How bloody was it?" she asked.

With new life and blood flowing through his veins, Sam said, "There was blood everywhere!"

"Which means it probably had a hole in it somewhere especially if it was hit in the heart or the lung. Usually when a deer gets hit by a car the bleeding is internal and would probably just come out of the mouth. Woo! I'm fuckin' good," she said. "There have been so many poaching incidents lately, it would make sense to at least cast doubt on the two of you. But, these judges are very eager to make a fool out of someone and could stick it to you. I need to get a hold of this broken arrow."

Denny sat up straight in his chair. "Wouldn't they still have the meat somewhere? We kept the offals too. We buried the bones. Maybe they have that and..."

"YES!" Humphries said, "I didn't even think. Yes!" She pointed at her head and thought, *he's thinking.* "I'm going to take a formal statement from the two of you. I'll record it on my phone. This evening, I will type it up and draft the statement. I'm going to reach out to someone I know and see if they can help me with this. I'm gonna need to see your car. I don't think the question is whether or not the deer was hunted, it was most likely already dying and you didn't kill it. If we can prove you hit it with your car, maybe there's broken ribs or bones on the carcass, and prove that neither of you have access to a bow, that will help. We can probably do a plea deal with a fine and maybe some time in The Cycles, but I'm going to push for just a fine and environmental service. Let's get this statement started."

Attorney Humphries turned on her phone and started the recording. The men started the story from when they left work and ended the story at the point where the police rushed into their homes.

Humphries listened intently, taking handwritten notes on the side. She wrote down anything she wanted to investigate further and questions she had. She didn't want to interrupt too much so she figured she would ask harder questions after they finished telling their side of the story. She nodded and wrote. She never looked up from the paper to look at the two men in front of her. She let them speak as if she was never in the room.

CHAPTER 5

KAYO & NAHLA BROOKS

Kayo was issued a mandatory leave to work from home for the following week. That following Friday evening around 6:20 pm, Kayo pulled up to the easement that led to the cabin on Nahla's homestead. Arrival at the property made her blood pressure rise and her heart race. She took a deep breath. It was raining and cold. At the entrance was a tree with a carving of four faces in the trunk one on top of the other like a totem. She, Orion and Ayrah made that carving over the course of four summers. Kayo looked at her bracelet with the compass and rubbed it with her thumb. Maybe it's been too long.

For months, Kayo and Nahla had been going back and forth about the twins working for Kayo instead of Marly. They preferred working with Kayo. She and Juno wanted to partner with them and start their own business. Kayo was family. She was fair. Kayo and Juno split everything evenly with them, even their own harvests, whereas Marly split 30/70 with herself taking the larger share. "They'll never get ahead like that," she reminded Nahla. But after India's death, Kayo's drinking spiraled out of control.

One evening, a week after the funeral, Kayo got drunk and furiously stormed into the cabin unloading her frustrations with Marly to Nahla.

Nahla stood by the bookshelf in the living room, wearing her glasses at the tip of her nose. Nahla was a dark, middle aged woman with locs in her hair. The grays were starting to show. Her locs were pulled into a bun at the top of her head with a headband wrapped around her brow. She wore an old cropped tank top showing her muscular shoulders, and stomach. On her left arm she had a dragonfly tattoo. She wore black sweatpant capris which displayed a tribal tattoo from her left foot going up her ankle and a short gold necklace with a compass as a charm. Her nose was pierced on the right side and she also had small gauges like Kayo. It was as if Kayo was staring into a looking glass that made her appear 15 years older.

"You need to tell Marly to back off!" Kayo shouted. She insisted that Nahla rethink allowing the twins to work for Marly, but Nahla wouldn't budge on the issue.

In a mildly dismissive tone Nahla replied, "Kayo, I know you're upset about your friend, but you've been drinking and you need to relax." Nahla pushed her glasses back up to the bridge of her nose. "Kayo, you and Juno don't have land for them to hunt and everything in the co-op is tied to Marly," Nahla warned her. Nahla didn't want Kayo to have that kind of drama with Marly but Kayo didn't care. "They can't cross her. She never plays fair. You're not ready for that kind of smoke, Kay! Slow down."

"You made an agreement with Marly, not me. Neither did the twins! They're unsafe with her. She only thinks about herself. She will throw Oree and Ayrah under the bus to save her own ass in a heartbeat. They're her top runners and best hunters and she disregards them like they're nothing. This family can't be stuck under her thumb forever."

Nahla continued looking at the books and finally pulled one off the shelf. Her disregard for Kayo's words disturbed Kayo.

"Maybe stop taking loans from her and she won't own you!"

Nahla tried to be patient but Kayo agitated her. She removed her glasses, placed them on the shelf, slowly turned around and said, "No one owns Nahla, baby girl. Let's be clear about that. It's only a matter of time before Marly finds a way to shut down whatever operation you think you got going on at the Danby's. She'll fuck you over and the Danby's too. They don't deserve that shit but she will teach all of you a lesson. Damn, I wish I never told you about that place. She's got men that will kill for her, police that will look the other way and judges that will wipe the slate clean like nothing ever happened. You have... what? Juno and a zippy bike? For the record, even though it's not your business, I don't owe Marly anything. I've taken care of that long ago. She did me a favor as a friend. The two of you need to worry about your own debt to Marly and stay out of my finances and business. "

"Our debt is almost done."

"But it's not done is it?"

Kayo's rage began to expand. "I don't get why you're afraid of her. Well, I'm not. I'll never be Marly's bitch," she stated with her chin up— cocky and confident.

Nahla got in Kayo's face and said, "Afraid?" Nahla turned around and giggled. "Bitch? This girl said, 'BITCH!'" Nahla turned fast and slapped Kayo in the face. "Watch your fucking mouth! I'm nobody's bitch!" Kayo flew back and fell against the couch. Her vision was blurry and lip was busted. "You want to take the twins and do what? How are you safer for them than Marly after what happened to India!?" As Kayo pulled herself together, she saw a baseball bat on the floor under the couch. She grabbed it and pounced to her feet. Nahla picked up a staff that was leaning against the bookshelf and whirled it around her body, spinning it and passing it from one hand to the next, daring Kayo to pursue a fight with her. Kayo huffed and foamed at the mouth but she knew better. She tested and woke the dragon that she heard so many stories about.

Nahla was deadly and was not to be physically tried by anyone. Nahla stood ready with the staff pointed at the ground. Her chin was down. Her chest moved up and down with every breath. Not because she was tired, but because she was pumped. She had a devious smirk on her face. She couldn't wait for

Kayo to make another move. Her heart raced and bumped against her chest but then, suddenly, out of nowhere, Nahla snapped out of it. Her body softened up and she dropped the staff on the ground. She looked at her hands, *What have I done?* she thought. "Kayo, I'm..."

Enraged, Kayo threw the bat and broke the window. She took her bag and stormed out of the cabin. She was done with Nahla and swore off hunting.

Kayo didn't know why Nahla never stood up to Marly. She never understood her reluctance to intervene on their behalf or their awkward on again off again friendship. Kayo also didn't know that Nahla had invested her money with Marly to help Kayo pay for college. Even though it wasn't Nahla's preference, Nahla didn't want to discourage Kayo from going to university, so she lied and told Kayo that it was money her parents left for her, but this was false. Two weeks after the argument, Orion was arrested for smuggling 100 pounds of venison into Vermont and spent a year in the Cycles. After that, Kayo and Nahla spoke a few times, but it was never pleasant, awkward and always empty.

Kayo hadn't seen Nahla in about two years. The slow paced drive down the driveway felt like walking the green mile. It was dreadful. Kayo didn't plan to stay, but she had a delivery from Marly to give to Nahla. *Why didn't Marly just give this to her herself?* she thought. Kayo parked in front of the cabin. She grabbed her backpack which had the package in it and threw it over her shoulder as she exited the pick up. *My stomach!* she thought. Her anxiety accumulated as she ascended the steps one step at a time. Regardless of the rain, the porch had a smell that was familiar. She could also smell Nahla was making bear stew. Lightning cracked above her head, pushing the rain into a full on storm. She knocked on the door and placed her hearing aids back into her ears. A few moments later Ayrah opened the door.

Ayrah grabbed Kayo. "I thought you were coming tomorrow!" Ayrah was more fair than Kayo, but also had locs. She was very lean but also fit. She had a runner's body, light brown eyes and freckles.

Kayo hugged her back and said, "No. It made more sense to come tonight. And you need to tell me about this guy you're seeing?"

"It's not that serious," Ayrah replied.

Kayo shook her head, "Well I wanna meet him. Where's Auntie Nah? I need to give her something and get out of here."

"Come in," Ayrah said.

"No. I kinda have to go. Can you get Auntie Nahla for me?"

Ayrah ran back into the house. A moment later Nahla came to the door and walked away. "You gonna leave my door open? Come in."

Kayo huffed and said, "Nahla. I'm not staying. I was asked to give you a package." Nahla didn't respond. She walked away and went back into the kitchen. "Nahla!" No response. Kayo walked further into the house when Orion came down the stairs.

Orion smiled, "Hey yo! Big cuz!"

"Oree! Look at all this hair," Kayo replied. Orion was her heart. She gave him a long hug. "Are you good?" She inspected his face, checking out his beard.

He let go and said, "I'm good. Thank you for sending me money and letters. They helped. I thought you were coming tomorrow."

"Where'd you guys get that rumor from?" Kayo asked.

"Juno. Maybe he said that so we wouldn't expect you. I dunno. He knows me. I'll show up to the cabin and kick in the door like, 'BOOM! Where's my big cousin?' I don't play about you, Kay!"

"Don't listen to Juno. And please don't kick in the door, Juno will kick in your ass!" They laugh. "Can you please get Auntie Nah for me? I have to get outta here," she claimed.

"No you don't, but I'll get her," he promised.

Kayo snuck back over towards the door, even though the smell of the bear stew kept calling her to the kitchen. *Maybe just a peek*, she thought. Thyme, garlic, onion, ginger, chili pepper, green peppers, potatoes, tomatoes... She could distinctly smell every spice permeating the air.

Orion came back into the room. "Dude. Can you please get your aunt?"

"I told her you were here. She's coming," Orion said.

Ayrah bounced cheerfully from the kitchen into

the living room and said, "Nah said 'set the table.'"

Kayo was perplexed and asked, "Who!?"

"You!" Ayrah said. "She said 'Tell Kay to set the table.' We always set the table, Kay," and Ayrah disappeared.

Kayo was frustrated and mumbled, "Oh my God. You guys are playing with me." She rubbed her hand across her face in frustration. She marched into the dining room and whispered to herself, "Where the fuck is Nahla? Why am I setting this stupid table again?" Everything was exactly where she remembered. Kayo put out three place settings. *I am not staying here for dinner.* Kayo put down the napkins, forks and bowls for the stew.

"Put down a trivet for me," Nahla said as she carried a big pot of stew to the table. Nahla seemed to come out of nowhere.

Kayo pulled a trivet from the serving table and placed it in the middle of the dining table. Harboring feelings, she could barely look at Nahla. "You cut your hair," Kayo said.

Nahla placed the heavy pot onto the trivet. She didn't give Kayo eye contact as she put a fourth setting at the table and said, "I did. About two years ago. After you left."

Kayo understood. "You don't need to set the table for me. I'm not staying."

Nahla ignored her, "Oree and Ayrah!" She sat down at the head of the table. Ayrah came in first and sat down. She began opening a bottle of wine.

Kayo stood there and asked, "Nahla, can we talk

for a minute. I have a package to give you, I'm not..."

"Oree! Let's go!" Nahla said.

Orion came into the room and plopped into the chair. He put his cellphone in his pocket.

"Nahla. I have to go." Kayo insisted.

"Sit Kayo. Take that jacket off and sit down." Nahla's face was serious. "I haven't seen you in two years, the least you can do is eat."

Kayo huffed. She took her jacket and hung it on the back of the chair. Orion smirked as Ayrah poured Cabernet for everyone at the table. Orion filled everyone's bowls with the stew. Kayo looked down into her bowl. It was nostalgic. She hadn't had bear stew in years and it was one of her favorites.

"You added boiled dumplings." Kayo's eyes lit up as a partial smile grew on her face. She ate the stew. The flavor exploded in her mouth. It was better than she remembered. So much time had passed between this moment and the last time she ate it; it felt like the first time. One spoonful at a time, Kayo scooped every morsel into her mouth and slowly enjoyed every herb packed into each savory bite. She tried not to be obvious that the food was enjoyable. She was still mad at Nahla and she had business to take care of. "Nahla. I have something to give you. Two things. One from Chopp. The other from Marly."

Nahla asked curiously, "Marly? Why are you talking to Marly?" She kept her eyes on Kayo as she ate her stew.

"I'm not. You know how I feel about her. I assume you're still working with her."

Nahla stopped and stared at Kayo and said, "I'm not. I haven't even... what the fuck is this about?"

"How would I know? She gave Juno something to give me to give to you. I've been trying to be private about the exchange but you haven't let me tell you anything since I got here and I have to leave soon."

"No you don't, Kayo. And, there's no reason to be secretive, so what is it?" Nahla asked as she scooped the last bit of stew from her bowl. She grabbed her glass and took a sip of wine with an expressionless face.

Kayo reached into her bag. "This should be explainable on its own. It's from Chopp. He said, 'Send whatever you can.'" She handed over the envelope. Nahla opened it and flipped through the money. She put the envelope on the table. "This package is from Marly. I have no idea what's in here and don't want to know."

Nahla took the package but was perplexed. Skeptically, she opened the package slowly. Orion and Ayrah watched intently. There was a folded piece of paper and a small box. She opened the box. There was a broken arrow with yellow and white fletchings with black stripes on the two yellow fletchings. Nahla unfolded the paper. It was a news article. "POACHING!" There was a picture of Sam and Dennis in the clipping and this was the main evidence of their case in Nahla's possession.

"Oh Fuck!" Ayrah said.

"What!?" Nahla and Kayo asked in unison.

"So... see, what happened was..." Aryah mumbled.

Nahla stood up from her chair at the table, "Ayrah! What happened?"

Ayrah put her hand on her forehead and closed her eyes.

Kayo joined in on the interrogation and said, "Just fucking say what happened, Ayrah!"

Ayrah looked at Orion for reassurance. It was clear he already knew the story but it wasn't his story to tell. Orion nodded giving her permission to proceed. Ayrah huffed. "There was this buck I had been watching for a week. A beautiful 10 pointer. He had to be about 200 pounds. I finally figured out his habits, so I went hunting. I knew I would see him. As I was walking to the stand he came out of nowhere following a doe. As soon as I had a clear shot, I shot him. Trust me. It was a kill shot but..." She looked at Kayo. Kayo gestured for her to keep talking. "He was too close to the road. I didn't want to miss my chance so I shot it. I followed him but he ran in front of a car. They hit it and those bastards took my deer. When I saw them I hid off to the side and watched until they drove off."

"Why didn't you tell me?" Nahla asked. No answer. Nahla looked at Orion.

"Don't look at me. I told her to tell you. Hiding it didn't make sense. So now what? Why is Marly sending this to you?" Orion asked.

"Blackmail," Kayo said.

Nahla banged her hand on the table and yelled,

"Fuck me!" Nahla grabbed her glass of wine, got up from the table and walked out the door.

Kayo glared at Ayrah and said, "No matter how big or small, you need to tell me these things!"

Orion got up from the table to follow but Kayo shewed him away. Kayo followed Nahla to the porch, gently closing the door behind her. "You can go ahead, Kayo. I won't hold you hostage any longer."

"I'm cool," Kayo said. She stood there with her bag over her shoulder.

Nahla pulled a joint out of her pocket and lit it. She took a long drag and started coughing.

"Slow down." Kayo warned her.

"No matter what I do, I can't shake this woman," Nahla added. She sipped her wine and took another smoke. She passed it to Kayo. "Don't be shy. I know you smoke."

"I've only ever smoked with Juno." Kayo took a hit of the joint, held it in and slowly blew it out. She hit it again and said, "I'm good." She passed it back to Nahla. The rain started to let up.

Nahla put the joint out and put it back into her pocket. She grabbed her wine glass and hung over the railing of the porch. She said, "You look like your mother, but you act like your father." She took another sip.

"And I fight like you," Kayo said. *I should fight you right now!* she thought.

Nahla laughed and said, "No one fights like me, baby girl. Remember that." Nahla looked up to the sky where raindrops were lightly falling. She watched the moonlight illuminate the dark clouds rolling by.

"It's getting cold. You should go inside," Kayo said. "I'm gonna stay at Juno's. He'll be here in the morning."

"Where are you going after that?" Nahla asked.

Kayo shrugged and said, "I'll figure it out." She picked up her bag and flung it over her shoulder.

"You can always stay here, Kay."

Kayo shook her head and said, "That's not gonna happen. We're not there yet. Dinner was good but I've had my fill of this place. I can only tolerate this place in small doses." Kayo descended the steps and said, "Might want to destroy that evidence and have Ayrah switch up her style of fletchings. Anyone that knows her knows those are hers." Kayo turned and walked towards the pick up.

"I only wanted to protect you, Kay," Nahla yelled out.

"Protect me? You fuckin' slapped me and busted my lip. How is that protecting me?"

"You called me a bitch!" Nahla reminded her. "Marly's bitch!"

"I didn't mean it like that, Nahla. I didn't mean you were Marly's bitch. I was saying I wasn't going to be her bitch," Kayo insisted.

Nahla walked down the stairs and said, "But that's how I took it." She looked at her hands and said, "Something about being called a bitch just... ugh... sets me off. I lose it. But you were right. I let Marly get away with too much. Kayo, I left the city because I couldn't control my temper. I was always fighting, involving myself in nightlife drama. The mafia would pay to see me fight or just tell me to fight someone that owed money and I would. Your dad introduced me to Chopp. He was running a boxing club and training calmed me down. Taught me how to actually fight. I got a job, but still would let my temper get the best of me. I met Marly through Chopp and she convinced me to leave the city. So, I came here to find peace and I found it. There's no in between for me. I'm either chilling down here or up there on 100. The city had too much going on. I couldn't hear myself think. Everything was happening all at the same time. The sounds. The smells. So, we started the market and when it was time to choose, I let Marly convince me she should be in charge. She was more level headed than me and good at numbers. Figured, I'll take a back seat and just chill. You know? I didn't come here to make noise. I even convinced everyone else to let her run everything. Now we see how that turned out." Nahla kicked the dirt around her feet and said, "That night, I lost more than just my temper. I was wrong and you were right. I didn't like hearing it. And for the first time in my life, I was afraid. I... I am... afraid."

"I think I understand that now, but that doesn't mean I'm ready for things to go back the way they were and you have to respect that." Kayo stood in the rain. She missed Nahla. She wanted to fight her and hug her immediately after.

Nahla nodded and said, "I know. I'm just happy to see you. I'll take what I can get for now." Kayo began walking away and Nahla yelled out, "Wait a minute!" She ran into the house and came back with a package. "Bear stew for the road."

Kayo smirked as she took the warm tupperware into her hand and said, "Why don't we stop by Marly's tomorrow so we can figure out her angle with this. She needs a visit. I can meet you there. Anyway, I gotta go. 'Til the sun meets the sea." She turned and walked away again.

"And the moon leaves the sky..." Nahla replied. Kayo got into her truck and drove off. Nahla continued to whisper, "Forever shall be, I'm bound to thee, our souls an endless tie."

The words were easier to say than "I love you, eternally."

Nahla closed her eyes and listened to the world around her. The crickets, the locusts, the frogs, water running off the roof down the gutters into the downspout. She let the tiny droplets cool her face and then she walked back into the cabin and closed the door.

Kayo arrived at Juno and her cabin 15 minutes later. She hadn't been there in a couple of years. The back road was muddy with potholes and small ditches full of water left over from the evening rain. She drove down the unpaved bumpy driveway. Juno must have recently covered it in gravel which made it more pleasant and easier on the pick up. She parked off to the side of the house. As she exited the truck, she grabbed her bags out of the back seat and took out her key to the house. It was quiet and dark. When she opened the door, to her amazement the place looked exactly how she remembered it. It even smelled the same, but was a little colder than she wanted it to be on this damp evening. She closed the door behind herself and immediately filled the wood stove with logs and lit a fire.

Once the fire was stable, Kayo texted Juno, "I MADE IT. STAYING IN THE GUEST ROOM." She peaked around in the kitchen, searching to see what food was in the cabinets and placed the stew into the refrigerator. After a quick examination, she went into the guest room with her things. It had just enough room for a full sized bed, a dresser and a wardrobe closet. There was also a small chair in the corner where she rested her backpack. She put the other bag on the floor and sat on the bed.

She scanned through her text messages and sent Monty and Beth a short text letting them know she had arrived and all was well. She saw that Patterson had texted her. She smiled and texted back, "I MADE IT. THINKING OF YOU. WANT TO SEE YOU WHEN I GET BACK."

Patterson replied, "COME BACK TO ME SOON."

Kayo looked at her watch. She decided to take a bath and started the water. Her bare feet pressed against the cold, smooth, black and white hexagon shaped tiles. She stepped into an old white cast iron tub that she and Juno salvaged from an abandoned home prior to demo and repainted. The water was hot. The steam filled up the room as she sat with her back to the edge of the tub. She completely submerged into the water for a few seconds and came up for air. *Breathe.* Her anxiety about talking to Nahla had mostly vanished. Even though Nahla violated her, she wasn't as angry as she thought she would be. She imagined a screaming match would ensue or that they'd get into a scuffle, but the encounter was unexpectedly refreshing.

As she relaxed in the tub, all she could think about was how healthy Nahla looked. She smiled, happy to have seen her childhood guardian doing well. *I let too much time pass*, she thought to herself. She loved that Nahla was taking care of the twins, and they also seemed healthy and happy. The homestead looked okay from what she could see, but she promised herself she would get back over there in the daytime and check it out again. As the water began to cool, Kayo knew it was time to get out and get to bed. She drained the water and got out of the tub.

By 9:15 Kayo was nestling herself under the covers in the unfamiliar bed. Though she had stayed in the cabin many nights, she never got acquainted with the guest room. The bed was stiff but the blankets were soft and clean. *It will do.* There was something off about staying in that room, but being that she and Juno were no longer together, it made sense that she didn't stay in the master. It was his space now. His domain. Soon enough, she would never have to come back here again.

The cabin hadn't quite warmed up, so she took an extra quilt from the closet and threw it over the bed before getting back in. A dim lamp lit the room. She opened a book called The Way of the Wild One. *This will be banned soon.* She was somewhere in the beginning. She turned to her last place in the book and read, "His eyes opened to see bloodthirsty fangs dripping of drool and flesh standing over his body." Suddenly a beam of light shone through the window and moved across the wall. She could hear tires pressing against wet gravel squishing them down into the mud. "You gotta be kidding me!" Kayo threw the book aside and jumped out of the bed. As she opened the guest room door, Juno came into the front door, wet with a bag thrown over his shoulder. Kayo folded her arms and leaned against the frame of the door. "I thought you were coming in the morning."

"I changed my mind," he said and closed the door.

Kayo was frustrated. "I don't really want to stay here with you. It's not appropriate."

Juno ignored her demeanor and threw his bag in the room. "What's not appropriate about it, Kayo? You're staying there. I'm staying here. There is a wall between us. You'll survive." He took off his wet jacket and hung it on the coat rack. He was dismissive of her and barely gave her eye contact.

"I know I will, but it's not me I'm worried about. You're always on the bullshit with me and I've had enough drama for the day," she continued.

"I barely even said anything to you."

Kayo agreed. "I just want to get ahead of your shenanigans. I'm not having it tonight."

"Then don't have it, Kayo. If me being here is that big of an issue, I can sleep in the car tonight." Juno grabbed the afghan blanket off the side of the couch and grabbed his keys. "You're fucking tripping for no reason."

As Juno headed for the door. Kayo asked, "Wait! Juno, did you..." Kayo wasn't used to Juno being anywhere near her without starting a fight. This time she realized she was the one starting one. She closed her eyes and took a deep breath.

"What, Kayo!?" Juno asked. "Did I do what?"

Kayo relaxed her posture. She couldn't get a rise out of Juno. It just wasn't working and she'd had enough of the drama between them. "Did you eat? Nahla made some bear stew. It's in the fridge." Kayo said.

Juno was surprised. He responded, "You already went by Nahla's?"

"As soon as I got here."

He walked over to the refrigerator and pulled out the foreign plastic container. "Figured you'd go in the morning." He unwrapped the package of stew and put it into the microwave and closed the door.

"I wanted that shit outta my hands as quickly as possible." She swiftly walked over to him, moved him out of the way and took the bear stew out of the microwave. She pulled a pot out of the cabinet and placed it on the stove. "There are some things that are too sacred for radiation waves. Wash your hands." She turned on the propane stove. Juno washed and dried his hands at the kitchen faucet and dried his hands with the towel that hung over the edge of the sink. Kayo turned and said to Juno, "Set the table."

Without hesitation, Juno grabbed a mat and placed a bowl, a spoon and napkin on top. He poured himself and Kayo a glass of wine and sat down. Kayo inspected the flames under the pot. When satisfied, she poured the stew from the plastic container into the pot. Kayo remembered where everything was. She grabbed a spoon from the drawer and slowly stirred the stew as it heated up. Juno passed Kayo the warm glass of wine. She took a sip and then asked, "Do you know what was in the package?" She took another sip.

"No. I have no idea what it was." Juno responded.

"It was one of Ayrah's fletchings. She shot a deer, it ran in front of a car and some guys got bagged for it."

"Ok. I saw something about that in my news feed. Didn't know that was her," Juno said.

"Marly could have just given it to Nahla herself," Kayo added. "Or you could have given it to her."

"She insisted I bring it to you."

"Why?" Kayo asked.

He shrugged his shoulders and said, "I don't

know." He changed the subject. "It's cold in this house. The stove needs more wood. Give me a minute." Juno walked outside and came back with a pile of wood in his arms. He walked back out and grabbed another.

Kayo stood there for a bit, watching him go in and out of the door. She stirred the pot again just as it began to heat up. "If you heard about it, then why didn't you tell me?" she asked, but Juno was distracted with sudden tasks that needed to be done.

Juno took off his crewneck, since it was now covered in wood chips and threw it in the room. He wore a white tank top underneath. He rinsed his hands off again in the kitchen. "I didn't think it had anything to do with us. As far as the delivery goes, people ask me to transport things all the time. I don't look. I just deliver. I wasn't sure what was in the box. Also, when I saw you I wasn't sober. You pissed me off and you had a lot going on that night. I honestly thought you would open it and call me, but you didn't call."

"You asked me not to open it," she said as she stirred the now simmering stew.

"When did you start listening to me?" Juno shrugged and sat back down at the table.

Kayo said, "I always listen to you. I *don't* always do what you say." She stirred more and said, "This is warm enough." She carefully used a ladle and scooped the stew into the bowl making sure it didn't splash onto Juno. As she reached over him, Juno eyed her body. He was eye level with her navel that showed between her shirt and shorts. Mesmerized, he watched her every move.

When she was done, she turned around to wash the pot. He stood up and grabbed her wrist and insisted, "I got it." Juno was now directly behind Kayo and his scent started to grab her attention. She could hear him breathing. She looked at his hand but didn't pull it away. Juno stepped closer. His body was completely pressed against hers. He said in a softer voice, "I'll take care of it after I finish eating." He reached beyond her and turned off the water.

Kayo turned around to face him. She looked him in the eyes and said, "We're not fighting."

"No, we aren't," Juno said. "You said you were tired of fighting and I don't want to fight anymore."

"I don't want to, but I need to. I need to be at odds with you, Juno."

Juno gently rubbed one of Kayo's stray locs between his fingers tips. "Why?" he asked her. "Why do we always have to be at odds? Why do we have to be so dysfunctional? I don't like it. I don't like that we do this to each other."

"I don't either but..." Kayo pressed her head and left hand against his chest. She took in the essence of his presence. He was strong, his body was solid and warm. She continued, "You were right, Juno. As much as I hate to say it, I *do* love you. An endless tie can never be broken. But it can be managed. I have to manage it." She looked at him again and said, "*We* have to manage it."

"Why, Kayo?" Juno asked. "Why can't it just be?"

"Because you remind me of everything I left behind, everything I lost and everything I no longer want to be. I can't live this life anymore."

"And being with Patterson is going to do what? It's who you are, Kayo. You cannot run from something deep inside of you," Juno said.

"I don't want to run. I want to bury it, forget and move on. Staying away from you is best and when you're around, fighting with you makes that easier. So please say something sarcastic or negative to me so I can have a good reason to be angry with you and shut my room door for the night." She looked at him again and said, "Because if I don't fight with you, I'm going to kiss you and then, I'm going to sleep with you and I don't want to do that."

"But I do." Juno gently grabbed her by the side of her head and said, "I want you, Kay. I'm not going to fight with you tonight. I don't want to fight ever again."

"Not even just a little bit?" she begged as her hand navigated to his waist.

"No, not tonight," he said as he pulled her face closer to his.

Juno and Kayo passionately kissed. Kayo suddenly felt enveloped in a whirlwind of recollections of their past. Their first kiss in the woods, memories from the Danby's Cabin and their first few nights on their own homestead flooded into her mind. She remembered being happy and fulfilled. She had no doubts in her mind that Juno was hers and she was his— at least for the night. She pulled him closer to her, and held him tightly. He gently pressed her back against the refrigerator as his hands navigated from her back, to her sides and up to her breasts. They continued to kiss when a tear fell down Kayo's face. Juno pulled away when he felt the teardrop run down over his cheek. Juno smiled and kissed her on the side of her head. They embraced one another for a few moments.

"Why did that feel like a goodbye?" Juno asked. Kayo didn't respond. "Is this when you tell me you have to go?" Juno asked.

Kayo nodded with her head pinned against his chest. "I have to." She pressed her hand against his chest again and pushed herself away from him. She quickly swiped her glass of wine from the counter, walked to her room and stood in the doorway. She said, "The door will be locked." She smiled and said, "'Til the sun..." and closed the door behind herself. She locked it.

"And the moon..." Juno said. "I'm locking my door too by the way!" he yelled. "Just in case you get any ideas!" He laughed.

"Get over yourself!" Kayo yelled. "Good night."

Juno went back to the table to finish the bear stew.

Kayo slid back under the covers. The bed was no longer warm. She laid on her back and covered her face with her right forearm. She then put her hands over her face and grunted. She thought about Juno's criticisms from the other night. *How dare he say I sabotage? I'm not the sabotager. He is,* Kayo thought to herself. She noticed how Juno always found himself around whenever Kayo had another love interest. He would ring her phone incessantly whenever she was on a date or randomly show up for some kind of emergency. *This is why I don't do boyfriends, because I can't!* Juno kept his car in her storage facility and would always beg for another week to retrieve it. Those weeks turned into months and months into a year. Now he shows up being "nice". *Please!*

Kayo couldn't figure out if Juno really wanted her back or if he wanted her miserable. *He's the one that ruined us,* she thought to herself. Kayo and Juno never actually gave each other a title, but everyone knew they were a thing. Kayo's blow out with Nahla pushed her to move to the city where she found a job working at the DCWS. Kayo felt that the move was necessary but also knew that her relationship with Juno would never make it, therefore she pushed Juno away and it was inevitable that he would move on. Juno started seeing Christa, but never lost his love for Kayo. They kept in touch for business purposes at first but then things reignited between them while Christa was still in the picture. Kayo hadn't expected much from Juno, but the pregnancy complicated what was supposed to be a simple love affair. When she found out she was pregnant, initially she wasn't excited about it, but Juno was. He decided he would leave Christa, but on the day he went to tell Christa, he found out that Christa had also been pregnant. He told Kayo, which was devastating, but to add insult to injury, Kayo lost their baby a week later. She couldn't do it anymore and didn't want Juno to miss out on being a father.

Kayo laid in the bed rummaging through her thoughts about Juno. It was all a jumbled confusing mess of emotions and stress. One thing she knew for certain was that her heart had always been with Juno and always would be.

CHAPTER 6

The next morning, at 4:00 am Kayo's alarm went off. She took her earplugs out and turned it off quickly so Juno could sleep. As quietly as possible, she got dressed, washed up in the bathroom and was quickly out of the door by 4:15am with a sidearm and her compact hydration pack strapped to her back. She hit the unpaved road and started jogging. It was dark out so she turned on her headlamp and kept running. It had been a while since she ran on uneven grounds but she didn't mind the challenge. She barely slept the night before and had a lot on her mind. Juno will be the ruin of me, she thought. Then she thought about Patterson and smiled. Her feet tapped firmly against the rubble as she steadily disappeared into the dark.

Between the tall trees and shrub lined road, Kayo's thin body carved through the darkness. She was unafraid as the quiet night opened its mouth and swallowed her with every step. She welcomed it. The quiet was so loud. She could hear the chipmunks scurry across the forest floor, the raccoons digging in the dirt, the crickets chirping to their mates and the owls interrogating each passerby. The twilight unveiled layered gradients of bubbly cloud bodies, one drifting above the other, moving at different speeds, while the moon reigned supreme as ruler of the early morning sky.

Thirty minutes in, the darkness had not let up nor did the cool air that brought numbness to Kayo's toes and fingertips. She exhaled a ghostly breath that stretched 4 feet behind her before disappearing. It would reappear with every expiration of air. This feeling was familiar. She was unaffected and focused. One foot in front of the other, Kayo made her way. She had no plans to turn around and no plans to stop. She pushed on through the pain of nerves firing in her thighs and stiffness of her joints. She looked at her watch. 43 degrees. 4:54am.

Kayo continued the light jog until she approached the totem tree which was the marker to Nahla's land. She ran down the driveway splashing through small puddles of mud left over from the previous evening rain. The cabin was in the distance but instead she took a left over to a barn-like structure about 50 yards from the house. As she approached she slowed down. She walked up to the door and waved her compass bracelet past a keypad on the door. A small red light turned green. Click. The door unlocked. Kayo opened the door and walked in. She shut the door behind herself and the lights came on one row at a time.

Kayo hadn't been to Nahla's gym in a few years but it looked and smelled the same. To the left Nahla had heavy bags, punching bags and kicking pads.

To the right there were weights, a smith machine, an elliptical machine, a bike and a treadmill. In the back half of the gym were grappling mats and the wall was covered with staffs, bows and spears. Kayo dropped her backpack and walked up to the mat. She took off her shoes, walked onto the mat and grabbed a staff off the wall. *Let's try this again*, she thought. Kayo started to slowly spin the staff and gradually increased the speed. She spun the staff around and around, tossed it in the air, caught it behind her back and whipped it around her body. She switched from one hand to the next, around her head and neck when she heard a noise and dropped it. It bounced on the floor and rolled.

"Rusty," Nahla said. Nahla emerged from a back room. She patted her neck with a towel and stepped up onto the mat. She grabbed a staff and started twirling. "Don't look at it. You're in charge. Not the staff." She spun the staff around her body and switched from hand to hand keeping her eyes on Kayo. She suddenly stopped with the staff pointing at the staff Kayo had just dropped. "Try again."

Kayo picked up the staff. "What are you doing here?" She popped her earplugs back into her ears.

"Meditating as I do every morning. Nothing new. Did you not expect me to be here? What are you doing here?"

Kayo shrugged and said, "I have to settle my business with Juno. You know this."

Nahla walked in a circle around Kayo as if she was stalking prey. "No, Kayo. Why are you here?"

Nahla spun her finger around pointing at the gym.

Kayo hesitated before answering. "I don't know," Kayo said as she watched her aunt circle. She gripped her staff firmly. Her heart was pounding.

"No? Hmm. I think you do." Nahla slowly paced around Kayo.

"I'm just here to train, and then I will settle business with Juno." Kayo insisted, but her eyes did not match the explanation of her intent.

"Your breathing has changed, Kay. Your veins are bulging in your neck. There's something deep in your eyes that concerns me. Is there something you want to say? Anything you want to do?"

Kayo's eyes were red. "I told you, I have business."

"It seems that business is with me." Nahla stepped back and gave the staff a quick spin.

Kayo slipped the staff into the other hand and spun it around. She clenched her fist as she began to fill from head to toe with rage. Her chest rose up and down as she inhaled and exhaled.

Nahla smiled and said, "There she is. There's the one that's been looking for me." Nahla started taking slow side steps around Kayo and said, "Do what you came to do!"

Without hesitation Kayo whipped the staff towards Nahla. Nahla used her staff to block it and they fought. Both spinning and blocking strikes from the staff. Nahla paced herself, while Kayo fought hard and fast. Kayo lunged at Nahla and Nahla gracefully stepped aside. Kayo rolled into a somersault and landed on her feet. Kayo charged back at Nahla again, full force spinning the staff and throwing strikes with the staff until she was close enough. She caught Nahla off guard and punched her in the face. Nahla blocked the next one and the next one, but Kayo hit her two more times in the face. In return, Nahla punched Kayo in the face then the ribs and Kayo fell back, dropping to one knee. She grunted from the pain of the blow. The staff hit the ground and rolled out of reach. The pain was intense. She had to catch her breath.

Click, click! The door opened and the twins entered the gym for their morning workout, but were stunned by the altercation taking place before their eyes. Orion went to stop it and Ayrah grabbed his arm and shook her head, "No." The twins stood back. Kayo stood up. Kayo pulled her hoodie off and threw it aside. The two panting figures stood in front of one another for a moment.

Noticing that the staff was no longer in the game Nahla tossed hers to the side and closed in on Kayo. "I don't need your mercy, Nahla.

Nahla shrugged, walked back over to the staff and picked it up. Kayo put her fists up, but it was clear to Nahla that the pain in Kayo's ribs was preventing her from advancing. Nahla began to spin the staff again, just as she tossed the staff in the air to catch it again, Kayo charged and tackled Nahla to the ground. Nahla's back smashed against the mat. The two fought, rolling around on the ground, flipping and striking one another. Blow for blow, the two women brawled. Nahla surprised Kayo with a few punches to the jaw. They rolled again. Kayo ended up on top of Nahla. Nahla wrapped her legs around Kayo's waist and used her legs to control Kayo's distance. Kayo punched Nahla repeatedly. Nahla blocked most of her punches but a few landed. Nahla trapped Kayo's arm and rolled her over. She now had her opportunity and landed a few more punches.

Kayo saw the staff a few feet away. She reached for it. It was at the tip of her fingers but Nahla pushed it away.

Orion was scared and told Ayrah, "That's enough!"

Ayrah pulled him back and said, "They will fight again if you break it up. They're not fighting each other. They're fighting themselves."

"They're going to kill each other." Orion insisted.

Ayrah shrugged, "Then they'll learn a lesson won't they."

At that moment, Orion realized how much Ayrah had become like Kayo.

The two women rolled on the floor. Nahla's age began to catch up with her. She was getting tired faster than Kayo and with every blow, her stamina waned. Kayo rolled Nahla onto her back. Nahla wrapped her legs around Kayo's waist even tighter than the first time. But this time, Kayo was able to get the staff. She pressed the staff into Nahla's neck and growled. Nahla pushed the staff away from her neck as much as she could but Kayo was too strong.

"Enough!" Orion approached the mat. "That's enough Kayo!" But to Kayo, Orion sounded like a muffled duck quacking on the far side of the pond.

Quickly Nahla was able to push the staff off her neck and over her head. To close the distance, she took her left arm, reached up over Kayo's head and pulled it to her chest, trapping Kayo on top of her. As Nahla did that, she reached for her ankle, pulled out a knife and poked it into Kayo's neck.

Kayo immediately froze.

Nahla asked, "Are you done? Or should I finish this right now?" Nahla meant it. Kayo stopped fighting. They were both breathing hard.

"I asked, 'Are you done?'"

"Get the fuck off me!" Kayo attempted to pull herself away.

"Auntie Nahla!" Ayrah said. "Let her go!"

Nahla held Kayo for a few more seconds then finally let go. She pushed Kayo back and rolled over her shoulder and got up onto her feet to quickly make space between them.

Nahla was visibly tired and out of breath. Kayo crawled and pulled herself up onto her feet. "Where'd you think this would go, Kay? We fight. Someone wins. Someone loses and then what? Revenge? Round two? Three?"

Kayo walked away to catch her breath. She put her arms up on her head and turned her back to Nahla.

"How many times do we need to fight for you to

let it go?" Nahla asked.

"I'm good!" Kayo said as she paced the mats.

"How many times? I need to know, because I'm getting old and I don't have time for this bullshit. I don't want this kind of energy around me where I feel like I have to watch my back from you. You want me dead?" Nahla walked over to the back room and pulled out a gun. She brought it back with her and loaded it.

Orion ran up to her, "She gets it Nahla. Chill out. Please, auntie." She walked over to Kayo. Kayo straightened up.

"MOVE!" Nahla said to Orion as she held onto the gun.

Ayrah kicked off her shoes and got onto the mat and stood between them. "Auntie. That's enough."

Nahla pulled the slide back and racked the bullet into the chamber. "The gun's not for me. It's for you, Kayo." Nahla gripped the gun by the barrel and handed it to Kayo. Kayo swiftly grabbed it and pointed it at Nahla.

Nahla stood firm with the gun pointed directly at her face and said, "I raised you three the best I could. I was young, I was not ready for children, but I've done my job. I have made plenty of mistakes but I'm at peace. I'm sorry I hit you. I'm sorry for what I said about India. That wasn't your fault, but I'm not carrying any of that as a burden anymore."

"Don't say her name," Kayo instructed.

"Fine. So, do what you came to do or fuckin' drop it, Kay! Because if you're going to come back again to fight me, I'm gonna end it the easy way. There won't be another fight," Nahla promised.

With the gun still pointing at Nahla, Kayo hit the magazine release, dropped the magazine, racked the slide and removed the bullet from the chamber. She threw the gun across the room. She then marched over to her bag and snatched it off the ground. She then saw her hoodie and grabbed that and wrapped it around her waist. "If I wanted you dead, I would have done it last night!"

"So are you content with the outcome?"

Kayo got in Nahla's face. Nahla didn't flinch. "You think I care that I lost?" Kayo smirked, "I don't. I know you can kick my ass and I can live with that. I don't care. But since you asked why I'm here, I'm here because you need to know that you'll never get a free hit off me ever again. You do that shit again, I'm getting something too."

"Fair enough. Are you satisfied? Are you done!?"

"Yes! I said, 'I'm good!' I'm done! Let that black eye on your face remind you what I said."

"Great. Now get the fuck out of my face!"

Kayo stood there for a second, but knew not to test Nahla for another moment. Kayo swiftly turned around and charged towards the exit. Before exiting she asked, "Marly's at 11?"

"I'll be there," Nahla said.

"Put something on that eye while you're at it."

"And you take care of that lip," she said as she smirked as if she was proud of Kayo's performance.

Kayo marched out of the door and Orion

followed.

Ayrah looked at Nahla and said, "Auntie you're getting slow."

"Oh my God I almost died." They both laughed. "Grab me that towel please. My back hurts."

"Oh hell no. You wanna be young. You go get it."

"You little shit!"

Ayrah laughed as she grabbed the towel off the floor. She threw it at Nahla and hit her in the face. "No more fights." Ayrah inspected Nahla's face and said, "Yikes! She got you a few good times too, Nah. Look at your face. You have a black eye, auntie."

"Well, if I knew she just wanted to give me a black eye, I would've let her punch me and be done with it. I deserved it."

"She needed to fight for it," Ayrah said. "She'd have it no other way. Neither would you. I hope you're both done with this. We should be fighting for you, not with you. And the drama between you two just makes everything weird. Oree and I don't like it."

"I don't either."

Ayrah grabbed her aunt's face and lifted up her left eyebrow with her thumb. "Both of you let your ego get in the way. Both of you. Kayo doesn't want this life anymore and you and Juno have to accept that. Besides her not being over what happened to India, which she blames herself for, the two of you remind her of dysfunction. She loves you both but you both disappointed her. Her, Juno... you and Chopp... You both have toxic relationships. She's trying to separate herself and be different because she doesn't want to be like you."

"I don't want her to be like me."

"Seems you do. But if not, you need to tell her that because she doesn't know. You only show her that you're proud of her when she acts like you. You smiled after the fight. Kinda psychotic! You praised her more for successful hunts more than you praised her for getting a degree. Did you know Kayo owns buildings on the edge of the city worth over a million dollars."

"Of course I know, Ayrah. I know everything about her. I remember when she bought the place. She took over the loan from the previous owner. I remember," Nahla said.

"She paid it off a few months ago," Aryah added.

"She also had money from her parents' death," Nahla added.

"True, that helped but she also made her own money running product to the city and... working for Marly on the side. I know you didn't know but, she made it so she doesn't even have to hunt anymore. After everything that happened, she never wanted back in those woods again."

"She tells you all this? What was she doing for Marly?"

Ayrah replied, "I'd rather let her tell you. I know you don't realize but we talk almost every day. I'm learning a lot."

Kayo stomped away from the gym. Orion grabbed her arm and said, "Come on, Kay. Wait up." Kayo stopped walking and turned towards Orion.

"I'm good, Oree," Kayo said, as she was starting to get the rhythm of her breathing back under control. *Breathe.* She kept walking.

Orion followed. "This needs to be done."

"It's done!"

"Are you sure, Kay?"

Kayo stopped and looked at Orion. "Orion, It's over with. Doesn't mean I'm not going to be frustrated afterwards. I just need to cool off."

Orion said, "Fair." He kept walking. "You almost got her!"

"I know!" They laughed. "I haven't trained seriously in so long."

"Yeah your timing is off."

Kayo looked at him with a mean face.

"It is! To be honest, I couldn't even keep up with who was who at one point. It's like you're the same person. It's crazy."

"I'll never be Nahla." Kayo hated being compared to her.

"Why do you hate her so much?"

"I don't hate her, Oree. I hate this life. I hate it for you and Ayrah. I don't want this for you two. The old days are no more."

"Sounds like your job is changing you, big cuz," Orion said.

"It's not the job it's her. It was all good until Marly became fucking Don of the meat mafia. She had me in a mess! She got you locked up. She ruined everything. If we didn't owe her money, I would have never pursued that bear with... I don't want anything to do with Marly and Nahla never stands up to Marly when it comes to you two."

Orion said, "Well, they barely speak. I don't think I've seen them acknowledge each other when in the same space. Anyway, things were good when we were doing our own thing."

"Doing our own thing isn't safe anymore."

Kayo convinced Oree to use his e-bike to go back to Juno's cabin. As she started the bike, she looked up and saw a raven sitting on a branch. She squinted and it flew off. She drove away.

It was still dark outside when Kayo arrived back at Juno's. She pulled up and placed the bike on the side of her truck and parked it there. As she got closer to the front door she could smell that Juno was cooking. She opened the door and there he was standing in the kitchen over sizzling bacon and eggs. He looked at Kayo and could tell she had been fighting. He laughed and shook his head.

"Shut up!" she said as she marched through the living room into the guest room. She slammed the door shut. A few moments later she chaotically went into the bathroom with a bag and slammed that door behind her as well.

Kayo took a quick shower and threw on a pair

of sweats and a t-shirt. She tossed all of her belongings into the bag and threw it back into the guestroom. She walked over to Juno and watched him pour batter into the waffle maker. He had already set the table and he had black tea waiting for her. She took a seat.

"I only have local honey. No sweetener."

"That's fine. Thank you."

When the second waffle was ready, he put it on a plate for Kayo and placed it in front of her with a few eggs and two pieces of bacon. He placed his plate down and sat down. Maple syrup and butter was already waiting for them both at the table. Juno looked at her and tried not to laugh. He started to eat. The room was awkwardly silent. Kayo tossed around the eggs with her fork. The silence was exasperating.

Juno broke the silence and said, "You need to eat Kayo."

"I am. I'm getting there," she insisted.

Juno took a few bites and curiously looked at her face.

Kayo caught him looking with a smirk on his face. She said, "Go ahead!" She took a sip of her tea.

"Go ahead what?" he asked. He blew on his coffee and smiled.

She smiled and said, "You're so fuckin' annoying I swear to God. Go ahead and ask."

Juno pretended to be choking a bit on his food, "Ask what? I'm minding my business for a change."

Kayo nodded, smiled and took a big chunk of the waffle and shoved it in her mouth. "Stop looking at me and ask!" she insisted. She picked up a piece of bacon and bit off half of it and laughed.

"Did you win?" Juno asked as he smiled.

"Nope!"

They both laughed.

"But, but... BUT she has a black eye and that's what she gets and I'm good with that."

Juno raised his glass and said, "Well cheers to a black eye!"

They tapped their mugs and smiled.

"How do you feel?"

"The same. Not sure it was even worth it."

Juno pointed his fork at Kayo and said, "It's always worth it, Kay. But now we move on from it."

Kayo nodded her head in agreement.

"I can't even lie, there's something about you after you fight. I just..."

"You just what?" she said with a smile.

"You better stay away from me," he joked.

It was still early and the sun hadn't risen, but the eastern parts of the sky started to turn blue. They continued to eat when Kayo's phone buzzed. She quickly looked and it was Patterson. She quickly tucked the phone away. Juno noticed, but didn't say anything about it. "I'm coming with you to see Marly." Juno said as he sparked a joint.

"No, Juno. I don't want you involved in this. I need to see where she's going with this, then I can figure out how to proceed." She took the joint from him and smoked it. She blew the smoke out away from the table.

"I need her to know that I'm on your side. Not hers. I told you, your business affects my business because it *is* my business." He took the joint back and smoked it again. He held the smoke in longer than before.

Kayo smiled at him and grabbed his hand. She said, "I appreciate that." Kayo's phone buzzed again. She looked quickly and put the phone away. She leaned into him and pulled the smoke from his mouth as he blew it out.

Juno stood up and grabbed his plate to clear the table. "Give him a call, Kay."

"Don't do that, Juno."

He insisted, "No no. Go Ahead. I'll clean up."

Kayo stood up and blew out the smoke. "Nope! You cooked. I got it." She took the plate from his hands and placed it into the sink. "Go shower. I'll clean up."

"Okay. Are you gonna wait for me?"

"Right there on that couch." She pointed and folded her arms.

By the time Juno emerged from the bathroom dressed, Kayo was sleeping on the couch. She was exhausted from the fight. Her body was sore and throbbing in a variety of places. Juno grabbed the afghan from the back of the couch to cover her. As he covered her she grabbed his arm and pulled him down to lay with her. He slid his body under hers and pulled the blanket over both of them. She tucked her forehead under his chin and laid her head on his chest. *Mine,* she thought to herself as if Juno was a toy she kept on a shelf, only to be played with when someone else showed interest. It was selfish but it was somewhat true.

Juno gently rubbed her back. She fell in and out of sleep as she fought every urge to touch other parts of his body. "Jesus, you smell so good," she whispered. *Oh my God. I just said that outloud,* she thought.

"Don't tease me, Kay. I'm vulnerable."

She giggled and whispered, "Me too. But, can you just lay with me? If it's too much, I understand."

"I'll behave," Juno promised.

Juno continued to gently massage her back until Kayo fell asleep with her head against his chest. Juno laid underneath her, comforting her as she slipped away into a deep sleep. When he felt that she was completely under, Juno then felt comfortable enough to give into his own tiredness and fell asleep soon after. Their breathing was in sync. Their hearts rhythmically in tune. Their bodies melted into one.

If ever there was love, truly meant to be, one would understand why God, in His jealous nature, rarely permits such a union to exist beyond the realms of unreachable fantasy or the haunting shadows of imagination. Rest assured, at every attempt to achieve it, or in any endeavor to find romance anew, lovers encounter nothing but a lifetime of turmoil. Their paths are painted with obstacles, missed opportunities, and disappointment, forever destined to return to one another in an infinite cycle of torturous hellos and goodbyes.

There will always be an insatiable longing to reconnect, spawning unresolved conflicts that yield, at best, more suffering, resentment, and envy. In this world, whether above or below, in this life or any other, no feeling of love is felt more profoundly than that which is not allowed to peacefully exist.

◆ ◆ ◆

At 11:00 am, Kayo's truck arrived at Marly's butcher shop just in time for the meeting. Juno jumped out of the driver's side and slammed the door shut. Kayo followed from the passenger side. The air was crisp. Wispy clouds flowed above and the sun beamed from beyond their feathery white legs. A flock of ravens flew by overhead and disappeared beyond the hemlocks. Nahla drove her truck. Ayrah and Orion were already present, sitting on bikes waiting for Kayo's appearance. Oree borrowed Nahla's. "Let me talk," Nahla instructed. She made the first few steps into the barn door entrance. Kayo and Juno followed behind her and the twins behind them.

The butcher shop was on Marly's main property, which was the same property that her residential cabin sat on, but it was farther into the property, away from the road. Anyone trying to approach would be seen with enough time to react. The wooden structure used to be a shed, but over time, Marly upgraded it to a grade A food processing center with six part time butchers and four guards. Marly's office was in the loft. There was a large glass window where she could oversee operations, but butchering took place in a hidden underground processing center. Above ground, they processed local pasture raised chicken. Below, Marly processed bear, deer and game birds, packaged and froze them for black market resale.

Nahla was first to begin the ascension of the metal staircase. She knocked on the door. One of Marly's bodyguards opened it. Marly maintained a straight face from behind her desk and waved her hand for them to enter. Patricia Marly had her hair pulled back half into a messy bun with the rest flowing down her back. Long strands of dark brown hair with gray strands dangled over her stark blue eyes. She was a medium build olive colored woman with a button nose and freckles, about five foot six inches tall. She had on bright red lipstick to match her nails.

The guard let Juno and Kayo enter but made Orion and Ayrah wait on the landing outside before eventually making them go back down to the main level. Marly signed some papers and slid them into an envelope. She passed the papers to one of her workers. "Jensen, bring this to Femi Odemwingie.

He will meet you in North Adams at City Hall. I need it there no later than 3 so he can update the records for the purchase." Her voice was accompanied by a subtle accent.

Jensen gave Nahla a firm look, nodded and left the room. The guard closed the door. "Nahla. Old friend. I haven't seen you in a bit. Good to see you."

Nahla pursed her lips and nodded, "Marly. What do you want?" She folded her arms.

"I figured that package would get you here. Why did you bring the whole squad, looking like the PowerRangers reassembled for a reunion tour?" Marly hadn't quite given Nahla full eye contact as she spoke.

"Whatever concerns me, concerns them. Whatever you have to say, they need to know as well. We don't have secrets, Marly, so get to it." Nahla asked sternly.

"No secrets? Come on now, Nahla, you know better than that. This work thrives off of secrets. That's why you're here isn't it? I know something that you would probably prefer remains a secret. We have nothing *but* secrets. They keep people like you honest. It's power. People will kill to keep secrets locked away, and I like to keep them until I need them." She walks over to Nahla and whispers in her ear, "We have a few secrets of our own don't we, Nahla?" She winked as she rubbed the compass pendant around Nahla's neck between her fingers. "It's been a while."

Nahla yanked her head away from Marly,

grabbed her wrist and threw her hand away. "Get away from me, Marly. Don't touch me." Nahla was furious and mildly embarrassed. "I'm not here to play games with you."

At that moment Kayo understood what Chopp meant when he said that Marly came in between them. She should have picked up on it sooner, but it was never anything she would have recognized in her youth.

Marly surrendered and raised her hands, "I've never played with you, Nahla. Between avoiding me and ignoring my calls, it's you who plays games." Marly scanned Nahla from head to toe. "Hmm," she said as she squinted her eyes. Marly walked back over to her desk and leaned against it. She folded her arms and said, "What happened to your face?" referring to Nahla's black eye.

Kayo was over it. "What do you want with Ayrah?"

Marly smiled and said, "You mean the broken arrow? That was a mess I cleaned up as a freebie. Didn't need her reckless ass behavior bringing heat my way. But, that was really just a crumb to get you here. I don't want Ayrah, I want you."

"Me?" Kayo said. "What for? I don't owe you anything."

"I need you to do a job for me," Marly admitted.

Kayo scrunched her face and said, "Hell no!"

"Kayo's not working for you," Nahla added. "Forget it!"

"Oh, Nahla." Marly stood with a straight face and said, "Kayo and I used to be partners. Right, Kayo? She doesn't need your permission."

Nahla looked perplexed. Her head whipped back and forth from Kayo, to Juno, to Marly. "What do you mean by 'partners', Marly?"

"Nahla, remember after India died— the night the two of you fought? Kayo, showed up to your house plastered. I should've known you were too young, Kayo but I needed help and you owed me money. It was a win-win."

Juno interjected, "Marly, don't bring that up. Just get to your point and..."

"I know about the hunt with India. There's no secrets there." Nahla asked.

Marly said, "She's not gonna tell you. Kayo left your house enraged. I found her at the Latch. You're familiar with the place. We had a drink and nice chat and came to some agreements to pay off the debt these two owed me. The next day, she helped me manage a problem I was having with some runners coming in from Vermont. They were undercutting both our little operations we had going on. She eliminated the competition for us both. It went down a little messier than we both thought, but she handled herself well."

"What did you do Kay?" Nahla asked.

Kayo walked away from the group and looked out the window that overlooked the main floor of the butcher shop. She balled up her fists. *Breathe*, she thought to herself. Kayo knew that Nahla knew nothing about the killings. *Why is she bringing this up?* "You can't blackmail me with that! We are both guilty."

"True. But, Nahla would never imagine this and needs to know what you're capable of. I'm also sure she doesn't know they weren't the first, there were others before that..."

"Self-defense!" Juno shouted.

"And she didn't stop there, Nahla. Her debt to me was paid but Miss Kayo got herself an idea and took out a few more jobs from me. You could say we were silent partners for a bit. She was heavily compensated which may explain a few assets she has been able to acquire. We will get to that later."

Nahla was concerned. She walked softly up to Kayo and asked, "How many, Kay?"

Kayo turned around and looked at Nahla with a sad face. She was somewhat embarrassed and ashamed. Kayo said, "For Marly, seven."

Nahla was flabbergasted. "Seven?"

"And before that?" Marly asked.

Juno insisted, "Marly, chill."

Kayo shouted, "Two! What the fuck is your point Marly?!"

Nahla took a deep breath and walked away. She put both hands on her head and closed her eyes. "Kayo. Nine people? What the fuck were you thinking?"

Juno tried to help. "Nahla, they..."

"Juno, stay out of this. Nine!? Nine!? Are you fucking mad?"

Marly stood up straight and put her hands in her pocket and said, "Thirteen, Nahla. Maybe fourteen as of this weekend."

Juno, Kayo and Nahla spun around and faced Marly. Kayo knew then that somehow her cover had been blown. She glared at Juno.

"I did not say shit about that I swear," Juno promised her.

"Nine would be lightwork for this young lady. I thought after a few years she lost her pizazz but, no no. My girl is back! And I request... no no, I require your assistance in other matters or the security footage is going directly to Metro Police."

Kayo marched over to Marly with her fists balled up. Nahla stepped in between and gently put her hand on Kayo's chest. She looked into her eyes. Kayo instantly felt reassured and calmed down. "Look at me, baby girl," Nahla whispered. "Not here. Not now."

"The problem is, I didn't know you'd be there, but now I know why you were but there were some important people there that needed to be terminated and you fucked that up. I'm also going to need access to those delivery tunnels because if my theory is correct, I bet they go directly to and through your building."

"No," Kayo said firmly.

Marly said, "They do, don't they? You rascal. Smart girl." She tapped her forehead with her index finger.

Kayo glared at Marly and calmly repeated

herself, "No."

"My constituents are not happy about their plan being foiled. You're not exactly in a position to decline. They want you to hunt The Tank."

"The Tank!?" Kayo yelled. "Oh, Marly you are a piece of shit. I'm fucking outta here!" Kayo began walking to the door.

"He's made an appearance and they want him. Didn't you split his ear almost in half? That's definitely him." She picked up a photo off the desk and passed it to Kayo.

Nahla snatched it and flipped through the photos. One picture was a close up of his ear split.

"That's the deal," Marly insisted.

Kayo responded, "Marly, you know what happened. You know what that means to me. I told you I'm never going back in those woods again!"

Nahla butted in, "That is out of line. Marly, the answer is no."

Kayo turned her back and marched toward the door.

"Kayo, you know you have a bone to pick with The Tank. What he did to your friend and to you. Don't you wear his mark on your back? This could be your only chance for revenge."

Kayo froze as memories of The Tank rushed in and crashed like a tidal wave. A tear dropped from her eye and she wiped it quickly.

"I believe every part of your body is itching to kill that beast for what he did. But, if not for me, do it for India. Hell, do it for Ayrah before I have to reassess my thoughts about her. She hasn't been in trouble with the law yet, maybe they'll go easy on her. There are two men looking at a couple years in the Cycles because of her. And all this footage of the young woman in green who killed all those men while on a date with her new boyfriend and his position with ARPA... I'm sure that will go over well."

Nahla walked closer to Marly and spoke quietly asking, "What's wrong with you, Marly? We raised these kids and you have no reservations about using them and throwing them under the bus. They cared about you. What happened to you?" Nahla asked.

"You. You happened to me," Marly replied with a soft whisper. "Love doesn't matter. It doesn't move mountains. It sure didn't move you! It just haunts, lingers and clouds the mind with lofty ideas of bullshit. You showed me that regardless of how you feel, you must stay in line with the things that must be done."

Nahla walked up to her and asked, "So this is payback for something that happened years ago?"

Kayo and Juno stood quietly listening in. With her eyes wide, Kayo thought to herself, *What the fuck is going on?*

Marly replied, "This has nothing to do with that."

"It does. You and I were never committed and you knew about Chopp."

"You'll never commit to anyone, not even him. I've made peace with that. Now, this is beyond me. It's business. You'll have 24 hours to negotiate and set the final terms for our agreement," Marly explained without returning eye contact. She walked over to her desk and sat in the chair.

"We'll be back tomorrow," Nahla signaled to Juno and Kayo to leave.

With her head down buried in paperwork, Marly said, "I'll be home."

Nahla, Kayo and Juno left the office. The guard closed the door behind them.

CHAPTER 7

NAHLA BROOKS AND PATRICIA MARLY

The Fisticuffs MMA Academy was located on the second floor of an old factory building in the middle of town. The brick walls were splattered with posters, flags, championship belts and boxing match news clippings from students at the club. It smelled like a wet mop and gym socks and the air was humid, and the room was lowly lit, mostly from sunlight and vintage fluorescent lights which were no longer legal. Chopp was renting the space but had been warned many times by the owner that he had to move, since the town was taking over the facility due to failure to pay taxes. He had four months left so he hired accountant Patricia Marly to help him sort out his books prior to closure. He brought Patricia to the office. She was shy and quirky with long hair that had nowhere to go. Upon entering the gym, Patricia was out of place. Hard core rap music played in the background. Over that, she heard grunts and bags being punched and clanking chains. Jump ropes rhythmically slapped against the hardwood floors and weights dropped on top of the horse mats in the weight area.

Nahla was sparring in the ring. Every inch of her body was dripping with sweat. She was very fast and lean. She wore gloves as she punched and kicked at her partner. She soon swooped in fast, spun underneath him. Using her legs and momentum she swiftly swept him to the floor. She got up quickly, put her knee in his chest, raised her hand to punch him, then tapped him on the head. She took her helmet off and laughed while helping him up. The moment Patricia walked by and saw Nahla fighting, she froze. She couldn't help staring in awe. Suddenly the dim room became brighter. *My God, she's gorgeous!* Patricia thought as she watched Nahla's locs come unraveled. Still wearing her mouthguard, Nahla smiled widely and captured Marly's attention for life.

Chopp broke her concentration and asked, "See something you like?"

Patricia smiled. With a slight accent in her speech she said, "I can't see well without my glasses." She couldn't think of anything else to say since she was caught staring. *Embarrassing.*

Chopp smiled and said, "Sure. I understand. Follow me." Chopp walked her over to his office.

Nahla hadn't noticed Patricia at first, but she did see that Chopp went into his office followed by a woman whose face she didn't quite catch. She took out her mouthpiece and said, "Give me a minute," to the trainer. Nahla left the ring and grabbed a towel. She walked over to the office and went in where she saw Chopp and Patricia sitting at a table with stacks of paper on top. She wiped herself as she spoke. "Hello." She stood in front of them both in her black sports bra and shorts. Beads of sweat rolled down her flat stomach. Patricia was afraid to look.

Chopp jumped out of his seat and said, "Nahla, this is Patricia Marly. She's here to help me close out the books here, which are a mess. I can't get a loan for another business if I don't clean this up."

Nahla reached out her hand for Patricia to shake. "Nahla Brooks. Kinda sweaty but, this is no place to work if you can't get past that."

Patricia stood up and moved her hair from her face. She insisted, "The sweat doesn't bother me. Nice to meet you. My friends call me Patsy." She shook Nahla's hand.

"Since we're not friends, I'll call you Marly," Nahla said with a gentle smile. "You from around here?" She continued to wipe her arms and shoulders.

"No. I'm from Canada. I moved here for work right after college. Been here ever since."

"I knew I heard an accent in there somewhere. How do you two know each other?" Nahla inquired.

Chopp answered, "She's from my 'Conspiracy Crazies' chat group as you call it. She comes to our virtual meetings regularly."

"More regularly now that things have been changing," Marly added. "Maybe you should stop in and check it out."

"Well, if you're a member then maybe it's not so crazy. In exchange, maybe I'll get some gloves on you one day. Teach you how to box." Nahla put her hands up and threw a couple jabs and smiled. She then looked at Chopp and said, "I'm calling it a night. Want to walk me out? I need to give you something."

Chopp nodded.

"Nice to meet you Marly, and for the record, even if we do become friends, I'm still going to call you Marly."

Chopp insisted. "Patricia... Marly, whatever, take a look around. I'll be back up in a minute."

Marly explored the gym. She dodged as many flying drops of sweat as she could but every so often, one landed on her face. She inspected the room of fighting gods and goddesses from corner to corner and between. They came in a plethora of chiseled shades anyone could imagine. Virtually no one was out of shape. She was slightly intimidated but couldn't get the image of Nahla out of her mind. She made her way to the window that overlooked the parking lot where she saw Chopp and Nahla being playful. Eventually Nahla wrapped her arms around his neck and they kissed. Marly quickly turned away from the window. *I'm so stupid*, she thought to herself.

As time went on, laws changed, the city got more restrictive and Chopp's survivalist group, which Marly was a part of, decided to move to the more rural parts of the state. Marly found a cluster of properties Up Rural and brought the idea to the group. Chopp didn't have the money but would stay up there to help Marly get her farm started during the week and visit Nahla in the city on weekends.

One weekend Nahla got into a fight at a bar, broke a woman's jaw and got arrested. She called Chopp back to back from jail but he didn't pick up. She ended up calling Marly. When Marly picked up the phone Nahla said, "Hey Marly."

It was late, but Marly sat up straight and responded, "Hey, Nahla. Everything okay?"

"I don't mean to bother you. I've been trying to reach Chopp and I don't have anyone else to call."

"What's going on?"

"I'm in trouble. I need help," Nahla told Marly.

Without hesitation, Marly picked her up and drove her out of town to the homestead. Nahla's knuckles were bloody and bruised. Marly came to her with a warm rag, bandages and gin. Nahla took a large guzzle of the gin to numb the pain.

Marly gently cleaned Nahla's wounds and said, "Stay here with me for a while."

"With you? I can't live here, Marly."

"I don't...I mean, don't go back to the city. Chopp told me these hands get you into a lot of trouble. I hear you have a temper."

"Chopp says I'm a spitfire but he tries to help me with that," Nahla said. "He teaches me how to meditate and filter out the noise. I have trouble focusing on what's important and worth my energy."

"I know what you mean. You can stay in the loft of my shed if you want. That's where Chopp stays when he's here. It's a small loft but it's not that bad."

"I don't know. It seems like a lot," Nahla said as Marly dabbed her hands with iodine.

"You won't want to leave. It's quiet here." Marly began wrapping Nahla's hands. "At least stay a few days and get away from it all. I won't bother you but, I'll be here if you need me."

Nahla tucked herself into the bed in the loft. Marly never bothered her except to bring her food. She read an entire book in three days, went on walks by the creek and fell asleep a few times on a hammock between two maple trees nestled in the back corner of Marly's property. Chopp arrived for the weekend to find Nahla staying in his space. He didn't mind. They went for walks on the trails, helped Marly with her garden, chickens and goats. They foraged mushrooms from the woods and went fishing at the lake. Nahla never felt a sense of purpose as she did while on the homestead. She stayed another week and decided to sell her condos to buy land and build her own at a property not far from Marly's.

After the death of her brother and sister in law, Nahla took custody of Kayo and eventually the twins. She wasn't ready for the commitment but didn't have a choice. Time went on, a few years passed, Chopp decided to move permanently back to the city. Nahla and Marly became close friends as they formed the co-op and started the farmers market selling produce, herbs, honey and meats.

One Saturday, late in the afternoon, Nahla and a teenage Orion showed up to Marly's butcher shop after a successful deer hunt. They had two bucks and a doe in the back of the truck. She came into the shop dressed head to toe in hunting camo with a safety harness wrapped under her legs and over her shoulders followed by footprints left behind from her muddy boots. She used her bloody hands and pulled her camouflage headband off her head and her locs cascaded down her back. Her face was dirty but donned a huge smile from ear to ear as she was greeted by the butchers. Marly watched how Nahla's presence lit everyone up around her. She watched how the men flirted with Nahla and how Nahla instinctively juggled their gestures. Marly couldn't help but greet Nahla with a smile.

"The eight pointer is Oree's. He can negotiate that with you. The four pointer and the doe... make me an offer I can't refuse," Nahla said as she grinned.

Once they made a deal, Marly walked Nahla back outside and after a quick chat, they agreed to meet at the local tavern called The Latch for a drink to celebrate.

Marly sat at the bar waiting. She had already started drinking as she anxiously waited for Nahla to arrive. When Nahla walked into the room she felt the same feeling she had felt when she first saw Nahla. It was a feeling she had tucked away for a long time. Marly smiled when she saw her friend Nahla approach. Her hair was down. She wore a white sleeveless shirt tucked into blue jeans with a leather belt and cowboy boots. She had a brown leather bag thrown over her shoulder. They hugged once Nahla reached Marly at the bar.

"This is a huge change from how you looked earlier today. I can't remember the last time I saw you wear actual clothes," Marly said. "Probably even took a shower."

Nahla laughed and said, "Mm Hmm. Some nerve of you, but I will admit you look cute. A little lipstick going on I see. Who are you trying to pick up?"

"You're funny." Marly smiled and said, "You and Oree kicked ass today so, I'm buying tonight. What are you drinking?"

"I dunno. Surprise me. Oh anything but tequila. I can't. You'll be bailing me out of jail again," Nahla joked.

"Then I should definitely get tequila so you can get arrested. But this time I'll leave you in jail." Marly laughed and ordered whiskey straight up. "This is a big girl drink right here!"

"I can handle it," Nahla said as she took a sip. "What made you want to come into town tonight?"

"I wanted to do something different. I'm getting tired of chicken shit and dirty nails. Sometimes a girl just wants to feel pretty, you know? Not that I'm going to do anything but..."

"Understood." Nahla took a large swig of the whisky and made a face. "Look around. Do you see any prospects? I've never seen you with anyone. I'm starting to wonder if you're from another planet." Nahla made googly eyes and stuck her tongue out.

They both laughed.

Marly said, "You seem determined to set me up

tonight."

"Indeed! I'm here to be messy! Maybe you'll meet your match tonight," Nahla said. "You never know!"

"No one likes me," Marly said. "I'm too boring. There's nothing mysterious or sexy about me really."

"It's not that they don't like you. They don't see you." Nahla turned to the bar and asked for two shots of whisky. The bartender put them in front of the two women. Nahla drank hers quickly. Marly did the same. Nahla said, "Marly, you are kind of mysterious which any man would think is sexy, but men are visual beings. Sometimes you have to make them look." She leaned over the bar to the bartender and said, "Turn up the music for me," and winked. She grabbed Marly by the hand and pulled her to the dance floor.

Marly was confused, "What are you doing?"

"Making them look." Nahla began dancing with Marly in the middle of the floor. Marly was uncomfortable with the idea but couldn't break free from Nahla's commands. Nahla wrapped her arms around Marly's neck and whispered in her ear, "You're beautiful. Own it."

The two women seductively danced in the middle of the floor and almost forgot where they were. More people got up to dance, which made the dancing a little less awkward. As they danced two men approached them. Nahla spun Marly around to dance with one and she took the other by the hand and danced with him. By the end of the song, Nahla backed away but watched Marly continue dancing for another song with the guy she met. Nahla smirked and continued to drink at the bar as she watched her friend from afar. Moments later Marly looked up and Nahla was gone.

Marly excused herself and went through every corner of the bar looking for Nahla. She stepped out the front door and saw Nahla outside smoking. Marly released a sigh of relief. "I got scared for a second. Thought you left with some guy or something."

"Jealous?" Nahla laughed. "Don't be. I'm all yours," she joked. "Sorry, I just came outside for a smoke." She passed the joint to Marly.

Marly declined. "I'll throw up."

"Shit. I've already done that," Nahla said as she laughed. "You get his number?" she asked as she put the joint away.

Marly covered her face and said, "I did."

"Good! He was cute too. But let him call you. Don't call him."

"I didn't plan on it," Marly reassured her. "He probably won't call, but it was just for fun anyway."

"If he doesn't call, he's an idiot. You're a catch. Anyone can see that." Nahla brushed Marly's hair away from her face. "Hopefully you're enjoying yourself. It's still early but do you want to call it a night?" Nahla asked.

Marly thought for a moment and said, "Not really. I'm enjoying my time with you."

"Then buy me another drink!" Nahla insisted.

"How about I make you one? I have a full bar at

the cabin," Marly said.

"I'll meet you there," Nahla smiled.

Around 20 minutes later, Nahla and Marly arrived at Marly's cabin. They walked into the front door. The place smelled like peppermint. Marly went to her bar, pretending to be a mixologist. She laughed at herself as she clumsily spilled the spirits on the counter. Nahla made herself at home. She removed her shoes and walked over to the record collection. "Vinyl? Nice." She was impressed. "This collection is A plus!" she told Marly. Nahla pulled out the album *Morning After*, released in 2017 by DVSN and placed it onto the bluetooth record player. As the music played, Nahla listened for a while and hummed one of the songs. When Nahla turned around, Marly was standing there with a drink in her hand. Nahla grabbed the drink. They tapped glasses and both took a sip. Nahla asked, "How long have you been watching me?"

Marly shyly responded, "Since I met you."

Nahla looked curiously at her friend. "I meant here and now, since I started trying to sing." Nahla put down the glass and said, "Maybe we should stop drinking," Nahla said. "I don't want either of us to say or do anything we don't mean."

Marly was embarrassed and said, "I'm sorry, Nahla. I..."

"You ok? You want water or something?" Nahla questioned but she knew Marly wasn't drunk. It was her attempt to try and give Marly a way out of what she had just admitted.

Marly looked at Nahla and said, "I rarely say things I don't mean. I meant what I said. Because of Chopp and our business relationship, I figured it was best to be quiet about it, but I've always had a crush on you. How do you not see it? Nahla, I can barely look at you. I'm sorry. I didn't mean for it to come out this way or to make you uncomfortable."

"You don't. I just want to make sure you're sober so I'll know what to do next," Nahla said.

"I'm sober," Marly said. "I wish I wasn't."

"But I'm not and one more drink and you won't be either," Nahla reminded her.

Marly was embarrassed. "I've completely overstepped. It's okay if you want to leave," Marly said abashedly.

Nahla tipped her glass back to drink and said, "I don't. I just wanted to make sure you're sober."

Marly turned away with her glass and asked, "Why does it matter?" Marly walked away, turning her back to Nahla.

As Marly tried to drink from the glass, Nahla took it from her hand and drank it. "Marly, it matters because I need you to be clear about what you're saying to me and I need you to be sober for what may happen." Nahla stood in front of Marly and stared at her. "You want me to stay the night?" Nahla asked.

"Nahla. Please, I beg you, don't joke with me. I can't emotionally handle that."

Nahla stepped closer and said, "No jokes. No games. I'm asking you if you want me to stay with you? You can say no."

Marly nodded. "Of course I do, if you're serious."

Nahla leaned against the desk in the living room. "Then just tell me to stay, Marly," Nahla instructed her.

"I want you to stay with me tonight," Marly said.

"No. Just... just tell me to stay and I'll stay," Nahla said.

"What about Chopp?" Marly asked.

"I don't belong to Chopp. Chopp knows the rules. He created them."

"What are the rules?" Marly asked.

Nahla gently approached Marly as she spoke. "One. Only come when I call. Two. Don't ever use the "L" word. Three. Don't ask me about my affairs with anyone else, especially Chopp," Nahla said as she approached Marly. "These are my terms. If you're okay with that, I'll stay. If not, I'll go my way and this never happened. I don't want to hurt you."

Marly grabbed a few of Nahla's locs into her hand. "I won't let you hurt me, Nahla." Marly looked Nahla in the eyes and said, "Stay with me tonight."

Nahla nodded and said, "Okay."

Marly moved Nahla's locs away from her face, leaned in and kissed her. Marly had never felt anything this amazing in her life. She melted into Nahla's hands, even though she was in control, at the same time she was powerless. Marly felt more fragile than ever. Her heart raced and pounded in her chest. Nahla's mouth was perfect and tasted like the evening rain— refreshing and warm. It was all surreal. Marly tightly held Nahla, lightly brushing her nose across Nahla's neck taking in her scent as if it was hers to devour. Then she kissed it and slid her hand between Nahla's thighs. Nahla softly moaned and Marly almost lost her composure. She whispered "I want you."

Nahla whispered back, "Where?"

"Come with me," Marly directed.

Marly gently grabbed Nahla's hand and walked her to the room. She shut the door behind them. It was the first night of many nights to follow with secret rendezvouses on Freedom Day and random weekdays in between. Marly kept her end of the bargain and let Nahla continue her affairs with Chopp without recourse. When Chopp was around she backed off and gave them space. She made excuses for Nahla's disappearances and anxiously awaited her reappearances after spending time with Chopp. Many times Marly felt that Nahla preferred Chopp, but much of that was her own insecurities. Nahla needed them both. She never wanted them together. She dared not let Marly touch Chopp nor Chopp touch Marly. There was never a thought in her mind to enjoy them together at the same time. They were so different; she preferred them individually. These times were difficult for Marly, so she buried her nose and her jealousy in paperwork and building the cooperative, her business and the black market.

A few years went by before Chopp realized what was happening. He drove up to Marly's cabin to deliver cash from a buyer just as Nahla was leaving.

He saw them embracing and kissing goodbye with a level of passion that completely threw him for a loop. Many things started to make sense. Nahla hadn't called for him as much as she had in the past. When he was around she talked less like her mind was elsewhere. Whenever the three of them were in the same space, things were awkward, like there was an inside joke he didn't understand. She was less playful and sex between them felt routine. It was enjoyable, but something was off about it. Something was missing. Nahla was slowly disconnecting from him. He expected and knew that Nahla would have friends and see other people. He had his own, but seeing her with Marly felt different. Maybe it was in his head.

Chopp didn't say a word. He didn't understand why Marly would tell him to come at this time knowing that Nahla would be there. He felt she did it on purpose. Nonetheless, he got out of the truck and walked over in the direction of the butcher shop. He didn't interfere. He was bound by his own rules. Nahla and Marly were caught red handed but there was also a relief felt amongst them now that he knew.

Marly began to panic.

"I'll talk to him," Nahla said.

"I fucked up, Nahla" Marly said. "I'm really sorry. I forgot I told him to come by today. I got lost in spending time with you." She had been friends with Chopp for many years. They never talked in depth about his relationship with Nahla, but everyone in the co-op knew they were together. Marly knew her friendship with Chopp would be ruined forever and she worried if business would be affected since he brought her so much of it.

Nahla embraced Marly and kissed her on the side of her head. "Look at me." She promised, "I'll handle it."

As Marly became in charge of operations and focused on the black market distribution of products, her nights with Nahla became fewer and farther between but more intense as if they were catching up for lost time. Marly wasn't around as much and traveled a lot. Nahla didn't push for her to come around. She focused on the twins and the homestead. Nahla had become less accessible emotionally and was more focused on the safety of the kids as they worked for Marly. Unfortunately, the twins kept getting themselves into trouble. The conflict of interest was putting a strain on their relationship. Nahla was also getting more frustrated with Marly as Marly became more secretive and more unavailable, letting Nahla into the business side of the operation less and less. Nahla was no longer reaching out to request Marly's company. Marly summoned her instead. Nahla didn't mind. She preferred it this way. If she didn't want to go, she would just say, "Not tonight." Apart, they were in their own worlds, but together felt like they were in a third dimension.

"Come see me." The text came through to Nahla's phone as she was cleaning the kitchen one evening. Though they were going through a rough patch, Nahla genuinely missed Marly. She packed a bag and went over. It was an emotional evening that was long overdue. They spent the first two hours on the couch watching a movie. Nahla laid her head on Marly's lap while Marly fondled her hair and gently kissed her on the forehead and lips. The rest of the evening was a standard release of sexual tension they both had pinned up from not spending time together. Late in the night, Nahla laid in the bed naked with her back turned to Marly. Marly played with her hair and kissed her back as she laid still.

"Are you awake?" Marly asked quietly as her soft lips connected with Nahla's smooth skin.

There was no response.

Marly liked to listen to and watch Nahla sleep. Marly snuggled in and held Nahla closer then whispered, "I'm sorry, Nahla. I can't help it. I've been avoiding you because I'm in love with you." Marly quietly teared up. "I always have been." She knew the "L" word was a deal breaker, but she had to say it. She only let it out because she thought Nahla was asleep. However, Nahla was wide awake. She heard everything. She laid still, stiff as a board, pretending to only wake when she felt Marly's lips pressing against her back a second time.

Nahla turned to face Marly with her eyes barely open. Nahla smiled and looked into Marly's watery eyes. She said, "Marly, I want to do something I've never done before and I need to do it now."

Marly kissed Nahla on the forehead and said,

"What is it?"

"Let me... I want to..." Nahla was anxious. She couldn't get the words out. Nahla was never at a loss for words.

Marly laid patiently beside her, holding her closely. She smiled at Nahla and said, "It's ok. Tell me in the morning. I'm not going anywhere."

Nahla nodded and closed her eyes and whispered, "I want to make love to you. I know it's against the rules but..."

Marly heard all she needed to hear and didn't waste another moment. She grabbed Nahla and pulled her into her.

"Wait. Let me do this," Nahla said. She gently traced Marly's face with her finger tips. She studied Marly's face with her eyes. She kissed Marly softly. For the first time Nahla took her time and made love to Marly. She was emotionally locked in and didn't hold back. "Patricia Marly, I love you," Nahla whispered softly in Marly's ear as they touched. It was so different from anything Nahla had experienced with Chopp or anyone else. Nahla needed this connection to happen but deep inside she knew she had made a mistake.

When Marly fell asleep, teary eyed and weary, Nahla tried to sneak out of the bed. Marly grabbed her arm. "Please come back to bed. Don't go," Marly begged.

Nahla said, "Marly, I have to go."

Marly sat up in the bed and asked, "Why? It's still dark out. Stay with me."

"I can't. Marly, I'm done."

Nahla pulled away and started dressing. She packed her small bag, frantically stuffing things inside.

"Done? What's wrong?" Marly jumped out of the bed and wrapped herself in a sheet. "What do you mean, you're done? What are you saying?"

"The terms of our agreement have been broken," Nahla confessed. "I violated them."

Marly was crushed. "What do you mean? You never... How did you..."

"I heard you. The "L" word, Marly. I heard what you said to me and I could've almost dealt with it because I knew, but hearing you say it... I had to make love to you or I was going to explode. I'm in love with you too, Marly. I love you so much I feel like I'm holding my breath until I get to see you. I'm not used to this. It's making me crazy! I'm so in love with you I'm fucking drowning in it. I'm losing myself and I can't do this," Nahla said as she grabbed her bag from the floor. "I didn't mean for this to happen, I'm sorry."

"No No. Don't you do this to me, Nahla! Please don't, Nahla. Please," Marly begged. "Tell me what you need me to do?"

"Nothing. There's nothing you can do. It's me," Nahla insisted. "I can't. I can't do it."

"You can do this. You can, Nahla!" Marly pleaded. "Give us a chance." Tears fell from Marly's eyes but each one was futile. "Please, Nahla."

Nahla couldn't do it and Marly could never do

what was needed. There were too many conflicts between Marly and the kids. There was a conflict of interest that Nahla didn't need hanging over her head and she still had Chopp who she cared for very much and didn't want to lose. She had already neglected him to quietly deal with her feelings for Marly. She didn't mean for her emotions to get out of control, but they had taken root in a place she never expected.

After the break up, they continued to see each other every Freedom Day of the month when the weather was right. Nahla would venture off to the creek to forage or read to clear her head. Marly would make an appearance. She would help Nahla forage or just sit and watch her read. Sometimes they would just stare at each other while Nahla smoked a joint against the oak. They wouldn't speak but by the last hour, they would find themselves sharing a gentle touch with fingers interlocked together or in some kind of embrace, but never made love nor kissed again. Nahla would always leave first and text Marly a "moon" emoji. Marly would text back a "sun" emoji with a heart. This went on for a few months after the break up until, one day at the creek, instead of finding Marly, Nahla found a blue little box with a hunter green bow on it. Inside was a gold necklace with a compass pendant and a small note. "Maybe one day you'll find your way back to me."

Nahla wore the necklace everyday ever since. Since then, Nahla completely avoided Marly, only seeing her in passing. It was better this way. Marly's business ventures were becoming more sinister. Nahla knew that Marly was spiraling, yet the twins were working for her and Kayo hated her. Nothing would be more devastating to Kayo to know that Nahla was in love with her archnemesis. As time went on Nahla and Marly's resentment towards one another multiplied. All Nahla could do was focus on why they needed to stay away from each other. Marly put the business over everything. Marly was Kayo's biggest threat. Marly created problems for the twins. Marly was a thorn in Nahla's side. Marly ruined what Nahla planned to be a life of peace. Since the break up Nahla had endless feelings of deep sorrow and brokenness. She felt empty. Regardless of all the reasons Nahla could muster up to stay away, Marly was Nahla's endless tie.

The next afternoon, Nahla anxiously rang Marly's doorbell. She shivered a bit from chill air that easily slipped down the openings of her brown leather jacket. She wore a knitted hat with a scarf wrapped around her neck. She looked around and saw a few guards walking the premises, but none were near the house. *Let's go, Marly*, she thought to herself. *Hurry up.* Nahla was ready to go. *I don't want to be here!* She hadn't been to the house in a couple years and just the thought of being on the porch reminded her of the nights Marly summoned her for company. *She wants to torture me.* Nahla heard the door handle turn and stood there with her hands in her pockets.

Marly opened the door with her glasses on. She took off her glasses and stood there for a moment. Marly had on house clothes and a long sweater. Her face was clean with no makeup and her hair was tucked under a Blue Jays cap. Marly froze, as this moment was nostalgic for her as well.

"Marly. It's cold," Nahla said.

"Then you should feel right at home."

Nahla rolled her eyes and huffed. "Please Marly. Let's just get to it."

Marly gestured with her head for Nahla to enter the cabin. Nahla walked past Marly into the cabin looking at her as she passed. She hadn't been there in years. It was warm and cozy. The fireplace crackled. She had upgraded the kitchen but the place still smelled like peppermint just as she remembered.

"Whisky?" Marly asked.

"Please," Nahla responded. "I love the upgrades."

"Figured you would." Marly took out a bottle of Japanese Whisky and poured them both a glass. Marly spilled a little on the counter. "I've never been good at bartending." She passed Nahla the glass.

They tapped glasses and drank. "Yikes. Whisky is trouble." Nahla smiled and shook her head. She took a sip. "You know, Marly, I came here to curse your ass out but I don't even have it in me." She took off her hat.

"I thought we would be kicking and screaming by now, but eh. Fuck it. How have you been?"

"Good. Trying to keep quiet and stay in my lane. How about you?" Nahla wondered.

Marly swirled around the whisky and said, "Busy... tired... I spend most of my days working or making and closing deals."

"Not much has changed. You look good. I'm digging the longer hair," Nahla said as she unwrapped the scarf from around her neck. "It's grown a bit since the last time we spoke."

"Thank you," Marly laughed. "You look... fuck it. I want to say something smart but you look amazing." Marly took another sip. "As always." Marly shyly looked at Nahla from head to toe and she sipped more whisky from her glass. "Are you still working out every day? Looks like it."

Nahla blushed, "It's hard work, trust me. I'm always sore, but thank you."

"What happened to your eye?" Marly inquired.

Nahla giggled. "Kayo," she confessed. "She's a lot. I have no idea where she gets it from."

They both laughed.

Marly joked, "I would never guess where or who." She said sarcastically, "She's a complete anomaly!"

"She is, but," Nahla continued, "I deserved it."

"That's probably true." Marly couldn't help but to ask, "Seeing anyone these days?"

Nahla bit her lip and smiled, "You know those questions are against the rules."

"I didn't know they were still in play. We broke those a long time ago. I figured we already crossed the line."

"Why not keep going then?" Nahla smirked again. "To be honest, not really. Not yet. I mean you know Chopp has always been in and out of my life but, I haven't seen him in a while. I just prefer time to myself now. Meditation helps me focus and keep any animalistic urges I have in check."

"Animalistic sounds about right."

"Since we're officially breaking rules, what about you?" Nahla asked. "Anyone keeping you busy?"

Marly exhaled and said, "Yes, actually. It's hard but I'm trying to do better this time."

Nahla paused for a moment then said, "Good for you. They're lucky to have you. I mean it. You're a great lover and you should know that. The way I treated you may not have made that evident, but you are." *And I miss you.* Nahla knew better than to say it outloud but for a moment she and Marly locked eyes and she forgot the purpose of her visit. She caught herself fiddling with the compass and quickly moved her hand away from it.

Marly smiled and nodded then, "I appreciate you for saying that." *I miss you too.* "I'm sorry that I outted you in front of Kayo and Juno. I was being petty. That was wrong of me and..."

"You can't out me if I'm not hiding. I'm just private and I really don't care what people think. I was a wild child, Marly. You're not my first experience with a woman. Plus, I told the twins."

"You told the twins?" Marly asked. Marly tried to hold back a smile. It delighted her to know that Nahla felt strongly enough to mention their relationship to them. "What'd you tell 'em?"

Nahla sighed, "I told them our friendship had become a little more than platonic and they may see you around more. They understood. I figured you would come by and stay the night at some point and I didn't want it to be weird."

Marly smirked and said, "All those years and I never stayed over."

"I wanted you to. I had some crazy idea in my mind to change that but things kind of fell apart and I wasn't ready to tell Kayo. I guess she knows now but she's going to be more upset with the who than the what of this. She hates your guts." Nahla smiled. Nahla knew the small talk between her and Marly had gone too far. "So, what do you want to do, Marly? Kayo isn't budging much. We talked all night."

Marly sipped the whisky and asked, "So, why'd you come if she wasn't ready to negotiate?"

Nahla looked up and said, "Truthfully, I wanted to see you alone."

"Teasing me isn't going to change anything, Nahla," Marly reminded her.

"No. Not like that, Marly. I wanted to talk to you about a lot of things and when people are around, we're too busy being snarky and we aren't listening to each other. The way you talk to me, the way we speak to each other... I don't like it. So I'm trying to be civil so I can understand all of this. I understand why you hate me, but taking it out on the kids..."

"They're adults, Nahla. They made choices they have to live with," Marly said. "You should have sent Kayo. Why are *you* here? " Marly was getting frustrated.

"Ultimately to negotiate or cut a deal. Kayo is more stubborn than you and it doesn't make sense to drag this out."

"I'm listening," Marly said. She could never let a good deal pass her by.

Nahla finished the whisky before answering. "Let's be honest. Ayrah and Kayo made mistakes that affected you, but really your issue is with me. Both Kayo and Ayrah belong to me. They're my responsibility. If you've ever truly cared for me, I don't get why you'd follow through on this. I feel like you're trying to punish them for what happened between us years ago."

"No, Nahla. You want this to be about you and me because that's easier for you to understand. It's not personal."

"It is. And this is why I couldn't do it." Nahla was angry. She stood up from the stool she was sitting on.

Marly asked, "Couldn't do what?" She stood up straight, posturing back at Nahla.

"Us, Marly. Your business always came first. And you thrive off of exploiting other people's needs and mistakes. The kids worked for you and I would never want to be in a position to choose between them and you."

"I would never have asked you to choose."

"Every time you brought up some debt they owed you. Every time your business placed them in harm's way. Every time you and Kayo would get into disagreements... You may not have said it out loud, but you were asking me to choose and you're doing it now. This is why I couldn't do it. And just so we're clear, I will always choose them first, without hesitation. Not a second thought will come to my mind."

"I don't expect you to make a different choice than that. And Nahla, you have means for them *not* to work for me and yet you pretend you don't and make them think their only way to get ahead is to hustle."

Nahla agreed, "It's true but they need work to build character. I trusted you with them but this is getting to be too much. I need you to understand that our past should have no bearing on how you handle this."

Marly was bothered and said, "Ok. Whatever, Nahla, I don't know how many times I have to say it's not personal. I don't really want this. You have no idea the decisions I have to make every day. I have no choice but to follow through on this. My reputation is on the line. This business doesn't only affect me. I have distributors and partners that want answers and I don't have them! I'm sorry but Kayo was in the wrong place at the wrong time. There are people who will be looking for Kayo if I don't deliver The Tank's fucking head on a platter. They know that I know Kayo and already questioned if I set this up. If I could have covered for her, even for your sake, I would have! Sometimes there's nothing I can do."

"Nothing you can do!?" Nahla clenched her fists then yelled at the top of her lungs, "Patricia Marly, you should have fucking called me!" she turned around, lunged forward and punched the wall leaving a dent in plaster. "Fuck!" she said as she shook her hand from the pain. It started bleeding. Nahla's chest pumped up and down as she breathed trying to calm herself down. She took a deep breath. Then she took another.

Marly stood firm. She wasn't scared, but she knew it was better to give Nahla time to calm down. She poured more whisky into Nahla's glass, poured more in her own glass and took a sip. "Take a breath, Nahla." Marly grabbed a roll of gauze from the cabinet and gently placed it in front of Nahla. "You called me Patricia." In a soft voice, almost under her breath she said, "You've only called me that once before." She gently grabbed and quickly inspected Nahla's hand. She rubbed her thumb lightly over the back of it and said, "It's broken."

Nahla winced. "It's not. It's fine!" She snatched her hand back from Marly, rubbed her hand from the pain then swallowed down all the whisky. She began wrapping her hand. Her ego wouldn't let her expose just how badly her hand was hurting. In a calmer voice she said, "You could cover for her if you wanted to. You know exactly how to clean these things up, but it was more important to you to exploit this situation for your benefit. You have a choice. Everyone has a choice, Marly. We all choose our actions."

"But someone else chooses our consequences," Marly added. "This time, I am the messenger. It's not my call."

Nahla regained control of her emotions and asked, "So there's no way out of this?"

Marly nodded. "No. My only part in this is to make sure she takes care of it?"

"No. She's not going to do anything. I'm going to take care of it. I'll handle it."

Marly was upset. "Fuck that! No!"

Nahla said, "Yes. I am. If it's about the job and not personal, then the work is the work. Why do you give a shit who completes it?"

"Because I don't want you to," Marly said. "Your ass is old and your hand is fucked up anyway."

"I don't care, Marly. All of this is because of me and you. The market, the co-op, the smuggling business started with conversations I was involved in. I let her work for you and accumulate debt when she didn't have to. I will complete the task. I will hunt The Tank. When I'm done, you leave Kayo the fuck alone and tell your friends the same or they're dead."

Marly didn't like the idea of this. "Nahla. You've never killed anyone. You..."

"You don't know me, Marly. Why do you

think I left the city? What scared me the most when you told me that Kayo killed 13 men was two things. One, the trauma this woman must feel with no one to talk to and help her through that. Trauma is the portal that lets the demons inside. Taking lives is not easy. Sure we hunt but a human being is different. A part of you goes with every life you take. And two, that she's more like me than I thought. I knew she could fight like me, even better, but I never thought she had the strength in her to take a life like I have and I have taken many. I was wrong." Nahla smirked and said, "Furthermore, let everyone know, it is not beyond my call of duty to slit every throat of anyone who threatens Kayo. The job will be finished. After that, never speak to me or my family again. They will not work for you. They will have nothing for you."

"That's not up to you, Nahla."

Nahla looked at Marly as if she had two heads and said, "It is. And if *you* ever threaten Kayo or any of them again, even Juno, I will lose my life to take yours. There will be nothing you can do to put the dragon back in the mountain. She'll be out forever."

"Nahla, you have to understand, things are more complicated than..."

"Forever, Marly! I will kill anyone for her. I will not stop until it's done!"

Marly didn't flinch. Instead she nodded in acknowledgment of Nahla's threat. She was too business oriented to take the terms personally. On the other end of this deal, Kayo's life would be destroyed. It was only fair. "Just so you're aware, Tank is suspected to have killed a hunter and two hikers this month alone. Seems he has a taste for human blood. The Department of Wildlife and Fisheries have tagged him for monitoring which is how we found him. I'll get you the coordinates where Tank was last seen and the terrain is pretty rough so that signal is only hitting those towers once every two to three days. Sometimes he stays put for a few hours but then we lose him again. Once I send you his last location, you have a week from that day. If it's not done, they won't take it easy on her. Or me."

"What do you mean or you?"

"I keep trying to tell you. You don't listen. This doesn't just affect Kayo. They don't trust me now."

"Marly, I don't trust you either. Believe me, I'm going to find out who your friends are and when I do, they'll regret they ever came for Kay. And if I find out you're lying to me or in any way behind this, I'll fucking kill you myself." Nahla ripped the chain off her neck and threw it on the floor. She then walked over to the bar, grabbed a brand new bottle of whisky and walked out of the cabin. She slammed the door on the way out.

"You killed me a long time ago, Nahla," Marly said to the back of the closed door.

Nahla climbed back into her truck. She drank directly from the bottle letting it spill over the sides of her mouth and breathed heavily. She wiped her mouth and took out her phone. She selected Chopp's number from her list of contacts.

Chopp answered, "Nahla? Everything okay?" He knew something was up. He hadn't received a call from Nahla in a long time.

Nahla sped off down the easement and said, "Not really Chopp. I'm going to need some help."

Chopp stood up from the shock, "I can get there in the morning if you need me."

"Thanks but not yet. I have to get more information but we should definitely speak in person."

"Does this have anything to do with Marly?" Chopp asked.

"This has everything to do with Marly," Nahla said. "Listen, I may even come there tonight. I'm not sure. I will call you back." Nahla hung up and continued driving down the patchy roads and within 10 minutes she arrived at her cabin but wasn't expecting to see Kayo waiting there on the porch. *Fuck!* Nahla thought. She got out of the truck and marched up the steps.

"What'd you do to your hand?" Kayo asked, "and why didn't you tell me about you and Marly?"

Nahla opened the door and marched into the house. Kayo followed. She shut the door behind them. When Nahla entered, she walked over to the kitchen and slammed the bottle of whisky she took from Marly's house on the counter.

"I wasn't going to discuss my affairs with a teenager, Kayo. By the time you were old enough to understand, it didn't make sense to talk about it."

"I wasn't always a teenager," Kayo said. "You should have said something!"

Nahla went into her room and started packing a bag. "Ugh! Seriously?" She said, "Kayo, you were coming and going. I didn't know what you were doing with Marly. It didn't seem relevant."

"What do you mean? We got into a whole fight about her. You could have told me then. Were you seeing her at that time? Were you seeing her when Oree got into trouble?" Kayo asked.

Nahla paused for a moment and said, "It's complicated, Kayo. You fucking hate Marly. What was I supposed to tell you?"

"You were seeing her weren't you? So when's the last time you were with her?"

"Excuse me, baby girl. I don't ask you who you're fucking and when. That is none of your business."

"So the night we fought, you were definitely seeing her. You knew she was fucking up this family and you kept seeing her?"

Nahla looked at Kayo and said, "Kayo, whatever it was, it's done now. There's nothing to discuss."

"Tell me the truth." Kayo took a deep breath and calmly asked, "Nahla, I couldn't see it before but now that I've seen you two together... Are you in love with Marly?"

Nahla didn't respond. She paused for a moment and then started throwing more items into her bag.

Kayo turned her back to Nahla and put her hands on her head. "For goodness sake, Nahla. You've gotta be fucking kidding me! You're in love with her. Great!"

"Marly was the biggest mistake of my life. She was my friend. I pretended I couldn't see it but I knew she had a crush on me. I was actively seeing Chopp. Sometimes I flirted but I never thought I would act on it. One night we went out. We'd been drinking and she told me how she felt. I thought one night wouldn't hurt. One night became another then turned into months then years. I also didn't expect to fall in love with her. The night I told her I was in love with her was the same night I ended it. I was fucking asshole for that. She wanted more but there was so much going on, I knew it wouldn't go any further. I left her there crying, begging me to stay. We met up a few times at the creek after the break up, then she left me the compass and never came back."

"The one you wear every day," Kayo remembered.

"Well not anymore. I just ripped it off my neck and threw it on her kitchen floor as I threatened to kill her." Nahla rubbed her injured hand and said, "I ruined our friendship. It was wrong of me to open that can of worms. Chopp and I have never been the same since he found out. It completely altered our friendship and my relationship with Marly, it's been tumultuous ever since." Nahla's eyes began watering. She looked away.

Kayo noticed her aunt was emotional and said, "You still love her don't you?"

"I deeply care for her, yes. I do. But here we are, Kay."

Kayo folded her arms and said in a softer tone, "Dang, I always thought it was Chopp."

"I let everyone think it was Chopp. Chopp even thinks it's him." Nahla giggled, "He knows about Marly. He caught us. I do love Chopp. He's always going to have a place in my life. Always. So badly, I wanted it to be Chopp, Kayo. I really did, but it's not. He's got too much going on anyway. He can't focus on me if he wanted to. This whole situation with Marly wasn't what I wanted for myself but... doesn't matter. Marly and I are over with. That chapter has been closed for a couple years now. Since... our fight. I knew I needed to end it and I did. I broke it off soon after you left. It just took some time, you know? But, we're done."

"That's not how endless ties work, Nahla. You're never done."

Nahla sat on the bed. She was exhausted. Kayo sat next to her. Nahla said, "You and the twins are the only ties that matter to me. I will always choose you three over everyone else."

"I understand but, you'll always find your way back to each other, Nahla. It can't be undone."

"I don't know if I believe that anymore." Nahla stood up and threw the bag on the bed. She packed a few items and zipped the bag.

Kayo asked, "Where are you going?"

"I dunno. I need to get out of here. Maybe a hotel or something. Maybe to the city to see Chopp. I have to let you know, since you won't do it, I told Marly I would hunt Tank."

"No! Absolutely not. I don't want you involved, auntie," Kayo said. "Look at your hand anyway. You're a mess. You can't fix my mistakes."

Nahla smiled and said, "I can't seem to fix anything. I went off on Marly. It was pretty bad. But as much as I want to blame her, Marly can't fix this. She was being a jerk to us earlier because she's mad at me. This situation is bigger than her. They accused her of setting everything up. She doesn't know what else to do. You killed some important guys and thwarted an attack that took months to put together. Harvesting Tank is probably on the lower level of possible consequences. If we don't finish that job, there will be men looking for you. They know exactly who you are. They will kill you, and I wouldn't put it past them to go after the twins. She doesn't want me to do it, but I have to."

"Auntie. Someone else was in that room," Kayo finally confessed.

Nahla looked up and said, "What do you mean?"

"The night of the attacks at the Gala. I killed those men one by one and someone shot the last guy I fought and ran off. He had his red dot on my chest, we looked at each other and he ran off. I thought it was a cop at first but I dunno. I think he knows who

I am. I dunno, I didn't trust Marly enough to say anything. I didn't even tell Juno. Whoever it was, looked right at me and then eventually ran away."

"Should we mention it to Marly?"

Kayo thought for a moment and said, "No. We will get this done and figure that out later. For now, don't say anything. I can't be sure if it's a friend or foe yet. Right now, if the focus is Tank, if it has to be done then it has to be me. Tell Marly there's a change of plans. I'm going to Town Hall in the morning and when I come back we can hash it out. I'm gonna need a day or two in the woods. I haven't shot that bow in years."

"And with Tank you cannot miss."

"I won't."

Nahla asked again, "Are you sure you're okay to do this?"

Kayo grabbed her backpack and a bottle of water from the counter and said, "I'm not, but I don't have a choice." Kayo packed her back with the intention of heading out. As she fiddled around for her keys, she was suddenly taken aback by Nahla's disposition. She watched Nahla pace back and forth in the living room. She played with her hand and paced as if she had a whole discussion going on in her head. Her lips were moving but not fully forming words. She stopped to scratch her head a few times and continued to pace. Kayo walked into the living room. She said, "I have to go back to the city tomorrow. I have some things there that I need and I need to see Patterson before I do something stupid with Juno. We're either gonna make love or fight. But really what's the difference between the two? Plus I need to get my bow." Kayo asked, "You okay?"

Nahla shrugged and said, "Not really. I said some things to Marly I kind of regret. I don't want to leave it like that. I know you hate her, and..."

Kayo walked up to Nahla and hugged her tightly. She held on for a while and finally said, "Just go, auntie. I understand."

Nahla let go, took a deep breath, turned around, and walked towards the front door. She jumped into her truck and sped off.

Kayo locked the door on her way out. She got into her pickup and drove away leaving Ayrah and Orion in the cabin.

Fifteen minutes later, Nahla arrived at Marly's cabin to three guards circling the premises. She ignored them as they watched her ascend the stairs. Partially wet from the rain, she softly knocked on the front door. Part of her didn't want Marly to answer while another part did. *I should leave.* She didn't wait long before Marly opened the door and leaned against the frame. Her long wavy hair was split down the middle and divided over her shoulders. Nahla stood there for a moment with her head down with her eyes shamefully glancing up at Marly. Marly held out her hand with the broken compass necklace in her palm. Nahla reached out and took it into her hand and slipped it into her pocket. Marly reached out and lifted Nahla's chin.

Nahla then gently grabbed Marly's hand by the fingertips. Marly carefully guided Nahla inside and shut the door behind her.

Kayo arrived at Juno's place, opened the door and immediately jumped into his arms. She took off her shirt. He lifted her up and carried her into his room, shutting the door behind them.

CHAPTER 8

After a late night, Juno and Kayo still managed to arrive at Nahla's gym at 4:15 am Monday morning. They decided to drive due to the rain that continued to fall overnight into the morning. Juno unlocked the door with his bracelet and held the door for Kayo to enter. He shut the door and they got right to it. Kayo stripped down to her leggings and a sports bra. Juno took off his hoodie. He had on gray shorts with black compression shorts underneath. His upper body was completely chiseled. Kayo couldn't help but touch his chest as they walked over to the power cage. Juno connected the music as Kayo set up the interval timer for 1 minute rounds with 35 seconds of rest. Kayo put on gloves, watching Juno's every move like a predator to its prey. Mine.

Once they were settled under the cage Juno asked, "Three rounds?"

Kayo said, "Let's go!"

In unison, they jumped up, grabbed the bars and started with hanging leg lifts. The workout routine was one they had done for years. Kayo continued to do the same routine in her personal gym at the Solemn Oak building. Neither one of them forgot the order. Juno had been regularly using the gym over the years to clear his mind and stay in shape. Nahla didn't mind. She always looked at Juno as family.

After three rounds they transitioned to medicine ball slams, then medicine ball passes, then push ups. Kayo struggled to keep up and laughed. Juno smiled widely when she took a break and asked, "What you doing, Kay?"

"Shut up!" she replied. She started doing push ups again, barely completing one more before the timer stopped. Juno kept doing push ups past the buzzer to tease her. She jumped on his back and wrapped her arms around his neck putting him into a choke hold.

He laughed and said, "You always cheat!"

She let go and flopped to the ground from exhaustion.

He crawled on top of her but instead of kissing her, said, "It's just the warm up. You owe me two more rounds. Three if you wanna get spicy."

"I bet you'd love an extra round," Kayo replied sarcastically.

Juno laughed and said, "I would actually." He leaned in to kiss her, but she gently put her hand against his chest. Juno smirked, stood up and helped Kayo off the ground. They returned under the cage for round two. After three rounds of the warm up, they made their way to the bags, engaged in a punching bag workout for five minutes then hit the weights.

It was like old times. Kayo's conflicted soul

felt stable again. For the first time she and Nahla weren't at odds and she and Juno weren't fighting. These two things never usually occurred at the same time and even still, she knew that these euphoric moments were short lived, ended chaotically and soon followed by long periods of strife and toxic interactions. But it was futile to dwell on the inevitable collapse of these cherishable moments with Juno. Kayo remained pragmatic, even though her heart wanted this feeling to continue forever, it would not— the high before the crash.

As their morning workout session came to a close the door opened. It was Nahla. She headed directly to the back room. She gave a quick glance and beelined to the door.

Kayo looked at her watch and sarcastically asked, "How'd I beat you here? Long night?" She laughed as she threw her hoodie on.

Nahla stuck up her middle finger and said, "Zip it!"

Juno used his hand to sign as if he zipped his mouth shut and threw away the key.

"Did you get your compass back?" Kayo teased.

Nahla continued to walk towards the back. Keeping her back turned, she reached into her pocket, pulled out the necklace and dangled it from her hand. She quickly shoved it back into her pocket.

Kayo giggled and said, "We're about done here. After we take care of things at Town Hall, I'll stop by before I head back home."

Nahla nodded. "Meet me here."

Kayo and Juno left the gym. Kayo left a piece of the protein bar on the wooden post again. They got into the truck and drove off.

Nahla went into the back room and shut the door. When she entered the room she leaned her back against the door and gasped. She had a long night with Marly. It had been almost two years since their last private interaction and Nahla's emotions were in a tailspin. Last night, they made love, drank chai tea, laughed about the past and present and made love again before bed and once again in the morning. She felt satisfied yet conflicted. She took the compass from her left pocket and clutched it close to her chest. She closed her eyes and breathed softly in and out as her mind began to reminisce about her love affair with Marly over the years. Charging through her head were flashes and recollections of the times she and Marly spent together gazing into each other's eyes, kissing and making love in secret— in Marly's cabin, room to room, from the back of the truck to hotels, to the woods, by the creek but never in Nahla's bed.

She remembered a getaway they took to a ski resort in New Hampshire and a cabin they visited a few times in the Catskills. Dinners and lingerie, surprise gift exchanges, random cupcake and flower deliveries— all the activities that sexual flings did not engage in, they did it. She and Chopp never did those things. *Chopp never loved on me this way,* she thought. Nahla wasn't used to these types of activities with her lovers. Marly was extremely intentional in selecting how they spent their time together. Beyond occasionally showing up in lingerie, or a friendly dinner, encounters with her lovers were exciting and fun but strictly business. No dates, no playful or passionate kisses, no emotional arguments. Marly was different. She made Nahla feel like their affair was special and every argument was worth the stress. After looking back on everything, Nahla realized that she and Marly were in a full blown relationship and Nahla was finally recognizing this to be the case. They were messy, happy and although by their own rules, they could not openly admit it, they were in love.

The evening encounter was an emotional setback but also a rejuvenation of lustful desires and longing. *We're worse than Kay and Juno,* she thought. She cursed Marly to hell and an hour later was laying in her bed wrapped in her arms. Toxic. But she didn't regret it. She smiled and thought, how badly she needed last night to happen; her body yearned for it. She couldn't move as she fantasized about the evening, wishing it would happen again tonight and the night after. She thought, I have to figure this out, but Kayo first. Then I will fix everything with Marly. She grabbed her phone and sent Marly a "moon" emoji.

Moments later, Marly texted back, "CAN'T FOCUS. UR ON MY MIND" followed by a "sun" emoji. Marly couldn't resist but to call.

Nahla smiled and picked up, "Hey." She was anxious to hear Marly's voice.

Marly exhaled. "Hey. Sorry to call. I dunno if you can talk, but I need to hear your voice."

Nahla felt relieved. "Yes. It's fine. It's good to hear your voice too. I've been thinking about you all morning. I can't stop thinking about last night. I really enjoyed you."

Marly smiled and said, "Same. You were so amazing. God, I've missed you." There was a short pause. They both needed it. Marly anxiously responded, "I need more of you. I want to see you. Can I see you later tonight?"

Without hesitation, Nahla replied, "Yes! Yes, of course. I want to see you too. I need to." She took a deep breath and asked, "How about dinner?" Nahla was nervous to ask. The circumstances weren't ideal.

"Sure. Where do you want to go?" Marly asked.

Nahla hesitantly responded, "How about my place?"

Marly was completely taken aback. "Your place? Nahla, are you sure?" Enemy territory.

"No but, YOLO!" If love was a cliff, Nahla was jumping off head first. "Marly, I want to see you, I want to cook for you and... I want you to stay the night with me." Nahla knew she was opening a can of worms. "It's okay if you don't want to. I understand if it's too much."

Marly was a bit overwhelmed but said, "No! I'd really love that, Nahla. It would mean a lot to me actually."

Nahla exhaled. "No pressure. I don't even know

what I'm doing right now. If you say yes now and back out later I won't be upset. Even if you walk up to the door, change your mind and leave. I'll understand."

"Stop. Please. I admit I have a lot going through my mind right now, but I've always wanted you to bring me home. So, don't give me a reason to second guess myself." Marly's heart raced.

"Then, no surprises. The twins will be there and... I invited Kayo. I don't even know if she will be back in town, but..."

There was a brief silence, but Marly was up for it. "I'll be there. Allow me this privilege and I'll take whatever comes with it."

"Okay." Nahla acquiesced. *I love her.*

"Okay. Need me to bring anything?"

Nahla closed her eyes and said, "Just yourself. Oh and wine. Bring something good. You're gonna need to bring a peace offering," Nahla laughed. "The twins will be your biggest allies. Ayrah likes a good red wine."

Marly smiled at the phone and replied, "Done. Anything for dessert?"

Nahla thought, Yes, you! but instead said, "No. Unless you want something, we should be fine. Is 6:00 okay for you?" Nahla was still nervous expecting to be rejected.

"It's perfect. I can't wait to see you."

"I can't wait to kiss you. See you then." Nahla hung up.

Marly hung up, leaned back in her office chair

and dropped her glasses on the desk. She thought about their night together and slipped away into her memories of that evening. Her love for Nahla had awakened from dormancy. As much as she tried to suppress it, the feelings had resurfaced and were more pungent than ever. *What am I doing?* Marly thought to herself. Reality was always a moment away. She reached into her desk, pulled out a diamond ring and placed it back onto her finger. Marly was engaged and didn't know how to tell Nahla. Marly had confessed to seeing someone, but was never clear about the seriousness of it. Even though she was fully committed to someone else, she also couldn't resist the lure of Nahla's presence or any remote chance they could be together again. Her sexual attraction to Nahla was uncontrollable. They were so deeply connected, Marly couldn't help but go back to her.

Being invited over for dinner was an even bigger deal. Nahla was presenting her to the pack as if to say, "Mine!" Marly was about to completely encroach upon Chopp's territory which possibly meant Chopp was out of the picture or at least she was going to be Nahla's priority. Staying over would be the nail in the coffin. *But why now?* she thought. It was a gesture that Marly longed for, but their timing couldn't have been worse. *Maybe I shouldn't go,* she thought. But of course she was going to go. *Maybe I will have dinner, but won't stay the night,* she lied to herself. She longed to experience Nahla in her room, knowing it was a sacred place for Nahla to share with anyone.

Marly received a text message the previous night but hadn't responded. She was so wrapped up in her time with Nahla that she hadn't even looked. She completely forgot to check her phone until she hung up with Nahla. She looked through her messages and replied to someone named Jessie, "SORRY I'M JUST SEEING THIS. WAS REALLY BUSY LAST NIGHT. SOMETHING CAME UP AND I GOT SIDETRACKED. I CANNOT MEET TONIGHT. CAN I COME VISIT THIS WEEKEND INSTEAD?"

Rain beat down against the windshield of Attorney Jessica Humphries's state-issued electric SUV as she sat outside of the courthouse in the parking lot across the street near the charging station. She thumbed through some papers and shoved them into a folder. She received a text, checked her phone and smiled. It was someone named Patsy. She replied, "BUSY TOO. THIS WEEKEND WILL BE BETTER FOR ME! SEE YOU THEN. LOVE YOU." Looking at the time on her dashboard, she noticed it was 8:53 am and she only had a few minutes to speak to her clients before it was time to speak with the magistrate. "Shit. Let me get my ass inside," She whispered to herself. Humphries grabbed a short umbrella and jogged through the chilly wet air, from her vehicle up the front steps. She took the steps up to the second floor where she saw Dennis and Sam waiting for her arrival. They were escorted by two police officers. "Things may not be as bad as they seem. Let's find a room where we can talk."

The room was located on the second floor next to the elevators. Humphries escorted the two men into the room. There were no windows, a conference table and five chairs. The police officers stayed outside. She sat down first. "Please sit," she directed them.

Denny and Sam looked at each other eager to hear what the deal was. "What are they saying?" Sam asked.

"I'm not feeling very optimistic," Dennis added.

"Well... no deal is perfect. The good news is that the weapons charge was dropped. Can't have a weapon charge if there's no weapon. As far as I'm concerned they found this fletching image from the internet or it was AI generated to coerce you to confess. They had no choice but to drop it since there's no evidence of it."

Dennis said, "But I saw it. We both did.

"Well, I don't have it. They don't have it. I didn't see it. It's not our problem. If they were serious, they'd still have it and I don't see them delaying this to find it. Anyway, the not so good news is that you're gonna get stuck with third degree poaching since they can prove you hit the deer with the car and took it without reporting the accident. We are looking at a charge for a salvaged carcass without a permit with intent to distribute."

Sam said, "We were going to eat it, not sell it."

Humphries added, "Distribute. They didn't say sell. Distribution includes sharing with or giving to family and friends."

"What does this mean for us?" Denny asked.

"It's looking like some time in the Cycles," Humphries warned them. "I can try working on that intent to distribute, but they're saying the way you had it bagged up looked suspicious."

Denny, "Bagging up meat and freezing it is suspicious?"

Humphries added, "They're going to ask for 2 years or 1 million watts between the two of you. That's 500k watts each."

Dennis asked, "How long does that take?"

"Depends on your fitness level but average is about 100 watts per hour on a bike. That's 5,000 hours give or take.

"I'm gonna lose my job," Sam said with disappointment.

"Well, I tried asking for a lighter sentence, but they mentioned past moving violations... Sam! Seems you've had some issues with racing in the past."

Sam was embarrassed. "I was racing trails on an ATV, overshot a jump and skidded out onto a public road."

"That's one. You have two other infractions that seem vague but you were cited and paid the fine."

"It cost too much to appeal and I couldn't get out of work," Sam said.

Jessica Humphries was empathetic but it didn't matter. "I understand but if you've had moving violations in the past, it doesn't help much and you were driving. Dennis, I may be able to get yours down a little."

"What do you recommend?" Dennis asked.

Humphries tapped her index finger nail on the table. "I'm going to make some calls for you. I'm hoping that today we can delay your sentencing, keep you out of the Cycles and get your bail down to a reasonable amount so we can get you out of here by the end of the day. I'm thinking we can do a plea deal and see if we can get time in the cycles a little lower, but there will be a consequence. My job is to help minimize it. There's so much going on with that terrorist attack, I don't think they're worried about you two as much. Sit tight. I'll be back."

Jessica Humpries grabbed her papers, stood up and fixed her skirt. She walked out of the room leaving the two men in total and utter confusion, but with a little hope.

Humphries picked up the phone and made a call. The phone rang. Someone answered and she said, "Hi. Judge Conway. This is Attorney Jessica Humphries. Sorry to bother you, but I have a loose end that needs to be tied up here. Please call back when you get a chance."

Kayo and Juno left Town Hall with their signed

papers in hand. Kayo drove the truck with Juno in the passenger seat. On their way back to Nahla's, they didn't speak. They barely looked at each other. Kayo kept her head and eyes straight on the road and did not flinch. The quiet was deafening. The regret was profuse but the task was done. Signing over the property was the final tie to sever between them. Kayo felt an overwhelming sensation of nausea and a slight sense of grief. The homestead was their childhood dream and she was giving it away for Juno to continue a life without her. She didn't want any money and nothing in exchange. She only wanted to move on.

Kayo and Juno had just made love the night before and this morning the energy they radiated could have shattered walls. But they were both liars, lying to themselves that turning over the house to Juno was a necessary job to complete before their final departure. It was Kayo's idea, but Juno agreed that it should be done only to appease Kayo. He always gave in. He always let Kayo have her way, deciding their next move. Like a toothbrush in the bathroom, a key on a ring or night slippers left behind by an ex at the end of the bed, the homestead was always a reason to reconnect back to one another and now that was gone. They could sign their lives away and pray this would be it but there would be no separation. *We've tried this before,* Kayo thought. She was afraid this move was just another vain gesture. Another attempt that with time would fail.

Juno couldn't stay away from Kayo. Like a ghost, he always appeared just when she was most vulnerable. He was always around lurking in corners and watching her from afar. Sometimes she knew, but pretended she didn't see him. She was sure he was staying with Chopp or had a woman in the city somewhere and Kayo was so routined, it wasn't hard to assume her next move. He could predict her exact location on any day of the week at any given time. He'd show up at the most random times sitting in the back of the same cafe or on a bench in a park she was running through. But she secretly loved the attention and adoration she felt from Juno. She liked that she felt protected, knowing Juno would kill for her and he had. It was another secret they shared that connected them to one another.

Kayo made her way back to Nahla's property and pulled up outside of the shed. She sent a text, "WE'RE BACK. OUTSIDE AT THE GYM."

Nahla replied, "I'M HERE. COME IN."

Before getting out of the truck they both sat in silence. Neither of them moved, knowing that they needed to talk. Juno finally broke the ice and said, "I didn't want to do that, Kay. I didn't want to take your name off the property."

Kayo looked straight ahead and said, "It is what it is, Juno. It's what we planned to do."

"No. It's what *you* planned to do," Juno insisted. "You decided this."

"Juno, We need to move on. This is an emotional rollercoaster neither of us can handle."

"Why not?" Juno asked.

"For one, we aren't together anymore and we don't work. We can't get it together. Secondly, I'm seeing someone and... I'm not like Nahla. I can't sustain ongoing love affairs with multiple people. It's confusing," Kayo added. "I care about you. I love you, but our time has come to an end and we have to be honest about that. Now I have this shit to worry about. I don't even know if I can keep up with Patterson to be honest. The poor guy is a great guy and I've been ignoring his calls. He doesn't need a woman like me fucking up his life too."

Juno asked, "I don't give a fuck about Patterson! You laid in my arms all night, kissed me and made love to me. What the fuck was that about?"

Kayo sat for a moment. She knew she was wrong, but made an excuse in her head. "The plan was to sign the property over to you. We didn't discuss anything different than that. It's the only reason I'm here. I didn't come here to salvage a relationship."

"Why would you do that, Kay!?" Juno insisted on an answer. "Why?"

Kayo looked at Juno and said, "I don't know, Juno. Maybe I was in my feelings. This place messes with my head. I got lost in old emotions for a moment. We are both at fault for that. Don't put this all on me. It was just sex."

Juno was frustrated and said, "Just sex? You don't know the difference between intimacy and sex, Kay?"

Kayo replied, "Well, if you felt I was taking advantage of you, I'm sorry. I didn't mean to confuse you."

"I know what I want. You don't confuse me. You confuse yourself." Juno opened the door and got out of the truck. He slammed the door shut.

Kayo huffed and exited the pickup truck. She stopped to listen for a moment and turned her head towards the trees. She looked around but didn't see anything. Together, she and Juno entered the gym. Nahla was waiting for them. She could see that the energy between them had changed. She asked, "You guys ok?"

Kayo hesitantly responded, "Everything is fine." *Lie.*

"Hmm." She was not convinced. "Backroom now," Nahla demanded.

Nahla had never invited anyone except Chopp into her back office. They all walked in and shut the door. At the desk, Nahla had three computer screens and two large surveillance screens on the wall across from the desk. There was an eight by eight foot rug and a two seater sofa against the wall. Nahla locked the room after they entered. Kayo was confused. They could have conversed in the main room. It's private and the door is always locked. She asked, "What's going on?"

Nahla said, "I had a long talk with Marly. Kayo, maybe I'm being biased but there isn't anything she can do. I want to be clear. She wasn't lying about that. She showed me the text messages and played the voice memos she received and they weren't nice. Her approach was all wrong but she was also mad at me. Either way, we agreed that moving forward Ayrah and Oree will no longer be working for her. That's over and done with. I know Ayrah and Oree will be frustrated."

"We will figure something out," Kayo added. "It's better for everyone this way to cut business ties with Marly."

"We discussed that and we both agree that it's time. It's better this way." Nahla raised her hand and said, "I wanted to show you my meditation room."

Kayo looked around and said, "Ok. Looks comfy." Kayo wasn't sure why the room was so important.

"This isn't it," Nahla said.

Nahla pulled out her phone, opened an application and started pressing in a code. She pulled the rug up on one end and a trap door opened underneath. The door lowered into the floor and exposed a steep staircase that resembled a ladder. Nahla held out her hand for Kayo to descend. Kayo went down first. She went down backwards holding onto the sides. Juno followed immediately after. Nahla descended the stairs last into a small 10x10 foot area. On the other end there was a door.

"When we moved here, we all built bunkers and put sheds on top of them." Nahla walked up to the door which she opened with an eye scan. "Marly eventually converted a portion into the butcher shop. Mine... come see for yourselves." Nahla looked into the eye scanner. They all heard a light buzz sound and bolts unlocking from within. Once the door unlocked she was prompted again to punch a 7 digit code into the keypad. She heard a few more bolts turn and then a light on the door turned green. The door opened.

As they entered, one by one a row of lights lit the room. On the left wall there were racks of guns, rifles and crates full of weaponry and ammunition. Kayo's eyes grew. She turned and looked at Nahla with astonishment. Nahla shrugged. "I thought a revolution was coming."

One by one Kayo scanned the ammo crates with her eyes: 9mm, .203, 5.56, 30.06, .38... Kayo knew her aunt had a few guns in the safe in the house, but she had no idea that Nahla had an arsenal hidden away underneath the gym they trained in for years. On the right wall was a small desk with four monitors showing cameras covering every corner of the property. One even showed the farmers market. There was a shelf with books and magazines. Kayo picked through a section of road maps, atlases and resource books: rebuilding engines, solar electricity, basic medical procedures. At the back of the room was another door. There was another safe in the corner by that door. It was open. There were stacks of cash, gold bars and silver bullion in crooked stacks. "Who knows about this?" Kayo asked.

"Just Chopp." She escorted them to the next door. She pulled a key from her pocket and said,

"This is what I wanted to show you." She opened the door. The room was dark with black lights that lit the room turning everything white a purplish glowing hue. The room was moist, cool and fans were running. Nahla had been growing and selling psychedelic mushrooms. "I grow four varieties. I've created and have been testing a strain that maximizes the trip to about an hour but the average trip is about 40 minutes. I call it the Dragonfly. Best seller. Chopp has been helping me move them through the bike shop."

"Cycledelics," Kayo said, "Kind of bold but makes sense."

Juno said, "So that's what's in these packages you've been giving me. I didn't know."

"You had no reason to know. I paid you well." Nahla smiled and said, "Sorry I never told you but it was probably better you didn't know. I didn't want Kayo to know, and didn't trust you to keep a secret from her. But I do trust you to get stuff to Chopp without trying to skim off the top. I know he still gets wild game from Marly, and I'm okay with that, but this has been a lucrative alternative without the competition."

Kayo asked, "So Marly doesn't know?"

Nahla answered, "No. I don't intend to involve her but, now the twins have a way to make money without the conflict of interest looming over my head. You guys can help me run this until you figure out what you want to do. It's up to you." Nahla stepped aside for a moment and grabbed a package.

She handed it to Juno and asked "By the way, can you get this to Chopp for me?"

Kayo snatched the package and said, "I got it. I have to go to the city in a few. I will make sure he gets it. To be honest, I don't like this for the twins or you either, but it seems safer than running game. Working for Marly is a major conflict of interest for you Nahla. You two need to sort that out."

"I know. I'm working on that," Nahla agreed. "She's got her hands in so many things. I don't think she's going to smuggle wild game much longer. Anyway, Kayo, once this is over with, and Tank's head is in a bag, we will make a plan for the twins. I would prefer your involvement, but it's your call."

Juno added, "I'm down to help wherever I'm needed. I'm glad you trust me to do that. I appreciate hearing that. Whatever you want to do Kay, I'll support it."

"I can't make a decision right now, but I can commit to reviewing your ideas and offering suggestions. I think Juno and the twins can handle this with or without me. My access to the delivery tunnels may help. Anyway, I can't stay long, I need to get back to the city but will be back later tonight. Tomorrow I will spend the day practicing. The next morning, I will be looking for Tank. Just get me his latest coordinates so I know where to focus. Juno, I will need you on standby."

"I planned on coming with you," Juno said.

"No," Kayo insisted. "I need to do this alone. If I fail, I need you to get the twins and Nahla out of here.

Nahla smiled, "You know I'm not going anywhere, baby girl. I don't run from anyone."

She looked back at Juno and said, "Okay, so Juno, I'm gonna need you to knock Auntie upside the head and put her in the truck and get her and the twins out of here."

They all laughed.

Nahla grabbed Kayo and hugged her tightly. They didn't share many embraces but when they did they were always meaningful. "Kayo. You won't fail. I can feel it," Nahla said emotionally.

Kayo replied, "I'm afraid, Auntie. I'm afraid I will fail. If I fail, I'll lose much more than India."

Nahla let go and said, "That's why you won't fail, Kay. You are smarter and more calculated than before. I've never seen you miss a target. Tank is older. Slower. He hides high in the mountain for a reason. It's your time. You'll get him. Remember everything you know about him."

Kayo closed her eyes and said, "He sounds like a truck. His vision on his left, my right, is gone. He..." Kayo dropped a tear and quickly wiped it away. "I have to go." She quickly spun around, left the grow room, charged through the safe room and climbed up the steep stairway. Juno and Nahla stood for a while before heading back into the safe room.

Nahla said to Juno, "You're the only person I trust with her life." She pulled a duffle bag out and placed a 30.06 inside. She put in an AR15 and a couple handguns. She opened the ammo cases one after the other, throwing in ammo for each of the guns. "On the day of her hunt, wait three hours, then head to the location. I don't care what she says. She's going to need help getting Tank out of there. He's tagged. It's gotta be removed and the body has to be gone. Most likely no one will look for him until the next morning, but you never know. Sometimes they send drones once they can no longer detect a pulse. Stay out of sight and earshot of her. She will hear you with those damn bionic ears if you're too close. You're going to have to track her."

"I can do that," Juno said. He took one of the handguns and pulled at the slide. He tossed it back into the bag.

"If you see Tank, mow his ass down," Nahla insisted.

Juno asked, "Wouldn't that defeat the purpose?"

"If it comes to that, I won't care." Nahla froze and stared at Juno. "Juno, Kayo isn't going in there as a predator. She's going in as prey. She wants him to come out and hunt her." She said, "So, if you see Tank, that most likely means she's gone, he's picked up your scent and he will kill you too if allowed. Tomorrow, I'm sending the twins out of town until further notice. Don't ask where. Chopp won't know either." Nahla paused again and asked, "Juno. Ayrah said you mentioned seeing Paul in the city not too long ago."

Juno responded, "Yeah I saw him. I saw him about a month ago in the city, but he avoided me, so

I just left him alone. Why?" Juno asked curiously.

"Kayo said someone else was at the gala and shot the last guy she was fighting. That's how she got away. She said that the person took aim at her but then ran away. I dunno. She said she didn't tell anyone about it, not even you. When Ayrah told me you saw him, I didn't care too much about it because it was meaningless. Now, I'm starting to wonder what he was doing in the city."

"Hmm. When did she tell you this?" Juno asked.

"A few weeks before the attacks. I didn't think much of it but recently it popped into my head so now I'm wondering about it. Anyway, let's keep an eye out on him. I may need to talk to him later," Nahla said.

"Absolutely! So now what are you going to do?" Juno asked.

"You'll know when it's done." Nahla locked the safe room and ascended the stairs. Juno followed soon after.

Kayo stood outside the gym waiting for Juno. She saw the raven again lurking in the higher branches of a pine tree. *Shadow?* She wondered. She reached into her bag, but noticed on the wooden post a nickel. She smiled and put the nickel into her pocket and said, "Thank you." She reached back into her bag and took out a small piece of the protein bar. She put her hand on top of the post but left her hand open. She looked up to the raven. Leaving her hand open, the raven flew down to the ground but soon after he flew away.

Kayo smiled and took a deep breath. She closed her eyes, taking in the sun and the fresh air. Kayo left the broken protein bar pieces on the top of a wooden post. The raven swiftly came back and pecked at it, perched at the top of the post. Kayo watched and said, "Well, you're not Shadow." She noticed all of his toes were present and accounted for. "Do you know him? Do you know Shadow?" She asked playfully. "Probably not." She put more food in her hand and slowly reached towards the bird. "You can trust me." The bird quickly snatched the food away and jumped to the ground about 15 feet away from Kayo. He pecked at the food. She smiled and said, "I don't know if you're a boy or a girl so forgive me. But I will call you Frank after Frank Abagnale, you little thief!" One of Kayo's favorite movies, *Catch Me if You Can*, was a movie about the cunning thief Frank Abignale who, as a teenager, led the FBI on a wild goose chase over fake checks. "If I find out you're a girl, I'll call you Abby. Deal?"

Frank flew away with a morsel of food and more waiting on the post. *I'll probably never see you again, Frank,* she thought. Just as she turned away, Nahla and Juno emerged from the gym. Juno walked up to Kayo. Nahla nodded and walked away towards the cabin.

Juno asked, "When are you coming back?"

"Hopefully in time for dinner. I'm not sure," Kayo replied. "I may need to stay at the cabin tonight. I hope that's fine."

"Of course. Let me know if you need anything else. I've got some errands to run, but I will be home this evening." Juno kissed Kayo on the forehead and walked to the back of the truck. He pulled the e-bike from the back and placed it on the ground. "Sorry about earlier. Right now isn't really the time to lay my emotions onto you."

Kayo felt guilty for being selfish. "Juno. I shouldn't have done that last night. I was being selfish. I'm really sorry."

Juno nodded his head and looked away. As he mounted the bike, he took a deep breath, quickly looked back and drove off. There was no talk of a moon or the sun. That never happened, even after an intense argument. Kayo watched with guilt that once again, she was leaving Juno in a fragile emotional state. Nonetheless, her focus was on Patterson, her bow and possibly her last week alive.

Truthfully, she didn't expect to return after the hunt. She wanted to tie up all loose ends and end with zero regrets, but last night went a little too far.

Internally, Kayo was mentally preparing herself for the final chapter of her life and made peace with the fact that it would be in the woods doing what she truly loved more than anything else. She intended to make these last few days count. Her plan was to get to the city, visit Patterson, grab her things and depending on how much time she spent with Patterson, maybe swing by to see Monty or Beth. Nahla invited her over for dinner and she couldn't miss it. It was possibly her last meal with the twins.

Just before getting off Route 2, heading onto 91 South, Kayo texted Patterson, "I'M HEADED TO THE CITY, BUT HAVE TO HEAD BACK HOME EARLY THIS AFTERNOON. WILL YOU BE AROUND?"

"YES," Patterson replied. "I CAN BE AVAILABLE IF YOU WANT TO SEE ME."

Kayo smiled and wrote back, "OF COURSE I DO. PITCHFORK AT 2:30?"

"COOL. IT'S A COUPLE OF BLOCKS AWAY FROM MY FLAT. I'LL MEET YOU THERE," Patterson responded.

CHAPTER 9

KAYO BROOKS, INDIA ALEXANDER & THE TANK

Kayo convinced India to help her hunt the Tank. She was still indebted to Marly and any opportunity to shave off some debt she took it. Every hunter in the co-op and surrounding towns had heard rumors about him but only Kayo and India caught him on the trailcam. Marly put out a bounty on the Tank of $2000 and double his weight in credits. If the rumors were true, he'd be over 500 pounds. Marly would have a $6000 payday selling the meat, and maybe another $5000 for the hide.

India and Kayo planned on splitting everything down the middle. They had his latest location on record and it was an opportunity of a lifetime. They could estimate his size based on their familiarity with the area and comparisons to other bears caught on the trailcam and the rumors seemed to be true. The Tank was massive. It was going to be an exciting hunt and both were ready for it. India wasn't as good a shot as Kayo, but was certainly proficient and good enough to take down a bear. They rarely missed a target, aiming for the heart or lungs was key for a fast kill. A gut shot would require time and tracking. It's a deadly shot but was not preferred.

India and Kayo spent a few days practicing. Nahla helped them work on their form and made sure their bows were fine tuned and waxed. They practiced in the woods from various angles, shooting from treestands, straddling tree branches, hunting saddles and on the ground through shrubs which was difficult because the smallest twig could send the arrow heading in the wrong direction. Kayo's camouflage colored compound bow was set at a 55 pound draw. She only needed to pull it once. It had a matching quiver and a 4 inch black stabilizer on the front. India's bow was all black with a similar set up but only a 45 pound draw. They both used carbon fiber arrows, but their broadhead preference differed. Kayo liked to use triple blade stainless steel fixed broadheads. India was a fan of broadheads with retractable tips — equally as deadly.

The afternoon prior to the hunt, Kayo, Juno, India and her boyfriend Paul went to The Latch for a few drinks and an early dinner. Kayo insisted that India eat more protein but India refused, sticking to a basket of curly fries and rootbeer. "I guess I know how you stay so lean," Kayo taunted. "You need to eat more. We have a long day ahead tomorrow."

"I'm not really hungry," India said. "Kinda anxious about tomorrow."

"Are you afraid?" Juno asked before taking a large bite of his cheeseburger.

India responded, "Not really. Just a little jittery and excited. Ready to get going."

Paul added, "Well, you should eat more than just fries." Paul cut a piece of his chicken tender and fed it to India and kissed her as she chewed it.

Juno looked at Kayo and smiled.

"Don't even think about it!" Kayo said, assuming Juno was going to try and feed her.

Juno laughed and said, "I'm not sharing my food with you! But, I'll take a kiss."

Kayo giggled and said, "Aww you feel left out. Come here." She leaned over and kissed him lightly on the lips. Then she grabbed one of his fries and shoved it in her mouth.

Paul asked, "You think he will come out?"

India replied, "I think so. He likes to move around for about an hour or two before sunset. I'm going to drop a pile of berries and hope I see a coyote so I can kill it and leave it out as bait. But truth be told, I don't anticipate being out there long. Tank is coming straight to me. He's going to lay down in front of me and say 'Take me home, India. I am all yours.'"

Kayo laughed and said, "He's actually going to come take my arrow and stab himself in the heart. I don't know what you're talking about."

"Just be careful babe," Paul warned. "I don't like the idea of bow hunting this thing."

"I'm always careful," India responded. "Trust me, love, I'd prefer a rifle, but that's way too loud. We'd get caught in no time. Bows and blades are real assassin's weapons. They don't snitch."

Kayo raised her glass and they tapped them together in agreement.

India continued, "Just be ready for the trophy photo we're going to take with me standing on his head!"

"Don't ask how we will get his ass outta the woods," Kayo added.

After dinner, the four friends drove up to the Danby family cabin and hung out a couple hours before calling it a night. The girls planned on getting up at 5 to head out around 6 am to their separate hunting locations. They had everything mapped out. Kayo planned to take the north side of the property, and India would take the south west section, closer to the trail cam that caught Tank in action. That evening before bed, they watched the movie *300* and cuddled by the fire. Kayo had a few sips of wine. She didn't like to drink too much before a hunt; however, the small buzz was enough for her and Juno to get flirtatious and handsy, so they decided to call it a night.

Juno got up and escorted Kayo to the room. He grabbed her from behind and kissed her on the neck. "Good night," Kayo said to Paul and India as they laid on the floor not far from the wood stove. As soon as Kayo and Juno were out of sight, India climbed on top of Paul and kissed him.

Juno shut the door behind them. He grabbed Kayo kissing her and whispered, "You think they'll hear us?"

Kayo smiled and said, "Depends on what you wanna do." She started unbuttoning his pants. "Wouldn't be the first time."

"I think I wanna keep them up tonight," Juno said just before he bit Kayo on the neck.

He pulled her shirt over her head and her hair fell down past her shoulders. He pulled his shirt off and continued to kiss her as he finished taking off her clothes.

The next morning everyone was up at 5am. Kayo took a shower while Juno started making breakfast. He made fried eggs with cheese and English muffins with sausage. Kayo finished getting dressed, walked over to Juno and kissed him, "Good morning."

"Good morning," Juno said with a smile. He loved looking at her face. He kissed her again as she leaned on him.

She reached over, grabbed the kettle and began making tea. She filled it with water and put the kettle on the stove for water to boil, then walked over to the table and put down placemats, plates and silverware. "What time are you guys leaving?"

Juno said, "We'll leave when you two head out this morning. Paul has to get back home and I have some errands to run for Marly. I'll come back this evening."

"No, don't. Wait until we call. I don't think we will see anything yet. I plan on watching from the saddle today. If we don't see anything we will pitch a tent and camp out for the night. I'll try tracking him tomorrow. You're only an hour away, so if we get something, I will call you and drop the location so you can help. Don't leave with our bikes in the trucks!"

India walked into the kitchen area and said, "Thanks Juno. Good morning." She had just got out of the shower and was wearing purple long johns.

"Good morning, You're welcome. Where's Paul?" Juno asked.

"In the shower. He's almost out." India looked around the kitchen and said, "I need coffee."

Kayo replied, "There's some instant coffee in the cabinet if you want to wait for the water to finish boiling. Should be another minute."

Soon Paul emerged from the bedroom. The party of four sat down at the table and ate breakfast. The girls finished first. As the guys finished up eating, the girls put on sweats, then started dressing in their hunting gear. They always wore regular clothes underneath hunting gear just in case something happened and they needed to look like hikers. Kayo's final act was stepping into and strapping her safety harness onto her body. She took her bow out of the case and walked it outside, placing it onto a mount on the front of her e-bike. She waited for everyone to exit the cabin. Juno came outside first. He threw his bag into the back of the truck. Leaving the door open he walked over to Kayo and hugged her. He whispered to her, "You look so sexy in this damn outfit." He kissed her as if he wouldn't see her again and said, "I wish I could come with you."

"We got it."

"I know you do. Be careful. Love you!" He walked toward his truck to leave.

"Love you too," Kayo said as she sat on her bike, pulled her backpack up over her shoulders and clasped the straps together in the front.

On the side of the truck India and Paul were hugging. Paul said, "You know I come from a family of trappers and hunting isn't really my thing, but I understand the risks. Please be careful. I need you to come back home to me. Maybe we can talk about you and me getting our own place together." He winked.

India smiled and said, "I'd love to do that. And I'll do something nice for you when I get back," and winked. She hugged and kissed Paul then climbed onto her bike.

Kayo signaled she was ready to go. India pulled up to her side. "Keep your location on. If by 30 minutes before sundown we don't see anything, meet me at the centerpoint. We will camp there and head back out in the morning. Bye bye my sunshine!" The centerpoint was the halfway point between their hunting locations.

"Tah Tah moonbeam," India responded.

Kayo put on her goggles and drove off. India followed suit heading west on a trail not far away. Kayo had to cut through a field behind the cabin first. As she was riding, along the treeline she noticed a ten-pointer grazing with a few doe. As tempting as it was, she wasn't there for him.

Next time, she thought to herself. She let him go. Eventually, the deer saw her and darted off into the woods.

She reached the trail and drove deeper into the dank forest. The sun was still low, leaving shadowy patches and low lit crevices throughout the woods. It was cold. The trail was covered in wet leaves from oaks, maple and birch trees that towered along the path's edge. Pine cones, fallen trees, random boulders and ferns dotted the view of the forest floor. Kayo removed her hearing aids to listen more carefully. She didn't like to wear them when in the woods. The tires and the motor of the e-bike were quieter than a traditional motor scooter, hence the preference for hunting. She could use all her senses to track Tank. Occasionally she stopped and listened, looked around for signs and smelled the sweet scented air. She looked for scat and scrapes or damage to shrubs that may be a sign of bears moving through the area. She saw coyote scat and deer droppings along the way. Most were fresh. She could hear a brook babbling somewhere in the distance and the cadence of woodpecker beaks against the trees. Kayo checked the map on her phone. 300 more yards, she thought. She tucked her phone back into her pocket and carried on.

India was closer to her destination. She also looked for sign as she traveled along the trail. She noticed scattered rabbit fur near a boulder and a few deer rubs on young ash trees a little off the trail. She suddenly came to a halt when she noticed a large claw mark on a white oak tree. She took a photo. She got off her bike for a closer inspection. "Not sure if you belong to the Tank but, you're definitely from a bear." She looked around for tracks. She saw one but couldn't follow the direction as it was lost over the fallen leaves. She took a few more steps in, picked up some leaves and smelled them. She couldn't tell if the bear urinated in the area because the leaves were wet from the recent rain showers that fell over the woods. She sent the photo to Kayo and got back onto her bike.

Not long after, both women reached their destinations. Kayo stopped at a tree she used in the past and had a hunting saddle set up where she could hang high in the tree and hunt. It was her preferred method of bow hunting. Before ascending, she covered her bike and excess supplies with camouflage netting at the base of the tree. Once in the saddle, she texted India a silly pic of herself along with the words, "MOON LANDING!"

India preferred a traditional stand. She put the stand up a year ago against an pin oak tree and it was still holding up sturdily. India also covered her bike with camouflage netting, climbed the ladder with her bow and got settled into the stand with her backpack. She sat quietly. She sent Kayo a thumbs up photo and wrote "SUNNY SIDE UP!" She took out her binoculars. She glassed the surroundings but didn't see more than a squirrel or two scurrying from tree to tree.

The girls communicated via text, "SEE

ANYTHING?" Kayo wondered. The signal was low but eventually made its way through.

"COUPLE SQUIRRELS, 3 DOE AND A BUTTON BUCK. YOU?" India's head turned to scan the area.

Kayo wiped her nose. It ran from the cold air. "I SAW A FOX AND A FEW HARES RUNNING BY. NOTHING INTERESTING. I HEAR TURKEYS NOT TOO FAR FROM ME."

India looked at the time. 2:35 pm. "WANNA HEAD TO THE CENTER POINT IN 30 MINUTES? IT WILL GIVE US AN HOUR AND CHANGE TO SET UP CAMP AND COOK DINNER."

"SOUNDS GOOD. YOU'RE ON FIRE DUTY. I'LL PITCH THE TENT."

"ROGER THAT!" India wrote.

Before leaving the area, India danced around. She had to use the bathroom and decided to go by the tree. When she was finished she got on her bike and rode off. Kayo left around the same time. About ten minutes into the ride, India heard a pack of coyotes running through the woods. They came from behind her and passed her, scaring her to the point she almost fell off the bike. "What the fuck!?" She stopped riding and looked back. She didn't see anything. She didn't hear anything. She assumed there must be prey ahead. She continued. Within five minutes India reached the center point where Kayo had just arrived.

"Did you hear those coyotes?" Kayo asked as she pulled the tent from the bag.

"Hear them? They almost knocked me off of my

bike! I didn't see what they were chasing. I couldn't believe how they ran past me. I've never seen anything like that."

Kayo listened as she removed the parts to pitch the tent. "Today was so blah."

"That's hunting. You sit for hours and nothing. Next thing you know a buck is under your stand."

"It's like they come outta nowhere," Kayo added.

"Or they wait 'til you have to pee to pop up on you! I had to take all my clothes off earlier to take a piss," India said as she began gathering sticks and putting them into a little pile. She took pieces of bark from a white birch and broke them into smaller pieces. She found a few flat stones and cleared an area to make the fire on top of them. "There was a berry patch between here and my stand. I didn't get a chance to look for bear signs. It was getting dark too quickly, so I will check on my way back to the stand in the morning." She used her flint fire starter to start a small fire. The sparks flew and she gently blew on the shavings she took from a birch tree. She added larger sticks as the fire became more independent.

It was dark and became colder by the minute. Kayo and India had sardines, crackers and venison jerky for dinner. Kayo used the fire to warm up tea in her stainless steel canister. They put out the fire and went to bed. The two friends snuggled together in the small tent and quickly fell asleep.

The girls woke up just before sunrise. Kayo climbed out of the tent first leaving India alone to enjoy her last few minutes of sleep. The forest was quiet. Kayo explored the area not far from the tent, looking for a private space to empty her bladder. The air smelled like wet leaves and pine cones. Mist rose from the warm forest floor into the crisp cold air and it only made Kayo's bladder feel worse. She pranced around looking for a place out of view from the tent. When Kayo found a spot, she squatted and leaned against a tree to relieve herself.

When she was done she took her time walking back. She stretched her back and arms after the long cramped sleep under India's wild movements in the night. As she turned the corner she saw him, circling the camp, sniffing around. It was Tank. India was still sleeping in the tent and Kayo had left it unzipped. Kayo gasped and ducked behind a tree. *FUCK!* she thought. She looked around to see all their equipment scattered. India's bow was crushed and Kayo's was on the other side of the tent with the Tank in between them. *Think.*

Kayo reached into the pocket of her camouflage bibs where she kept a curved fixed blade knife with a finger hole at the base of the blade in a sheath, a compass with a whistle and chapstick. She had to wake India and take Tank's attention away from the tent so India could get out and away. Maybe India can get to my bow, she thought. She hid behind the tree and blew the whistle causing Tank to turn and India to wake! India saw the Tank at the opening but his back was turned from his curiosity at the sound coming from the other side of the trees. He began taking heavy steps away in the direction of the whistle but as soon as India exited the tent, the Tank caught wind of her and swiftly turned in her direction. "Stand your ground!" Kayo yelled.

The excitement confused the Tank as he wasn't sure which direction to proceed. He growled and drooled, whipping his head in both directions. He wanted them both. Kayo continued to blow the whistle and came from behind the tree so Tank could see her. India slowly backed away. "Get my bow. It's behind the tent," Kayo instructed.

India grabbed the bow. She looked at it as if it was foreign. The quiver and arrows were all intact. "I can't pull your bow, Kay." India was right. Kayo's bow was specifically fitted to her and Kayo was stronger than India. India couldn't pull it back even if she tried and now was not the time to make a first attempt. India wasn't sure how but she had to get the bow to Kayo.

Kayo walked slowly toward Tank as India slowly retreated. Tank's attention was now on Kayo. India quickly grabbed the bow and hid behind the tent. "Throw me the bow, India."

"I can't throw it. It will break."

"Slide it towards me as far as you can and we will make him circle away from it," Kayo directed India. India pushed the bow in Kayo's direction but it wasn't close enough. The bow remained to Kayo's right about 15 feet away.

The two girls circled around, with Kayo heading in the direction of the bow. Tank became increasingly aggressive and decided his target. Tank stood erect and then charged towards India. Kayo ran to her bow, tucked and rolled, picked it up and quickly nocked the arrow into position. As she raised her eyes to focus, she saw the Tank with his claws pressing into India's chest. She screamed, "KAYO!"

The Tank roared in her face as blood streamed from her mouth. It was all so fast. Kayo had barely had a chance to get to her feet. She pulled the bow back. Her arms were still and her stance was perfect. India screamed her name again, but if Kayo's ears had failed her, this was the only time she couldn't hear. The chaotic forest morning went silent. The Tank left India bloody and shredded as she cried for help and turned his attention to Kayo. Kayo stepped back with Tank in her sights. He's too close, she thought. All she could hear was her heart beat, or maybe it was India's. Kayo wasn't sure. Kayo stepped back and just when she was ready to release the Tank jumped and her foot slipped into a small ditch she hadn't noticed. The slippery leaves and broken twigs gave way under her foot causing her to twist her ankle and miss the tank completely. She tried to run, but the Tank grabbed her in her lower back and pulled her back towards him. She screamed. She grabbed the knife from her pocket and jabbed him in the left eye and crawled away on all fours.

The Tank fell back and was even more furious than ever before. He looked back at India who was laying on her back choking on her own blood. The

Tank focused back on her and marched in India's direction. Kayo ran towards him, jumped on his back erratically stabbing and cutting. She cut a slit through his ear splitting it in half and with one connecting swing he tossed Kayo five feet away. She landed and hit her head on a stump. Kayo was knocked out.

Cold came over India, she was losing blood and the Tank made his way to Kayo. India pulled out a knife. With her last bit of strength she tossed the knife towards the Tank. It spun and stuck him in the back. When the knife landed, he stood up on his hind legs and growled, then ran off into the woods. India dropped her arm as she shivered and called for her friend with whatever would be considered less than a whisper, but Kayo did not hear her. Kayo did not respond.

The sound of chickadees and starlings carried over the breeze as the wind picked up along the trail. Overhead a red tail hawk circled for prey making its presence known as the air broke underneath its wings with each flapping motion. It was almost an hour when Kayo finally opened her eyes. Her ears were ringing, her head was throbbing and she could barely see. She touched her head and found a lump above her right eye. It was cold. The sun hadn't quite reached the treetops, but its beams shone between the trunks like spotlights presenting the main actor at center stage. This morning light landed on India. She laid quiet and still with her eyes open to the sky. Kayo panicked when she saw her friend lifeless with an arrow through her chest. I did this, she thought. She grabbed her friend and screamed a sound never heard in these woods. A war cry announcing loss of a beloved soldier and friend— her sun. The earth stood still. Not a bird, squirrel, mouse nor cricket dared answer that scream. Every living creature understood that cry. Kayo sobbed with her lifeless friend in her arms. Both were covered in blood. "JUNO, FIND ME. I NEED HELP!" She sent him a pin. Kayo stayed there and held her friend, shivering in the morning air, until Juno arrived.

Juno saw India and immediately cried. He couldn't believe what happened. He pulled himself together and helped Kayo remove all evidence of hunting. He removed the arrow from India's chest. Kayo couldn't dare touch it. "I did this, Juno."

Juno hugged Kayo and said, "It was an accident, Kayo. Look at her wounds. We've hunted long enough to know she was going to die no matter what." Juno tried to reassure her that India's death was due to The Tank but Kayo couldn't accept it.

When they got back into town, Juno rushed the girls to the hospital. Nahla, Ayrah and Orion were also there waiting. They convinced the authorities that the bear attack happened during a camping trip. Paul met them at the hospital. He was devastated. Even after India's body was removed, he stayed in the family room for a few hours demanding to be left alone.

Time passed and when Juno reached out to keep in touch, Paul wouldn't respond. Despite numerous attempts to connect, he never spoke to Kayo or Juno again. Occasionally Paul would be seen at the Farmer's Market with his parents to trade rabbit hides, but he wouldn't stop by Nahla's table. Even though his mother would frequent the table for homemade wine, honey, eggs and herbs, he dared not engage.

Eventually Ayrah and Oree approached him and he was reluctantly friendly. The first time he barely gave them eye contact. The second, Ayrah gave him a bracelet India had made for her. The third time he came around, he exchanged numbers with Ayrah after she promised to gather some of India's items from Kayo's room per Kayo's request. The fourth time, he finally shared a quick smile and wave with Nahla. She accepted it as a peace offering, but never approached him. He still wanted nothing to do with Kayo no matter how many times she tried reaching out.

Kayo arrived at the Pitchfork on Busy Buzzy. She parked it in the e-bike rack and chained it to the post. She wore a long black coat with brown fur around the hood. Bundled from the cold air chill, she walked into the establishment and saw Patterson waiting at the bar. *He's breathtaking.* His infectious smile made her blush. It was a work day but he couldn't resist catching up with Kayo for a late lunch date. She couldn't help but to smile when she saw his charming grin. He stood up to greet her. He gently embraced her leaving hints of his cologne on her collar. He pulled out a stool for her and said, "If I knew any better I'd say that's a new cut on your lip, but what do I know?" Regardless of the wound, Patterson was enticed by her glossy lips.

Before entering, Kayo used a lip gloss Beth had given her. They not only caused her lips to shine but did more to exaggerate the busted lip. Kayo pressed her finger tips against her lip and smiled. "How've you been?" She changed the subject.

"I've been good. It's probably good that you've been away. Work has been pretty crazy after what happened. Everyone's been swarming me about the attacks and... you." Patterson smirked and gently grabbed Kayo's hand. "How about you? How've you been holding out?"

As she pulled out her ear plugs and put in her hearing aids she responded, "Well, home is a stressful place but I'm managing. I have to head back tonight. I had to come back to grab some things I forgot to bring home." She pretended she didn't notice that everyone had been asking Patterson about her. She could imagine the questions. She was sure they were more curious about him choosing her as a date than they were about her surviving the attack. She was an awkward nobody. There was nothing special anyone could remember about Kayo, but there was talk that she cleaned up really well and was stunning at the gala. All the single women were put on notice.

"I missed you, Kayo. I couldn't stop thinking about you. I wondered if there was someone else."

There's everyone else, she thought but as her mind tried to run towards her problems, it gravitated right back to him. Kayo gazed into his eyes. She was lost, diving head first into the sunken place without a rope or a safety harness and no plan to abort the mission. "I missed you too."

There was an awkward silence of stares and smiles exchanged between the two. Patterson looked into Kayo's eyes and said, "I have to ask. Are we still trying?"

Kayo gently grabbed his hand and said, "Let's get out of here."

Patterson nodded. "Okay. Give me a minute. Let me call my job and let them know I'm out for the day."

"You don't have to do that," Kayo insisted.

"Yes. I do. Be right back."

As soon as Patterson was out of sight, Kayo walked outside, picked up her phone and called Marly. Marly was taken aback by the call. "Kayo?"

"Tell your men back down. I'm not running away. I came home to take care of something." Kayo whispered.

"What do you mean?"

"There are two guys following me and they need to back off!"

"I didn't send anyone, Kay. What do they look like?" Marly asked.

Kayo looked over her shoulder and said, "One is a red head. The other is a sloppy fat fuck that looks like a penguin. They walked in right after me. Not even subtle." She looked them right in the face as she said it. The two men were sitting at different ends of the restaurant.

"Ok. I think that's Antonio and Bruno," Marly assumed.

In a stern voice Kayo said, "Maybe your friends sent them. Tell them fuck off!"

"I'll make a call," Marly reassured her.

Kayo hung up and whispered, "So fucking annoying." *Let me enjoy my last day in peace!* She swiftly turned around and Patterson was standing right behind her. "Hi!" She didn't know what else to say. He caught her off guard. He seems to be the only person who could do that. She prayed he didn't hear any parts of the conversation, especially the last line.

"Who's got your attention while you're with me?" he asked. "I'm feeling jealous." He winked.

Oh it's just Marly who's responsible for my dysfunctional family and possibly trying to get me killed. "It's my Aunt Nahla." *Who's been fucking Marly for years and busted my lip the other day.* "She's just making sure I got here safely."

Patterson was curious. "What's your aunt like?"

Kayo thought, *Me.* And she hated that this was the first response that came to her mind. Kayo detested every comparison to Nahla more than anything in the world. When she was younger, she was totally convinced that Nahla was supernatural, but as she got older, she realized that her aunt was just as fragile and flawed as anyone else. "She's like..." Kayo thought of what to say for a moment but finally let the words come out unfiltered. "My Aunt Nahla... Drives me totally insane. I could kill her." She laughed. "But, truth is, she's the strongest person I know. I mean it. She's so strong it's unnatural. She is courageous, creative, disciplined and... and stubborn, and spiritual and resourceful. And she lies." Kayo smirked, "When she loves... she loves so hard... and deeply. I didn't realize she was capable until recently. She's had to tuck that away to raise us. Oh, and she's a great cook and demands we set the table and eat together every time. She takes really good care of my twin cousins. I love that about her. She would have been a great mother. When I look into her eyes... there's so much pain and... fear and questions. When she smiles, she gets a tiny moment of freedom and then is locked away again and she goes back into an empty place. She's fit and so damn pretty. I really don't know anyone like her. And I hate her. Well, I thought I hated her. I dunno if I do or if I'm just more comfortable hearing myself say it. I guess I want to hate her. She's... my sun and my moon, my teacher, my protector and... my rock. She wasn't my mother, she wasn't perfect but she saved my life." *I love her.* Kayo's eyes got warm and moist as tears started to form at the corners of her eyes. She described Nahla in all the ways she wanted to see herself, but never felt capable of all those things at the same time. Giving Patterson no chance to ask another question she asked, "You ready?"

After a brief deliberation on empty stomachs, the two decided to pick up gyro wraps from the deli and ate them on the way to Pattersons flat. Patterson pushed the e-bike as they strolled away. The short walk felt like hours. Two steps forward, and one step back, intentionally prolonging the distance between A and B. Patterson also insisted on stopping to buy Kayo chocolates which he playfully fed to her until she chose her favorite. He kissed her a few times, forehead, cheek, lips— as she let the flavors melt in her mouth. She put a piece of chocolate in his mouth and was fixated on his lips as friendly smiles turned into deliberate eye locking stares and flirtatious touches. He ran his thumb across her jawline. His hands were strong and cold but comforting. Patterson wrapped his fingers between hers and led her out of the shop.

Patterson's flat was a standard two bedroom, two bath pad. He was somewhat minimalistic. Everything was clean and white with natural wood accents. He helped Kayo take off her coat and hung it up. Kayo circled the place taking in every scent, shape, pattern and accessory in the living room. There was a lot of natural light and a large window with a few plants in front of it— a medium sized Monstera Deliciosa, a large Bird of Paradise, a small snake plant and bamboo on a stool. Kayo noticed they needed water, without asking, she helped herself in the kitchen and filled up a large glass pitcher. As she watered the plants, Patterson watched her gently move the leaves out of the way and pour water at the base of the plants. She looked over her shoulder and smiled when she saw him looking. "Are you watching me Hanzel?"

Patterson walked over to her and grabbed her from behind. "I'm always watching you, Kayo, but you never answered my question."

She turned around. "Which question is that?" She knew exactly which question he was asking about, but she wanted him to ask again so she could answer properly.

"Are we still trying?" Patterson looked into her eyes when he asked. The rhythm of his breathing, the moving of his lips, his cologne, the look in his eye... Kayo was trapped. There was something addictive about his intentionality and his persistence. It was as if he had initiated a mating dance that hypnotized Kayo into submission. It held her captive. She could have lost herself in his arms for months and wouldn't notice.

Kayo softened her body and said, "I'm so bad at this but this is me trying Patterson. I'm here." She reached up and passionately kissed him. Before Kayo knew it, Patterson picked her up, walked her to his room and placed her onto his bed. He swiftly removed his shirt as he kissed her. Kayo gave in, feeling not one ounce of guilt nor hesitation. He slipped off her shirt and gently helped her remove her jeans. Then he removed his slacks as he lusted over her body. He took a brief moment to take in the view as if he couldn't believe this was happening. *He's so sexy*, she thought. Patterson climbed on top of Kayo and she pulled him to her. Her lust for Patterson amplified as she explored his body with her naughty hands.

Kayo looked into his eyes. She was the predator pretending to be the prey. Pretending to not want to be captured, but she lured him into her. He couldn't resist but to take the bait. Kayo had wanted Patterson so badly and here he was delivering above and beyond her expectations. His tongue was more curious than his hands, meticulously exploring each part of her body. She wanted to explode.

She remembered her first spring on the homestead as she took in the scent of his hair and skin. They reminded her of honey, lavender and wildflowers from hikes in the cool spring forest. His tongue tasted like cotton candy at the local fair in June. His body pressed against hers and it was warm and soft as the humid summer air. He was inside of her, and as she watched the light flicker against the beads of sweat dripping down his body, it reminded her of the forest floor after a fresh autumn rain. She licked the sweat from his neck as he pushed deeper inside and she bit his ear. His cold fingertips evoked her memories of hunting and the frigid winter sting piercing its way past her bibs and through her bones. And suddenly Kayo didn't know where her body was. She was floating in an abyss of nothingness. Kayo was out of control and could only respond to the demands of Patterson's movements and requests. She couldn't catch up. She couldn't take over and she couldn't believe the sounds she was making. *Did I just say his name? What am I saying?* She couldn't help it. "Right there. Don't stop!" Kayo suddenly felt an electric and warm rush go from the center of her body to every extremity and she cried out loud. It was so intense, Patterson couldn't help but do the same when he felt her body vibrating from within.

Neither of them could move. Patterson laid still on top of Kayo breathing heavily. He was exhausted. He finally came around and kissed Kayo repeatedly on her face and neck. "Are you gonna pretend you don't know me in the morning?"

Kayo smiled and kissed him. "Yes. Can't have you catching feelings."

Patterson whispered, "Too late. This only makes me want you more. I wish you could stay the night."

"I really wish I could too but I have to be back home by six."

"You don't have to leave just yet." Patterson said as he fastened his mind to the idea of another round. This time he took her to his shower which felt like making love in the rain.

Patterson was very deliberate and calculated. He wanted to please Kayo and with every kiss and thrust he made his point. He was her puppetmaster. He didn't have to say much, and didn't tell her what to do, but she knew exactly how to follow his lead.

Right as she was about to climax the second time he looked her in the eyes and said, "Mine."

Mine? Yours? Wait. What? I don't belong to anyone. I'm not that girl. I have too much going on even though I want you so much. My life is in shambles and I may not make it through the next day. You can't look at me and say 'MINE' and think that's how it works. Who said I accept... even though I do, this isn't a negotiation. What are the terms? Plus, that's my line. I say what's mine and what belongs to me. How dare you talk to me like I belong to you, with your handsome face and sexy... You just got here and I'm not ready. I don't see how you can come into my life and claim me like I'm supposed to sit back and let you tell me what we are doing. The audacity of you to think I have feelings for you because I do and...

She was reaching her peak and Patterson could tell. He thrusted into her again and said, "Mine." He wasn't just talking. He wanted confirmation.

This wasn't fair. She may as well have been drunk. *What are the terms?* she thought. *What am I agreeing to?* "Give me a second!"

"No. Tell me it's mine," he said softly into her ear. "Tell me."

Kayo was holding on for dear life but broke, let out a moan and said, "It's yours."

"Tell me again!" He thrusted again.

He took the breath out of her. "It's yours!" she proclaimed and caught her breath.

"You promise?" His voice cracked. He was

almost there himself but needed to hear her say it before he could release.

She nodded. "Yes!" She meant it. "I promise." She felt an explosion of pleasure and her body collapsed completely onto Patterson.

He caught her and pushed into her one more time. He moaned loudly in her ear and stopped moving.

The warm water ran across Kayo's face, hiding her tears. She leaned into him as they both got their breathing under control.

As they dressed Kayo sensed Patterson had a question about the scar on her back. During sex, he kept running his fingertips over it as if he was reading it like a blind person would read braille. *What's the story here*, he thought.

"I would have preferred to warn you about it before anything happened," Kayo said.

"Warn me about what, Kayo?" Patterson put on a t-shirt and grabbed some sweatpants.

"The scar. I felt you touching it. Your fingers got stuck there, so let's get this out of the way. Come look at it," Kayo demanded. She took off her shirt and turned around. Patterson touched her scar with his cold fingertips. "I don't talk about it much and won't get into details today, but my friend and I were attacked while on a camping trip. She didn't make it. That's all I'm gonna share about that." Kayo quickly turned around and pulled her shirt over her head.

Patterson felt a little embarrassed. He had noticed the scar but didn't realize how much he focused on it. "Thank you. You've shared so much of yourself with me today. I'm honored."

"Please Patterson..."

"No. I really am." He smiled at Kayo and touched her hair. He said, "I see you're trying and that makes me happy. I like it. I like you." Patterson kissed and hugged her.

Kayo smiled shyly and said. "I kinda like you too."

"Kinda? Well, how do I get you from kinda liking me to really liking me? What do you need from me?"

"Time. Patience. Food," she joked. "Just be yourself. It's working."

Patterson pulled her close to him and said, "Thank you for letting me know."

They kissed again.

"Unfortunately, I have to go," Kayo said with a serious face.

Patterson walked away and came back with a white box. "I wanted to give this to you before you left, I just couldn't figure it out in time. But this is for you." Patterson always gave her a small token but she never took his gestures for granted.

Kayo opened the box. Inside was a leather bracelet with a gold four-leaf clover charm. He took it out and placed it onto her wrist. "No more clovers from the street. Now you'll always have good luck."

Kayo smiled as he put it on her. "Is this like a leash?"

Patterson laughed and said, "That will be the

next gift."

Kayo punched him lightly in the arm. She grabbed his face and gently kissed him again. She sighed and said, "I don't want to leave you."

"Just say you'll come back to me."

Kayo looked him in the eyes and said, "I'll come back to you. I promise."

CHAPTER 10

5:56 pm and Marly boldly tapped on the door. She stood nervously with a $400 bottle of Cabernet Sauvignon in one hand and a bouquet of flowers in the other. I feel like a dork, she thought. She looked back and waved off her body guard Jensen. He nodded, got into his car and left. Suddenly there was the sound of a metal lock awakening.

Ayrah answered the door. "Oh God this is really happening."

Marly smiled. "Yes this is equally as awkward for me as it is for you. Good evening, Ayrah. This is for you. I was told I better bring a peace offering."

"Thank you, but you didn't have to do that." Ayrah said with a smile.

"It's cool. I spent all day trying to find something I thought you'd like."

Ayrah had never seen Marly so vulnerable. She also hadn't really seen too many positive interactions between her and Nahla and wasn't sure what to expect. There was something about Marly that Nahla liked. Besides her being attractive, Ayrah was trying to figure out what it was. Ayrah took the bottle into her hands and inspected it. "Relax, Marly. It's all good. This is our home. You're welcome here. Come in."

Marly exhaled. "Thank you."

"I'll let my aunt know you're here."

Ayrah disappeared with the wine. This gave Marly a few moments to look around and take in the environment. She reviewed the pictures on the mantel, the knick knacks, the decor, the smells— rosemary, lemon pepper, chili.

Suddenly Nahla emerged from around the corner wearing a tank top and a long skirt. Marly felt a sense of relief. Nahla walked over to her. Marly said, "These are for you." She handed Nahla the flowers. Marly gently grabbed and kissed her.

"I love them. Thank you." Nahla pressed her forehead against Marly's and said, "I told you, I couldn't wait to kiss you. I missed you."

Marly said, "And I missed every part of you. I've been dying all day to see you."

"Let me put the flowers in a vase. Ayrah's almost done setting the table." Nahla kissed Marly again. She could feel the tenseness in Marly. "Look at me. Relax. The twins are easy going and Kayo's not here. If she stops by, it doesn't matter. You're here with me. You're good." She kissed Marly on the cheek.

Marly let her go and she disappeared around the corner again. Marly took a deep breath. *I can still leave. But I'm not.* She received a text message. It was from Jessie but she didn't read it. She put her phone on DND and slipped it into her coat pocket.

Orion peeked his head around the door and said, "We're ready."

Marly was startled a bit, but nodded. They entered the dining room where Ayrah had just finished placing the wine glasses. Orion placed an oven roasted pheasant seasoned with lemon pepper and chili in the middle of the table. Nahla pre-sliced a few pieces for easier serving. For sides she made sliced potatoes with a cream sauce and string beans. Every item on the table was from her garden and the pheasant came from one of Orion's spring hunts.

"This looks really good, thank you," Marly said. She smiled and took in the scent of the freshly roasted bird.

Orion directed her to sit at the end of the table. Nahla sat at the other end smiling. Marly winked as she ate the food. No one spoke. They looked around and smirked but no one dared speak until there was another knock at the door. Orion said, "Oh! I'd love to get that." He sprung out of his chair and went to the door. It was Kayo. Orion opened the door.

"Why is Marly's truck here?" Kayo asked as she pulled her bag off her shoulder.

Orion smirked and said, "She's our dinner guest tonight."

"WHAT!?"

"I'm assuming Nah's messy ass didn't tell you."

Nahla heard Kayo's voice from the other room, took a sip of wine and said, "Kayo's here."

Ayrah laughed with her glass of wine at her lips she sang, "Let the sideshow begin!"

"Quiet, Ayrah." Nahla looked at Marly and said, "Pay her no mind, Marly. You're my guest. Eat!"

Marly shook her head and whispered, "You didn't tell her I was coming?"

Nahla shrugged and said, "If I told her, she wouldn't have come and I wanted to see her as much as I wanted to see you." Messy! "She'll be okay. Oree is good with her."

Orion tried to calm Kayo down and said, "Kayo. Shhh. Just shhhh! You have a big day coming up. You need to eat. You can't take all these emotions with you into the hunt."

"I know and I just.... forget it. I had a great afternoon. I'm not going to let this ruin it and if this is what it's going to be, then I don't want to mess this up for Nahla. I want her to be happy."

"Thank you. Drink some wine and relax." Orion gave her a hug and a kiss on the forehead, "Your hair is soaking wet. Come on."

Kayo took off her coat, placed it on a coat hook and walked into the dining room. "Hey Auntie." She leaned over and kissed her on the cheek. She walked slowly over to her seat with a predatory glare and said, "Marly," as she nodded. She sat down.

Marly felt uneasy and said, "Good to see you, Kayo."

Nahla looked at Orion. He mouthed to her, "We're good."

Nahla nodded.

"Hey, Ayrah." Kayo adjusted her seat at the table and initially didn't budge. Finally, she reached for the bottle of wine and poured a hefty glass. Kayo was a wildcard and very unpredictable. The entire table was fixated on her next move.

"Hey, Kay. Let me make your plate." Ayrah smirked as she placed food onto the plate for Kayo. When she was done she put the plate in front of Kayo and said, "Eat something. You look worn out."

Kayo nodded her head and began eating. She was worn out. Patterson took all her energy from her and she was famished. The food was almost as good as her afternoon with Patterson. She couldn't get him out of her mind. She could still smell his cologne on her collar. Her phone buzzed. She looked at it and smiled then quickly put the phone away.

Nahla noticed. "How was your trip home? Did you get everything you needed?" Kayo didn't answer. "Kay. Did you get everything you needed?"

"Yes. Sorry my head is all over the place."

"Looks like it. What's on your mind?"

Sex! she thought. "I need to practice. I haven't shot that bow since... I'll spend the day practicing. Tomorrow evening, I will head to the latest location and camp there. Marly, I'll need the updated coordinates."

"You got it. Anything else you need. Let me know."

"I need you to take care of my Aunt." Kayo looked Marly directly in the eye for a few seconds and thought, *Or I will kill you.*

Everyone froze and looked at Kayo. Ayrah's eyes grew large. She looked at every face at the table watching for reactions. The only person unbothered was Nahla.

Marly understood. Nahla had given her that look so many times, but coming from Kayo she knew it was a serious silent threat. It wouldn't be the first time her life was threatened by one of the Brooks women.

Marly ate her last bite of food and said, "Nahla, this was really delicious, thank you for having me over. Thank you all for your hospitality."

Marly was on her best behavior. Kayo wasn't used to this.

Ayrah and Orion were finished eating. Ayrah said, "I'm gonna go out for a bit. I'll be back in a few hours."

"I wanna meet this guy, Ayrah," Nahla insisted.

Ayrah smiled but didn't respond to the demand. Instead, she grabbed her plate and the bottle of wine on her way out. "She said it was for me." She took it into the kitchen. No one cared. There wasn't much left.

Orion followed, "I have some errands to run. I'll be home late. Don't wait up." He walked over and gave Nahla a kiss on the forehead.

"Wash those dishes for me before you leave," Nahla demanded.

"Just leave them, Oree. I'll get it," Kayo insisted.

Marly blushed and mouthed to Nahla, "Thank you."

Nahla winked and flirtatiously scrunched her face at Marly.

Kayo felt like a third wheel but wasn't ready to leave. She sat at the table, hoping to make Marly as uncomfortable as possible before leaving, but eventually decided to let it go and said, "Why don't you two go relax. I'll clear off the table and do the dishes before I leave."

"Are you sure?" Nahla asked.

"I got it," Kayo said as she piled the plates into her hand. She quickly cleared the table while Nahla and Marly made their way back into the living room with their glasses of wine, Kayo cleaned up the table.

Nahla put firewood into the fireplace and Marly sat on the sofa watching. "I love making the evening fire." When Nahla was done, she sat on the opposite end of the sofa. After adjusting her oversized skirt, she reached over and grabbed Marly's hand which was stretched across the back of the sofa. "Thank you for coming by." She stroked the back of Marly's hand with her thumb.

Marly interlocked her fingers with Nahla's and said, "My pleasure. I didn't know you cooked so well. I feel there's so much I need to get to know about you." Marly nudged closer until her body was resting against Nahla's. Nahla crossed her legs, stretching one leg on top of Marly's lap and fondled Marly's hair. Marly rubbed Nahla's thigh.

Nahla smiled and said, "There isn't much to know. You know all the things that matter."

"No, Nahla. This matters. Watching you with the kids. They really love and respect you." Marly put her glass on the coaster on the coffee table. "They're such good kids."

"They are. They changed me."

"I can see that. You changed me," Marly admitted.

Nahla was curious, "How so?"

Marly rubbed Nahla's thigh and said, "You made me want to be loved. I never stopped looking for that feeling you gave me. Because I couldn't find it, I resented you. I took it out on the kids, especially Kayo. I tried to hurt you through them. I wanted your attention."

"You didn't need to do that to get it. I wanted you to choose me, Marly."

Marly leaned in and asked, "Is it too late to choose you, Nahla?"

The light from the fire reflected against the side of Marly's face and radiated in the background like a halo of flames. Her glossy lips looked supple, warm and soft. Nahla couldn't resist but to grab and kiss her.

Marly kissed her back, slipped her hand underneath Nahla's skirt and squeezed Nahla's thigh. Suddenly, Kayo walked in. Marly jumped back. *Shit!*

"Whoa. Ok. I uh... excuse me." Kayo fled back into the kitchen.

Nahla was embarrassed. She put her hand on Marly's shoulder and said, "Excuse me for a minute."

Nahla went into the kitchen where she saw Kayo leaning against the counter. Nahla giggled. "Sorry about that, Kay."

"This is so odd." Kayo laughed. "Looking back, those Freedom Days when you disappeared, you weren't always with Chopp were you?"

Nahla smirked and shrugged her shoulders.

"Auntie you're something else. Do you know what you're doing?"

Nahla shrugged and said, "Of course not. Who knows what love wants to do until it does what it wants to do? Listen, I know this is hard for you..."

"You're in love with the woman I hate. Maybe I don't hate her but I certainly don't like her."

"Well thank you for specifying." She smirked. "I want to ask you something. You don't have to answer but, do you blame her for India's death?"

"I want to blame her but I can't. It all comes back to me. I took the loan. I owed the debt. I convinced India to go. It was my idea to split up. I left the tent open. I fucked up the shot and I shot India." Kayo began to tear up. "I can only blame myself for everything that happened."

"And India had no say in any of it? India just did whatever you wanted? Would India blame you?" Nahla looked at her and said, "Is that how you want to remember your friendship? Through mistakes and pain?" Nahla picked up Kayo's chin with her hand. "India made you happy. She loved you and wanted to be like you. She celebrated your wins and complimented you every opportunity she had and all you talk about is this. This one memory. Five, maybe 10 minutes of your entire friendship. There's more to your friendship than that. India doesn't blame you. She saved your life with her very last breath. Didn't she? Even though you made a mistake, she made sure to save you. Because that one mistake doesn't define her love for you or yours for her. Don't let your love for each other be overshadowed by the bullshit."

"Like you and Marly?"

"Somewhat. Our entire relationship feels like one mistake after another but the good times are so good, Kayo. They always bring me back to her. She's my sun and I'm her moon. India was your sun and you were India's moon. The moon never leaves the sky. Even in the daytime the moon is always watching. The moon is the silent protector. The moon lets the sun rest because it brings the moon light and joy and happiness when they're together and enough to last even when they are not."

"I'm no protector. I failed."

"No, baby girl, the sun must set. Rising again should never be an obligation, so we celebrate when it does. Take no days together for granted. Maybe she knew you needed to protect someone else."

"Who?"

"Me. I used to be your moon but, Kay, now I'm just your sun. And I hope I give you light, joy and peace like you've given me for so long."

Kayo smiled and grabbed Nahla and hugged her.

"Now regarding, Marly, I love her. I wanted you to see us together, not fighting or pretending, but just being normal and open about how we feel. I dunno if this will last. I hope this time it does, but who knows. I'm going to take it in while I can. I've hid my feelings for Marly from you long enough. Letting you know lifted a weight off my shoulders and it's refreshing. I didn't want you going into your hunt worried about me. I'm happy. But like I said before, if this is too much for you, I will 100% let it go."

"No, Auntie Nah. It kind of feels like you woke up from a bad dream and I like that you're happier. The twins need to see you smile more often."

"I appreciate that." Nahla wondered, "Did you see your friend? That guy?"

Kayo's eyes lit up. "Patterson." She replied, "I did. I really like him. He's so perfect. He's smart, thoughtful and handsome. It's like I can't help but to do whatever he wants me to do."

Nahla smiled and said, "He must've put one on you today."

They both giggled.

"Trust me," Nahla added. "I fully understand. But... What about Juno?"

Kayo asked, "Why do I have to choose?"

Nahla nodded and said, "You don't, but between the three of you, one of you will."

Kayo thought about what she said for a moment, then hugged Nahla and said, "I'm gonna get out of here." Kayo walked out of the kitchen into the living room. She grabbed her things and went to the front door. Marly was standing in the living room. She looked at Marly and whispered, "Don't make me kill you." Before she stepped out of the door she said, "Coordinates please!"

Marly nodded.

Nahla shut the door and leaned against it.

Marly walked over to Nahla and wrapped her hands around Nahla's waist. "Empty house."

Nahla wrapped her arms around Marly's neck. She moved Marly's loose strands of hair off her face. "I can't resist you. Your eyes are so beautiful," Nahla whispered. They kissed again. Nahla's desire for Marly increased by the second. "Maybe it's time for dessert," she teased.

Marly grabbed and kissed the palm of Nahla's hand as it passed over her face and said, "First answer my question." She kissed Nahla on the space between her jawbone and neck. Then kissed her collar bone. She whispered in Nahla's ear, "Is it too late for me to choose you?"

"No."

"What do you want?"

"I can make a list of things, but right now I want you. Come with me." Nahla guided Marly upstairs to the master suite. She shut the door behind them. The room was cool and smelled of cinnamon and cardamom. The lights were dimly lit. Marly looked around quietly. Nahla said, "I'll be right back. Make yourself at home." She went into the ensuite and closed the door behind her.

Marly took off her boots and placed them by the door. She began walking around, looking at photos on the dresser of Nahla and the kids when they were younger. She had pictures of herself hunting, boxing and a few trophies she had won. Marly looked at the boxing photo and remembered that smile. There was a picture of the members of the co-op from 10 years earlier. Under the window was a small bookshelf filled with books and a pile of books neatly stacked to the side of it. Marly squatted down to look at the titles, but then Nahla emerged from the bathroom wearing a robe.

Marly stood up straight. Nahla's beauty always redirected and captured Marly's attention. Marly lustfully breathed and gazed at Nahla as she unwrapped her robe. Marly said, "Come here." Nahla walked over to her and ran her hand through Marly's long hair. She lifted the hair to her face and smelled it. Marly slipped her hands into the robe and followed the soft lace that clung to Nahla's figure from her hips to between her thighs. Nahla gasped and Marly seductively whispered into Nahla's ear, "Make love to me."

One passionate kiss led to another. They spent the night together making love and fell asleep wrapped in each other's arms, under the cream and white duvet cover swallowed up by the serenity of Nahla's sacred, fluffy, forbidden bed.

Kayo made her way to Juno's house. She walked in and it felt different, as if whatever was left of her had vacated the premises. She would have even thought it smelled different but she knew that was in her head. Juno was in his room and opened the door when he heard Kayo enter.

"How was the ride?" he asked.

"Good," Kayo answered. She could barely look at him. She had slept with him the night before and then earlier today was with Patterson. "Not sure I can shoot as well as before, but..."

"You never forget. You just need to practice good form." Juno walked over to her and stood behind her. "Feet parallel. Square your shoulders..." He moved her shoulders with his hands. "Arms up! Aim from the hip. Give me strong arms here." He touched her hips and ran his hands across her arms as he spoke. She lowered her arms and he walked away. "You just need time shooting outside. Your instincts will come back."

Kayo smiled at Juno. She knew he was aware of what she had done. The faint scent of Patterson's cologne hadn't gone unnoticed. Though faint, it was enough. "Thank you, Juno."

"What do you need from me?" Juno asked.

Kayo said, "Just protect my family."

"What about you? I've always protected you."

"You have, but it doesn't need to be your burden."

"No, Kayo. It's never a burden. It's my pleasure. It's all I know and all I ever want to do. Anyway, you should get some sleep." Juno turned away and asked, "Has the sun met the sea?" He kept his back turned away from her but listened for an answer.

Kayo whispered, "No." She hesitated then asked, "Has the moon left the sky?"

"The moon will never leave the sky." Juno walked into his room and closed the door.

Kayo walked into her room and plopped on the bed. She didn't know how to juggle these feelings. *I can't possibly love two men equally and individually.* She picked up her phone and saw a text from Patterson. "MY PILLOW SMELLS LIKE YOU. I MISS YOU ALREADY."

She sniffed her collar and closed her eyes. She smelled lavender and pine cones and cotton candy and autumn rain and... Quickly, Kayo was in a daze. Regardless of her feelings for Juno, she was falling in love with Patterson and couldn't help it. She was excited to hear from him. She didn't know what to text back. She didn't want to seem too anxious and didn't want to write something silly. She wanted to tell him how amazing he was and how much she wanted to see him again. She wanted to jump in the truck and drive back to him and climb underneath him or on top, whichever he preferred. But she was days away from her imminent death and couldn't imagine feeling safer around anyone but Juno.

She rubbed on the clover charm and wished this wouldn't be their last interaction even though she had already made peace with the idea. *Tank is going to kill me. I will never see this man again.*

She texted back, "YOU HAVE NO IDEA HOW BADLY I WANT TO SEE YOU AGAIN."

"WHY WOULDN'T YOU? DID I DISAPPOINT?"

he asked.

Kayo smiled and replied, "ABSOLUTELY NOT. I TOLD YOU... IT'S YOURS."

"AND I'M YOURS. ALL OF ME," Patterson wrote. "YOU DID SOMETHING TO ME. THIS FEELS DIFFERENT."

"IT DOES AND I DON'T WANT IT TO STOP," she texted. "WILL YOU WAIT FOR ME?"

"FOR SURE. YOU'RE WORTH IT." Patterson then wrote, "I'M FALLING, KAYO."

Kayo replied, "GOOD. ME TOO."

"OK. WELL, I'LL LET YOU GO. SLEEP WELL."

"YOU TOO. SEE YOU SOON." Kayo wrote. She put the phone on the charger, turned over and went to sleep.

In the middle of the night Marly woke up. Nahla's head was on her chest. She asked, "Nahla, are you sleeping?"

Nahla whispered, "No." She held Marly tighter and kissed her collar bone.

"If I tell you I love you, are you going to leave me in the morning?"

"No. I'm gonna kick you out though."

They both laughed.

"I love you, Nahla Brooks," Marly whispered anxiously. "I always have. I always will."

Nahla sat up and looked Marly in the face. "I love you too, Patricia Marly. You make me happy. I don't want to lose this feeling again."

"I don't either. I don't want to lose you. I'll do anything for you." Marly kissed Nahla again on her head. "Anything." She asked, "What else do you need from me?"

"I need names, Marly." Nahla said. "Give me the names of the people coming after Kayo."

Marly looked away. "Nahla." She slipped herself from underneath Nahla and said, "It's not that simple."

"You said 'anything.' I need to know who these people are who are threatening Kayo. My baby girl is terrified and I can't help her. I don't like feeling like this. How do I know it stops with the Tank? What if it doesn't?"

Marly moved to the side of the bed and put her feet down on the floor. She covered herself with a sheet. "Is this why you brought me here? Parading me around like an idiot."

"I would never do that to you, Marly. Do you understand the conversations I had with my family to even get myself to this point?"

"Are you using me?"

"What? No!" Nahla insisted. "Marly. I genuinely love you and I want to spend the night with you. I've been thinking about you all fucking day, my head is spinning. I want this."

"Me too but I thought discussions of business were off the table," Marly mentioned. "I thought we wouldn't discuss this any further."

Nahla sat up and pulled a sheet over her body.

"We won't when Kayo is out of trouble and when Kayo's life isn't on the line. If she doesn't deliver, then what?"

Marly stood up and said, "I don't know."

"You don't know. You have an answer for everything else but today, you don't know."

Marly got up and grabbed her clothes. She began putting on her shirt and jeans.

"And now you're leaving." Nahla grabbed her robe and put it over her body. "Marly, bringing you to my family was a lot for me. I enjoy you, and I so badly want to please you tonight, wake up in your arms in the morning and pretend as if none of this is happening. I've completely surrendered. I've never been this vulnerable with you, but I'm not gonna beg you to stay. It's your move."

Marly looked at Nahla and said, "Walk me out."

Nahla clenched her teeth and closed her eyes. She put on her robe and walked Marly down to the first level. She stood in front of the door while Marly put on her jacket. Marly walked up to the door waiting for Nahla to open it. Nahla said, "I've learned that lovers who start fights are running away from something that has nothing to do with me. Something else is going on. You go figure that out." Nahla opened the door and closed it behind Marly. She sucked her teeth and stood there for a while, then went into the kitchen where Ayrah was having a late night snack of cookies and milk.

"I thought Marly was staying the night. What

did you do auntie?" Ayrah inquired.

Nahla shook her head. "I don't know. It just feels like one step forward, two steps back with her."

Ayrah smiled and said, "Women seem hard."

Nahla shrugged and said, "Women are hard. Men are hard. I've had them both. Doesn't even matter. Choose your hard."

"Is it ever worth it?"

"When you love someone, every minute. I just think I jumped the gun a bit. We can't fix anything between us until we close this chapter with Kayo. Anyway, I'm going back to bed. I probably won't sleep but, what's new? Anyway, thank you."

Ayrah's mouth was full of cookies, "For what?"

"Helping me see clearer and being wise when I'm not able. Thank you." Nahla walked out of the kitchen and went back to her room.

The next morning Kayo was out early practicing shooting her bow. Orion and Nahla gave her tips to improve her posture. It had been a while and her posture needed some help. She still had no problem pulling back the bow but she was shooting low and to the left. Nahla adjusted her sight and she got back on target. They practiced shooting from standing, crouching and shooting from an elevated position. Nahla made Kayo take a break to rest her arm and shoulder which was hurting a little bit from fighting the other day. They hadn't heard from Marly after sending numerous requests for the coordinates. "I need to know where I'm going, Nahla. The Tank could be anywhere."

"Marly and I got into it last night. Nothing crazy but... I think she's annoyed with me; however, this is business. She needs this as badly as we do, so I don't know why she's not responding. I'll drive over and check in. I don't like showing up unannounced. I'll shoot her another text and let her know I'm stopping by. Hopefully she sees it before I get there."

As soon as Nahla walked away, Kayo noticed Frank sitting on the rooftop. "Frank!"

Orion asked, "Who are you talking to?"

"Give me some food or something."

Orion reached into his backpack and pulled out bear jerky. He ripped off a piece. She put the jerky on the porch rail and walked away. Frank snatched it and flew away.

"Frank is my little friend. India used to have a raven that would bring her stuff."

Orion said, "You know what. I remember that. Shadow right? Has Frank ever brought you anything?"

"A nickel." Kayo shrugged. "Our relationship is relatively new."

Orion laughed and said, "That's better than nothing. It's pretty cool. I want a raven."

"Yours will find you. Give without expectation of anything in return. That's what India told me."

Nahla had grabbed a few items from inside before leaving. She jumped in her truck and drove over to the office. She saw the truck was there. She walked into the shop and ascended the stairs. She knocked. "Come in," Marly said.

Nahla was frustrated that Marly hadn't been responding. She pushed open the door and said, "I've been calling..." There was a woman in the office. Marly and Nahla both froze. Nahla immediately knew something was off.

"Uh, Nahla. Nahla Brooks. This is Attorney Jessica Humphries..."

The woman confidently walked up to Nahla and stuck her hand out. "Hi. I'm Jessie. Patsy's attorney and luckily for her I'm also her fiancée. Nice to meet you."

A quick glance and Nahla noticed Marly's ring on her finger and smiled. Nahla shook Jessie's hand. "Oh hey. Nice to finally meet you. Sorry to interrupt. Patsy. I just stopped by to get those coordinates. I've been texting all morning but I see you're busy. When you get a chance please check your messages. We need those coordinates ASAP."

Nahla wanted to run out of there and Marly wanted her to leave as soon as possible. The two of them have never had a normal exchange in front of other people. "I got a little tied up. I'll make those calls and get them to you right away. Sorry I didn't see your text messages."

Jessica tried to help, "It's my fault. Patsy didn't know I was coming and I've taken up her entire morning with these wedding plans," Jessie said. "I can't make these decisions on my own, you know."

Nahla smirked and said, "Well, I'll let you two love birds get back to it. See you later, boss." Nahla walked out of the office and shut the door.

"She works for you?" Jessica asked.

Marly replied, "We partner sometimes but not often. Why?"

Jessica put on a big smirk. "Woo! She's freakin' hot! I'm gonna have to watch you around her." Jessica joked. She walked up to Marly and kissed her on the lips. "Or maybe I'll come around more often to enjoy the view. You may have to watch me!" Jessie joked. "I love when you get jealous." She leaned over and kissed Marly on the lips again.

Marly smiled awkwardly, but deep inside she was fuming at the idea of Jessica's openness about her attraction to Nahla. *Mine!* she thought. "Give me a minute, Jess," Marly said and left the office. Marly quickly jogged down the steps. She spoke softly and said, "Nahla, wait. I know this is bad, but let me explain..."

Nahla turned around smiling. She could see Jessica looking out onto the shop floor from the office window. "Do *not* make it look like we're fighting, Patsy." She knew that would sting a little.

"Don't call me Patsy!" Marly insisted.

Nahla conceded. She was being petty and now was not the time. "Fine. I will talk to you about this later. Your fiancée is looking out the window at us right now and I don't like it but I would never ruin that for you. You better pull something out of your pocket and pretend you forgot to give it to me. I'm gonna flirt with one of the guys and leave."

"I can't let you leave like this."

"You can and you will."

Marly refused to let Nahla leave, "Promise me you will talk to me later."

Nahla sighed and said, "I promise. Now let me leave."

Marly reached into her pocket but there was nothing but a wad of cash.

Nahla snatched it and gave her a fist bump. "See you around." She said with a big smile then she waved at Jessie watching through the window. As an extension of her performance, she walked over to Jensen and said, "Just go with it." She pulled on the brim of his hat and whispered in his ear. "Follow me out." She grabbed him by his belt and dragged him out of the shop in a flirtatious manner. When they got outside she said, "Sorry to drag you into that. I didn't want... you know."

"I understand. Our job is to protect her even when it hurts us. Even when it keeps us apart from the things we want and people we care about the most," Jensen stated.

"Jensen, I didn't know she was engaged. Did you?" Nahla asked.

"I figured you knew, but would it have mattered?" Jensen asked as he lit a joint. He smoked it and passed it to Nahla.

"Yes." She took a smoke and blew it out. "I have my lovers, but marriage is sacred to me. It's a boundary I won't cross, which is why I avoid it like the plague. Or it avoids me. I'm not sure I'm worthy of it."

"You *are* worthy of it. But I'm not sure anyone deserves you," Jensen flirted. Jensen took the joint back and smoked it. He passed it back to Nahla.

"Would God do that to me?" she said as she snatched the joint back from Jensen. "Keep love away from me?" She took a smoke and passed it back.

Jensen took another smoke and blew it out. He said, "Yes. If He could keep you for Himself or protect your heart until the one you need comes along." He touched her arm and said, "I kind of miss you, Nahla." Jensen and Nahla hung out a few times but he was significantly younger and it never went any further. They were attracted to each other but Nahla let the idea go. He also worked for Marly and the conflict of interest was too great. Instead, they formed a private friendship, shared secrets and smoked marijuana together. They'd find secret places to meet up. Jensen never got further than flirtatious banter and shoulder massages. No one else knew. It was how she privately kept tabs on the twins and Marly after Kayo left. "Would be nice to get some one on one time again."

"I know we haven't hung out in a while. When this is over, I promise I'll make time for you. I... We're talking too much now. Marly doesn't know we talk at all and I'd like to keep it that way. She's going to watch this video later and have you questioned," she said referring to the cameras Marly had posted around the property. Nahla smiled, tilted her head to the side. She adored Jensen. She took one last look at his cute face and said, "Give this money back to Marly when she's alone. I'll check in with you later."

Jensen whispered into Nahla's ear, took a smoke from the joint, and leaned into Nahla. He gently grabbed her face and exhaled the smoke from his lungs to hers. She held it in for a bit, closed her eyes and exhaled. Jensen bit his lip, smiled and said, "Let me know if you need anything else."

"I might. I'll call you later."

Nahla hopped into her truck and sped off. As she drove, she opened up the palm of her hand. Inside was a piece of paper she slipped from Jensen's pocket as he passed the smoke to her mouth. On it was a list of five names:

JASMINE SUMMER
CRANSTON ASHER-SMITH
FEMI ODEMWINGIE
ALEJANDRO SANTIAGO
VERNELL BAILEY

One person she knew. One name was familiar. The rest were ghosts to her. She would start with the one she knew— Femi.

Back on the shop floor, Marly checked in with the guys before heading back up to the office. She needed to cool off and get the jitters out. She finally went back into her office where Jessica was waiting, flipping through color samples for dresses. "By the way. I took care of that issue with the two guys?"

Marly was distracted but asked, "What two guys?"

"My clients with the poaching situation. They totally believed me when I told them I was assigned to their case."

"Oh yeah. What was the outcome of that?" Marly asked.

Jessie continued playing with the colors, holding them up to the light and placing them by Marly's face. "Well, as you know I had my buddy, who owed me a favor, pull the evidence. The time they faced was significantly dropped. I convinced the arbitrator to lower the sentence and have them participate in the Cycles from Home Pilot program. They can do their hours from home and still work. Takes twice the time to meet the hour quota, but costs the state less money. They can still see their families, work, pay taxes and generate electricity. Win-win for the state."

As Jessica was talking Marly picked up her phone and saw all the texts from Nahla and Kayo. She texted Nahla, "CAN WE TALK?"

"I think this lace pattern is sexy." Jessica noticed Marly's disposition was off and attention elsewhere. Jessica said, "Maybe I've overwhelmed you."

Marly was completely distracted, looking at her phone. She was caught off guard by the whole thing and didn't know how to fix it.

"Patsy, are you even listening? Who are you texting?" Jessica asked.

"Sorry I was just checking my phone. I haven't looked at it in hours and..."

Jessica was annoyed and asked again, "Who are you texting?"

"Jessie, I'm trying to take care of this thing."

Jessica turned her head to the side and gave Marly a stare. "Are you texting Nahla?" Jessica was serious. She put her hand on her hip.

A shock ran through Marly's body. She couldn't lie. "Well, yeah... Just saying I got the messages and..."

Jessica cut Marly off. "Patricia. How long have you been sleeping with her?" Jessica asked with her arms folded. Her intuition took a minute but she finally put the pieces together.

"What!?" Marly asked. Her heart jumped. Her stomach dropped. She was completely shaken up by the question. *I dunno what to say.* "What do you mean?" *I know exactly what she means,* Marly thought.

"Patsy, my job is to read between the lines, find clues and put them together for a living. Since that woman entered this room you've been disheveled. I saw her look at your ring as if she had never seen it before. She probably could've pulled off that stunt easily if your ass hadn't chased her down the stairs, and since you've returned, I can't even get you to look at me with a straight face. You're still chasing her."

"Jessie. I followed her because I owed her money. I forgot to give it to her. You saw me give her money. You know everything about me and this business and what we are planning to do in the next day or two, down to the details. You know and I appreciate and love you for everything you've helped me do but sorry. I'm struggling to focus on lace, colors and god damned party favors!"

"Fuck a party favor and tell me how long you have been fucking that woman!" Jessica slammed her hand on Marly's desk.

"Jessie... do not do this right now," Marly instructed.

"How long?"

Marly asked, "Why are you doing this?"

"You can't answer the question because you can't lie," Jessie told her.

"I don't want to lie, Jessie!" Marly replied with a shout. "But, I don't know if you want the truth. No matter what I say, you only want to hear the idea you have in your head. So what version of truth will suffice?"

"Start with the objective truth. That's what I want to hear."

"Sure you do, Jessie. You want to hear that I've been sleeping with Nahla off and on for ten years and we broke up two years ago because her kids worked for me and it was ruining our relationship. And in between that time I met you. I was falling apart, but you made me focus. You're beautiful and smart. You work so hard and you're sweet. You give me something tangible and logical as opposed to something that's always been inconsistent and confusing. You keep me in check. I love you for that and you love me. Then that poaching incident came up. It's Nahla's niece Ayrah who shot that arrow. Nahla and I avoided each other and hadn't spoken in years but she came to me in her niece's defense and pleaded with me. We argued and we fought and we couldn't help it but we kissed and... we made love over and over and it was amazing and wonderful, even better than I remembered."

"I tried. I fucking tried. We both tried to let it go but can't be in the same room as enemies or friends. We will always default to being lovers. And to add insult to injury, it was her other niece, Kayo that killed those men at the gala. You can't make this shit up. She had no idea an attack was planned. She was on a fucking date and had to fight for her life. She wasn't there to sabotage anything. They were shooting everyone and she's trained her entire life for that. She was just in the wrong place at the wrong time and because she used to work for me, the partners suspect that I may have sent her to fuck it up. Kayo hates me. She'd never help me. But fate has it, she was there. Fate hates me."

"From Kayo's perspective, imagine Nahla, the

woman you love more than anything, is in love with and sleeping with the woman you hate more than anything, me. Kayo was my best hunter until there was an accident that made her swear off it forever. Now my constituents made me threaten her and her family to hunt the same bear that killed her best friend. They all hate me— my partners, Kayo, Nahla... I am sure she's done with me. I know she is. She called me Patsy. That's not... that's not her name for me. My name is Marly."

"When was the last time you slept with her... Marly?" Jessica asked with tears in her eyes. "If you can stick your tongue in her mouth and God knows where else, and use that same tongue to lie to me, then you can use it to look me in the eye and tell me the truth. Just fucking tell me. When was the last time you fucked that woman, Patricia?"

"I was with her last night."

Tears ran from Jessie's eyes and she asked, "You said she was in love with you. So, let me ask this. Are you in love with her?"

Marly didn't answer.

Jessica didn't need a response. She knew the answer. She began grabbing her things off the table, shoving them into her oversized purse. She whipped the purse strap over her shoulder, took her ring and threw it across the room.

Marly tried to stop her. "We don't work. Nahla and me. We won't work but you and I will." Marly touched Jessica on the arm and said, "I'm so sorry, Jessie. I would never intentionally hurt you like this.

I was being selfish. I wasn't thinking." Marly felt terrible. "How do I fix this?"

Jessica snatched her arm away and said, "I'm not going to scream at you. I'm going to walk out of here with my dignity but you will always be a piece of shit! I fucking hate you! Fuck you both!"

"Maybe it doesn't matter, Jessie, but she didn't know. Nahla didn't know about you. I lied to her too." Marly stepped closer to Jessica and said, "Please. Jess. You don't have to do this."

Jessica looked back at Marly. She smiled and touched Marly's face. Marly closed her eyes and touched Jessica's hand. Jessica pulled away and said, "I was with Patsy and I was in love with Patsy. Not you, Marly. Marly belongs to Nahla. Goodbye." Jessica slammed the door on her way out.

CHAPTER 11

Nahla arrived at the cabin, sat in her truck and couldn't get out. Her legs wouldn't... her hands couldn't. She just sat there with her head against the steering wheel. Breathe. She felt an ache in her stomach. Why is love so complicated? Why is it always unreachable? There was no time to ponder the repeated triumphs and mostly failures haunting her experiences with love. Marly called Nahla's phone. Don't fucking call me. Nahla didn't pick up. She sent Marly to voicemail wishing she could just as easily send her to hell. She wanted to curse Marly out, but didn't have the words. Marly called again. "UGH!" she blurted out. Nahla didn't want to answer but she promised herself not to be noticeably angry. She reluctantly picked up the phone. "Hello."

"Nahla. Please let me see you," Marly begged.

"All I need from you right now are the coordinates. You don't need to see me to send them." Nahla needed this to stay about Kayo's task.

Marly made an excuse. "I would rather not text classified information to you."

Marly had a point but Nahla didn't care. "I have a pen and paper. Read them to me."

"Nahla, you promised to talk to me."

"Marly I will. But not right now. Not about us. Where is the Tank?"

"The last location we have is 42.647 North, -73.1659 West. Mount Greylock."

"I'm familiar. We used to hunt there," Nahla said.

"They received a ping around 8:15, 10:15 and another at 11:15 this morning. He's near the Roaring Brook Trail, staying within a mile radius of the peak. It's the only place they can get a clear signal. We believe the towers pull the tag info every hour. He has a tendency to stay in a location for two to three days before moving around. Getting into position tonight or early morning would be ideal."

"Thank you Marly. If there's anything else you think Kayo needs to know, you can contact her directly."

There was a moment of silence where they listened to each other breathe. Marly finally said, "I'm sorry I didn't tell you."

Nahla took a breath and listened intently.

"I know marriage is a boundary for you which is why I didn't tell you. I didn't think we would ever reconnect like this. I selfishly wanted you so badly, and once we crossed the line I couldn't take it back. I didn't mean to put you in this position. I... hello? Hello?"

Nahla hung up. *I can't do this right now.* She pressed the phone against her chest and began to cry. She cried as if someone had died. Her heart

felt hollow— like an empty bucket slowly filling
with drops of sorrow, drip by drip. She wanted to
punch the dashboard but her hand was already sore
from punching Marly's wall. *Get it together, Nahla,*
she thought. She couldn't let Kayo see her like
this. Nahla took deep breaths and remembered her
meditation techniques. She was high from smoking
with Jensen but that didn't help mellow her out. *I
need a drink.* She put the list of names into her pocket
and got out of the truck.

Kayo was in the cabin when Nahla entered the
house. She was packing her bag for the hunt. Nahla
went straight to the bar. *Whiskey!* Like a mad woman
she opened a bottle and threw it back, gulping down
ounces at a time. The whiskey ran down the sides of
her mouth.

"What the hell, Nah? You okay?" Kayo asked.
"What happened?"

Nahla snapped out of it. She didn't want Kayo
to know what happened. "Yeah umm. I'm a little
anxious, that's all."

Kayo gently grabbed the bottle from Nahla's
hand and said, "I doubt that's what's going on but
whatever it is, I need you sober." Kayo looked at her
watch and asked, "Did you get the coordinates from
Marly?"

"Yes. Mount Greylock."

"Greylock. We used to hunt up there a lot but it
gets windy this time of year," Kayo said as she folded
a few items.

"That's what I'm worried about. How's your

shooting?"

"Eh. Good enough I guess." It was actually spot on, but Kayo didn't want to be boastful. Once adrenaline and nerves kick in, one half a degree off and the arrow is liable to go anywhere.

"That wind may be a problem. You're gonna have to adjust your shot accordingly. Take a few when you get up there to feel it out. He's been hanging around the Roaring Brook Trail. You'll have a couple days before he's likely to move on, so you may need to cover some ground while you're up there. When do you plan to head out?" Nahla wondered.

"Tonight. I'm gonna bring my e-bike and a hammock tent. I have three days worth of water, jerky and emergency food ration bars. I don't want to cook up there."

"Good. I wanna give you something before you go, but don't open it until you get there." Nahla walked up to her book shelf and handed Kayo a book. It had a soft leather cover, like a personal diary. There was a green ribbon wrapped around it and tied into a bow. "Also something you should know. The tower pulls data on all the tags in the area fifteen minutes past every hour if he's in range. If they don't detect a pulse, they'll send a drone within 24 hours. Get him and let Juno know where to meet you to help you get him out of there. He won't be easy to move."

Kayo put the small book into her bag. "I'll be okay, Auntie Nah. Get the twins out of town for a bit.

That's all I ask. Baker is on standby if you need help. He's down for anything."

"Cool," Nahla replied. "I'm meeting up with Chopp tonight. He's gonna help me take care of some things while you're gone."

"Do I want to know?" Kayo asked.

"Probably not. He'll be here in an hour or two."

About an hour before sunset, Juno and Kayo reached the base of the Mount Greylock State Reservation and stopped on Route 7 near the start of Roaring Brook Trail. He helped Kayo take the e-bike out of the truck. The air was bitter as wind ripped across the landscape. The towering pines and oak trees whistled back at the gusting winds. Kayo had one backpack, a bow and her e-bike. She covered the bow with a wool blanket and strapped it around her backpack. "The main roads into Greylock are closed. This is as far as I can get you. You need to hurry into the woods. If anyone sees you with this bow..."

"I know. I need to get to Hopper Trail. I think that's where he will be. Between there and the summit." She removed her hearing aids and placed them into her pouch. She put her finger in her ears. They felt irritated.

"Try to stay on the trail as much as possible. Use the hybrid feature so you can get more time on the battery and send me your location once you settle in."

Kayo pushed the bike into the woods and disappeared into the brush.

Juno drove off down the road, but did not forget Nahla's instructions. He pulled off the road, tucked the truck into the woods where it couldn't be seen from the road, and waited in his truck. He called Nahla.

Nahla picked up. "How are we looking, Juno?"

"Moon landing," he replied.

Nahla nodded and said, "Ok. Remember what I said. It's gonna take her a little over an hour to get up there. Stay on her trail. You know she's not going to stay on the trail. We hunted there a few times and she knows some short cuts."

"She said something about hanging between Hopper Trail and the Summit," he informed Nahla.

"I think there's a berry patch up there. The morning India was attacked she said something about it not being far from a berry patch."

"Don't worry Nahla. I'll find her."

"I know you will, Juno. Keep me posted." Nahla hung up.

Juno reached into the glove box and pulled out a knife. He reached under his seat and pulled out a handgun. He checked to make sure it was loaded. Juno was prepared to remain there for a few days if necessary.

Kayo hit the trail riding as quickly as she could. The setting sun was half way between the trees and always feels like it wants to set faster than it takes to rise. She still needed to get somewhere and set up camp. She intended to get out early in the morning. She suspected he would move closer to sunrise or sunset and bed down during the day. Getting into position prior to sunset would be best.

Around 45 minutes into the ride she stopped to take a break and look around when suddenly a bird whipped in front of her face and flew away. She initially thought it was a bat, and waved it away, but upon closer inspection it was a raven. It perched itself on the limb of a young ash tree. She looked closer and said, "Frank? What are you doing here? You followed me?" Frank dropped something from his beak. She took out one of her emergency food bars and broke off a piece. She got off the bike and picked up the shiny gift. It was a paperclip. *What am I gonna do with this?* she thought and giggled. "Thank you, my friend." she said with a big smile. "I can't believe you followed me here." She stuck out her hand with the piece of the food ration. Frank swooped down and took it. He flew back and landed on her bike. She stuck her empty hand out and he jumped inside her palm. "You came all this way for food? Greedy bird." She pet the back of his head.

She gave Frank another small piece of the bar. She ate a small bit herself and said, "You gonna tell me where to find the Tank or you gonna tell him where to find me?" She giggled and looked back at the sky. Frank flew off and perched himself about 20 feet ahead of her on the trail. "You're right. I better get moving." She looked at the trail map on her phone. "I should be there in about ten minutes." She got back onto the bike and rode off.

Kayo found a spot she liked. She immediately made a fire, then pitched her tent above the ground between two trees just as the sun bid its final goodbyes for the evening. "This should hold." Using a fallen tree log as a bench, Kayo sat quietly next to the fire she constructed from twigs and branches in the area. Night had fallen. She was surrounded by evergreens and a variety of leafless deciduous trees. The fire crackled in the night and warmed the air that radiated against Kayo's smooth dark skin. She could hear running water nearby and small creatures shuffling through the leaves. Crickets, owls and fishers crying afar watched her in the spotlight created by the dancing flames. Her fingers were numb and the joints in her hands were stiff. She took out the book that Nahla had given her and turned it around in her hand, inspecting both sides of the cover.

Kayo curiously untied the ribbon and tucked it into her pocket. She flipped open the first page and could see the book was a series of hand written letters between Nahla and her father Kayron Brooks. They would write a letter on one page or two and send the entire book back to the other person to reply. There were about 30 back and forth letters between the two. The last letter was sent right before Kayron deployed to the Canadian border and never returned. Kayo closed the book. *Why would Nahla give this to me now?* She looked at her cell phone. The signal was shotty. She was alone.

It was getting late and windier by the minute. Kayo made tea, using the running water she heard about 20 yards away. She put out the fire and climbed into her hammock tent. Using a small LED flashlight she read the first letter:

Nah,

I am sending you this book so that our letters never get lost. I will write to you, you turn the page and write back to me and we will do this from now on. So far, things between Cornelia and I have gotten better. Less fighting, more talking. At least our breakups have gone from once a week to once a month. Progress I would say. I hate that we fight in front of Kay. She's getting older and I'm afraid she will begin to think this is normal. It's not. You'd be happy to know, I put her in boxing classes. She needs an outlet. There's so much she doesn't understand, but again things are better. Thank you for talking me off the ledge so many times. Also, Cornelia says, "Hello." The two of you should try speaking again. It would make me happy.

Enough about me. What about you? I need you to stay focused. I can't have you getting in trouble again. What are you doing? I want you to call a friend of mine. His name is Jeremiah Thomas. We call him Chopp. He was stationed at the southern border with me off and on for two years. He's a good dude. He runs a gym in the city called Fisticuffs. Look him up and tell him I sent you. I think he can help you with your temper. You have to fix that. One day the consequences will catch up to you. You have to get yourself some help.

I want you to know I love you. I am always thinking about you. We have to figure out what to do about Eve before she implodes. She said she's been sober for three months. Let's keep an eye on her. Please call her. It may be helpful to get to know the twins better. I wish I lived closer. Anyway, I look forward to hearing from you.

Love your favorite brother, Kayron

Kayo never pondered how intimate letter writing could be. The time and effort it took and how a person's words must be concise and deliberate. She studied her father's penmanship which displayed what she remembered about his character or what she imagined him to be. He slanted his Ls and Ts to the left. The loops in his Bs and Ds were left open. His lowercase Rs looked like capital Rs but smaller. Some words were written with letters smudged together, melting one into the other in an old style of writing they called "cursive". Surely her father put his own twist on it. Some words were hard to read.

She lightly ran her fingers over the lettering, feeling the indents every letter made into the paper— some letters deeper than the others. She wondered about her father's emotions during various parts of the letter. He was a calm man. Her mother, not so much.

> *To my favorite brother, by default because you are my only brother, Kayron,*
>
> *I miss you. Sorry it took so long to write back. My last case was thrown out (Sort of. I had to pay a fine.) and I decided to take you up on the offer to meet your friend. He's kinda cute. Lol. We get along very well. He started training me and it's helping me get my aggression out. I'm too tired to fly off the handle like I used to. Should've reflected on my temper before I kicked in my ex's door and busted his car windows. Ghetto!*
>
> *I stopped fighting at the club for money, made some space between me and my old friends, and have been doing some IT work from home*

for a company called StarPol. Who figured I would learn how to code from free courses on QuikFlix? They need code written for a navigation application in their products. I have some other renewable energy projects I'll be working on soon. We're coding fitness equipment to charge batteries, etc. Work is good because I can stay busy and away from the bullshit. OH! I bought a condo. Actually I bought two adjacent properties. I had some money saved up and figured why not. Maybe I will join them together and make a bigger place but for now I'm just renting the second unit.

I'm glad to hear about you and Cornelia. Kay needs to see healthy adult relationships. That's what I want more than anything else. I probably need to see them too, otherwise I have no faith left in them. Mom and dad didn't help either. Tell C I said "Hello." I'm really sorry I hit her like that. I was scared for you and Kay. Maybe next time a light shove? lol JK I will keep my hands to myself. Maybe!

Anyway, I will always be here for you. Eve, I don't know what to do about her, but clearly having kids didn't

make her grow up. FYI. She relapsed.
Oree and Ayrah are with their father
and he's a mess too. I will keep you
posted on the latest developments. Tell
me more about this boxing class.

Love always, Nah
PS, write me a poem.

Kayo smiled as she read her aunt's letter to her father. She examined the unique characteristics of her writing and how she made her lowercase Fs hang long— a bit exaggerated. To create her Gs, she made a separate loop and tail which sometimes didn't connect. She also wrote partially in cursive which made Kayo have to decipher a few words, but the chaos of her lettering, when zoomed out, faded into a precisely spaced series of symbols. It was artwork. It was nothing Nahla had done intentionally, but Kayo thought it was beautifully written.

She understood why Nahla hit her mother. Cornelia was violent towards Kayron, especially when she was drinking, but one time she turned her anger towards Kayo and hit Kayo repeatedly. It was beyond a spanking. It was abusive. She was angry. Kayo believed her mother suffered from a form of PTSD after her deployment to Puerto Rico. No one knew what happened but she was never the same when she returned.

Kayo flipped through to the next letter.

My baby sister Nahla,

I'm glad to hear you are doing well. I knew meeting Chopp would be good for you. You're in good hands. Kayo's been doing well. She's your twin! She looks so much like you it's sick! She's been having issues with her hearing and has been getting tests. We are waiting to hear back. She's been training regularly and has added mixed martial arts. She's pretty good. Maybe one day she can beat you up for me. lol. Things with Cornelia have been flat. Not bad, not great but manageable. She's in therapy. I will join her after a few sessions but I'm not ready for Kayo to join us. Not yet. But, Kay asks about you all the time. Visit soon?

I'm sad to hear about Eve, but she did this to herself. I wish one of us could take the twins so they could have a better life but I can't have them here with my messy situation. It's too unpredictable. Anyway, I wrote this for you:

*How sacred a love more holy than this,
One born, then the next, inherited
gift.*

A comforting soul, our secret is held,
From young until old, you never would
tell.

From father, to mother, to womb and
first breath,
To child, to teen, mid-aged, until
death.
My love live it deep, it burns from the
core,
Your heart ever gives, even when I'm
no more.

Through storm raging grief, you guide
me to shore,
Beyond heaven's reach, or hellfire
scorn.
'Til the sun meets the sea, and the
moon leaves the sky,
Forever shall be, I'm bound to thee,
our souls an endless tie.

Love always, Kayron.
PS, stay away from Chopp or I'll kill
you both! lol

Kayo closed the book. She never knew where
that saying came from but she'd said it so many
times, she couldn't imagine there being more lines
and yet she was   here reading it. She wanted
to imagine hearing the lines in her father's voice
but she could barely remember it. She remembered

hearing Nahla repeat it over and over when she first moved in. Probably due to the sadness of losing Kayron, her brother. *She never had a chance to grieve,* Kayo thought. Nahla would come into the room and kneel by her bed and say it to Kayo as she tucked her into the bed at night. Then somehow it became the mantra of the members of the co-op — a proclamation that they'd always be one. It seemed like everyone said it, but when Nahla said it, she meant it. *I am India's moon.* She knew right away that Nahla was her father's moon.

The intimate exchanges between siblings are rarely romanticized. Kayo imagined Kayron's love for Nahla, to be similar to her love for the twins — a sacred gift. Kayo tucked the book into her backpack after feeling she had violated her father's secret thoughts, even though Nahla volunteered the information. *What are their secrets?* she wondered.

Kayo was exhausted from hiking, riding and tent pitching. She was sore all over her body, but had to be well rested for the hunt. She briefly thought about Patterson and their night together. She smiled, making peace with the idea that it would be the first and last time she would touch him but it was a beautiful memory to fall asleep to. She leaned her head back onto her backpack and was quickly taken away by sleep.

Nahla and Chopp got down to business as soon as Chopp arrived. They sat and waited in the commuter lot where Femi parked his car. Femi walked fast. He couldn't help it. He was a dark skinned man with a large nose and wide mouth. He wore glasses and a peacoat with a gray scarf tucked inside. He reached his car and fumbled around looking for his keys. He got into his white BMW and started the car. Just as he began to pull off a truck blocked him. He beeped the horn and Nahla emerged from the back seat.

"Hello, Femi," she said as she placed a gun into his side.

Femi looked down at the gun. "What the..." Femi was shocked. "What is this?"

"Shhh." Nahla wore a black balaclava mask with a hood over her head. "Follow that truck. Don't be stupid." She dropped pictures of his wife and children on the passenger seat. "Flick the high beams once so my partner knows you understand."

Femi was shaking. He hit the high beams and Chopp pulled off. Femi followed. Once they left the parking lot they drove down the road, made a few turns and Chopp pulled over. Femi stopped. "What are you doing?" he asked.

"Just follow my directions. Pull over and get into the passenger seat." Nahla pulled out her phone and showed Femi video footage from the cameras inside his house. His wife was making dinner. One of his children, a little boy around the age of four, ran across the screen and quickly disappeared.

"Follow all directions. Don't speak unless I ask you a question."

Femi pulled over the car and squeezed into the passenger seat. He contemplated opening the door and making a run for it but he was afraid.

Nahla gave him handcuffs and a black cloth bag. She instructed, "Put the cuffs on and put the bag over your head. Do it now."

Femi listened as instructed. His breathing became erratic. He was panicking. His hands were cuffed and his face was covered.

"Lean the seat back as far as it can go," she told him.

He followed her directions and said, "Please. Tell me what this is about."

"I told you not to speak!" She lifted the mask up over his nose. She then took a cloth and stuffed it into his mouth and said, "Sit up!"

When he sat up she used duct tape, wrapping it around his mouth to keep him quiet. "Probably should've done that first." She pulled the bag back over his head and pulled the draw string tight. She wrapped the duct tape around his wrists. He took his hands and struck her in the face. She hit him repeatedly with the gun and put it against his head. "Don't make this harder than it needs to be. I will kill you. Now scoot to the back seat." As he started scooting to the back she yelled, "Stop!" She tied his feet together then said, "Continue."

Nahla got out of the car and got into the front. She raised the seat and put on the child locks.

"Femi. I don't trust you will be a good boy for me, so it's time to take a nap."

Femi tried to yell something but his mouth was stuffed and he couldn't. He tried to scream from behind the mask but it wasn't working. Nahla poked Femi with a needle and a few seconds later, he passed out.

Femi woke up tied to a chair in a small cold room. His head was pounding and was bleeding. The blood ran over his left ear down into his shirt. The walls were made of red brick with white mortar stuck between the blocks. There was one small window at the top of the wall to his left, a steel door in front of him and a steel gray garage door behind him. Two chairs were about four feet in front of him. Under his feet was a drain and there was a hose rolled around on top of itself, attached to a spigot in the wall. Femi's glasses were missing. He focused his eyes as well as he could. Four figures walked in. Chopp, Nahla, Baker and Diggy. Diggy's mouth drooled as he growled. Nahla handed Baker the keys to Femi's car.

"Take all the time you need," Baker told them as he and Diggy left the room. "I'll be outside."

Chopp responded, "Don't go far. We won't be long."

Both Chopp and Nahla stood in all black tactical gear. Chopp dropped a bag on the ground and shut the door behind Baker. They took off their balaclavas and dropped them to the floor. Nahla shook out her hair which reached her shoulders, and pulled it up into a ponytail.

Femi squinted his eyes. "Nahla? Chopp? I don't understand."

"You busted my lip, Femi. Not a good idea." Nahla licked her lip and touched the bloody area.

"What did you give me?" Femi asked as he squinted from the pain shooting through his head.

Nahla smiled and said, "A psychedelic tincture. Puts you out for about an hour. You were doing too much."

Chopp took an AR15 that was strapped around his neck and placed it against the wall. He responded, "Before you start lying I want you to think." He hit Femi in the head. "Think. What beef would Nahla and Chopp have with you Femi?"

Femi opened his mouth.

"Nope! Don't talk yet, because I can see you want to play stupid. Take a moment, breathe and think." Chopp said with a straight face. He sat down in one of the chairs in front of him. Nahla stood there with a Sig p226 in her right hand. She said nothing. They waited. Chopp went to his bag and grabbed a pair of rusty shears.

"I have money. I can get you money," Femi pleaded.

Chopp said, "If we wanted money, you'd be at the bank. We want information. Now!"

"I'm trying to focus...think, think, think! Ugh.

Okay..." Femi said. "Kayo, yes. She's in trouble right? Ok. Kayo. Big mistake. Big. She shouldn't have been there." Femi squinted. Wondering what Chopp planned to do with those tools. "What are you going to do with that?"

Nahla asked, "Keep talking or you will find out."

Femi squirmed and said, "Nahla, I'm not involved in this. Please!"

"Give us some info, Femi," Chopp said as he played with the shears. "Or you're gonna find out why they call me Chopp."

Femi swallowed his spit. Nahla went over to the hose and turned it on. She sprayed Femi in the face. Although it was painful, he was thirsty. He tried to lap up what he could. The water made him colder. Femi was soaking wet. Watery blood from his head ran down into the drain beneath his feet.

"Talk, Femi," Nahla said as calmly as she could.

Femi said, "They're going to kill me."

"And I am going to kill your family, Femi. Your options are limited and my time is being wasted." Nahla looked at Chopp and nodded.

Chopp kneeled in front of Femi and asked, "Left, right, hand or foot?"

"What?" Femi yelled.

"You choose or I do. Left. Right. Hand or foot!?" Chopp asked. "I won't ask again."

"No, no, no!" Femi begged, "Please don't. Please!"

Chopp ignored him, grabbed his left hand and chopped off the tip of his pinky finger. Femi bellowed out a loud howl that echoed off the walls of the chamber. Blood squirted everywhere. Neither Chopp nor Nahla were affected by the blood nor the scream. Femi almost passed out.

"No, no, chin up, Femi." Chopp pushed Femi's head back.

"I would've said left foot, personally," Nahla teased.

Femi screamed, "I curse you! I curse you dammit!" He cried and foamed at the mouth. His breathing was labored. His head fell to the side.

"That's only the first half of the finger, Femi. I can chop this down to the knuckle before moving on to the next finger. Talk," Chopp said.

Femi spit blood from his mouth and said, "You're going to kill me either way."

"Yes," Nahla said fearlessly. She walked over to Femi and squatted in front of him. "You are going to die here tonight, Femi. We will kill you, burn the body and wash the ashes down the drain. Your missing body will never be found. So you are here to save your family. You have plenty of nails, teeth, fingers and toes... a dick. We can go on all night. I would prefer not to do that so I assume that we should move this along faster."

"FUCK YOU!" he spit in her face.

Nahla closed her eyes and used a cloth to wipe her face. She took the black bag that was over his head earlier, folded it in half and taped it above his nose and around his neck, enough for him not to choke. "At least he didn't call me a bitch."

"Oh yeah. Don't do that!" Chopp joked.

Nahla looked at Femi and said, "No more spitting." She looked over at Chopp and nodded.

Chopp took the sheers and chopped off the tip of his ring finger.

Femi screamed, "Argh! Mother fucker. You son of a bitch!" He tried to break free from the chair. "Fuck you!" Femi cried, "God help me! Help me, God! Please!"

Nahla and Chopp stood over Femi watching him, waiting for him to calm down. Nahla sat in the chair and crossed her legs. She lit a joint and took a puff. She passed it to Chopp. He did the same and passed it back. Nahla knew it was a matter of time. *He will break,* she thought. She puffed from the joint again and put it out. She placed it back into her pocket. She glared at Femi as if she was staring into his soul. She waited. Chopp took out a flask and passed it to Nahla. She took a sip and gave it back.

Femi began to mumble what she believed to be a prayer. Then he whispered, "Water. Please."

Nahla got up and turned on the hose, but this time, the stream was gentler. She put the end of the hose through the mask and Femi gulped down as much water as he could. She took back the hose and turned it off. She pulled her chair closer and sat down. "Femi let me help you. I'm going to give you four names. You're going to tell me how these people are connected, what they have to do with Kayo, you,

Marly... Tell me everything. Then, you're going to tell me where to find them. If there's anything else, or anyone else I need to know about, you're going to tell me that too."

Femi began to cry.

Chopp pulled out the shears and Femi yelled, "Please! Abeg. Abeg! No more. Please! I will tell you everything, but please promise me you will not touch my family."

Nahla squatted in front of Femi again and looked at him. She said, "If it ends with you, I promise they'll be fine. No harm will come their way. However, if any of them, just one of them, tries to seek revenge, I will kill them all. I will make your children watch me gut your wife from the inside out and I will slit their throats and burn them in the house you built for them. Ask Chopp, I love to play with fire. After I burn them, I will fly to your home country and hunt down your mother, your father, and slay every sister, brother, aunt, uncle, cousin and blood relative or married into your family. I will not stop until your entire bloodline is eradicated off the face of this planet. Do you understand?"

Femi nodded his head as he cried.

Nahla stood up with her gun in her hand. She leaned against the wall and put the gun into a holster in the front of her pants. She crossed her arms and said, "Jasmine Summer, Cranston Asher-Smith, Alejandro Santiago, Vernell Bailey. Start with Jasmine. Go!"

Femi shook his head. "No, Nahla. This... This

story starts with Vernell. That bomb wasn't for him. It was for the new kid. The young guy. I... I'm trying to remember his name... Pat... Patterson. Hanzel Patterson."

Nahla leaned forward and walked toward Femi. "Say more!"

"He was supposed to speak after Vernell Bailey but the bombs went off too early. Someone fucked it up. He was poised to take Vernell Bailey's job in about three to five years and Vernell was pissed about it. The board wanted Vernell out. They said he lacked innovation and spending was getting out of control. But Vernell wasn't ready to go. Vernell was supposed to emerge a hero after the attacks and figured they would beg him to stay another 10 years."

"But now he's dead," Nahla concluded.

Femi looked up and said, "No. No. He's in the burn unit at the hospital in Palmer. He can talk but he's in bad condition. He's the one who set up the blasts. His nephew insisted on getting his hands dirty and Kayo killed him. The police have been covering up the names of the suspects because they're all involved. They scrambled the drones that night."

"So, Vernell Bailey planned the attack?"

"Yes. Him and Cranston Asher-Smith. He's the President of the ACPP board of Directors. They're best friends. He's the only one that wanted Vernell to stay. He was getting kickbacks from contractors too. The general public has been complaining about the amount of power and influence of the ACPP and spending has raised alarms. The governor proposed absorbing the work of the ACPP into the ATF, since they consider meat a controlled substance. The ACPP needed the work to look different and needed a crisis to exaggerate the need for a separate institution." Femi was out of breath. He licked his dry lips and said, "Water. Please."

Chopp went and got the hose this time. He turned it on and gave Femi a few more gulps of water. "Keep talking, Femi," Chopp instructed.

Femi nodded, "They plan to say the attack came from mercenaries Up Rural. They even have a "manifesto" Vernell probably wrote himself. His agency stays in power as long as there's a crisis. Climate crisis, bird flu outbreak, meat factory bombings... The ACPP needs more clients to distribute vouchers to and if they expand Up Rural, they can cut poaching even more and put everyone on the voucher system. Control the food, control the people. They manage the meat supply but they eat as much as they want. They've been extorting Marly for years."

"Hmm." Nahla sat down in the chair in front of him again. She pulled out a knife from her boot and pointed it at Femi. "What do you have to do with this?"

"I do real estate, Nahla. They make me help with land grabs, finding tax liens to buy and transfer properties from older folks. They want to make a 15 minute city, E-City 104, not too far from the land owned by the co-op and expand the delivery tunnels to reach it. I did some research and found the blueprints of the delivery tunnels and saw they pass right under the Solemn Oak campus. I told Marly about the place because it presented a good opportunity. Marly put me on the task to figure out who owned it. It was Kayo. Kayo used a trust to try and hide it but I figured out she owned it. When I told Marly it was Kayo, Marly told me to back off. Said she would take care of it and see if Kayo would negotiate use of the tunnels. But... I didn't listen. I told Vernell and now he wants that property for himself."

"Wait, Marly told me that Kayo killed someone important."

"Vernell doesn't care about that kid. He would have never sent him in there. That was so Marly would back off. He exaggerated it to make an excuse to go after Kayo and take over Solemn Oak. He's planning on using eminent domain or tax liens, safety hazards, whatever he can use to acquire it from Kayo. He doesn't care about Kayo killing anyone. He cares only about Solemn Oak. Marly hates Vernell and he hates her. She was trying to buy up as many parcels as she could before he took them all. Most of Marly's conversations with Vernell, from what I know, haven't been pleasant. He's constantly threatening to expose her."

"So why are they making Kayo hunt the Tank?" Nahla asked.

"Huh?" Femi shook his head and said, "Nahla.

I don't know anything about the Tank. I've heard stories about the beast but the plan for her to hunt him is above me. I don't know anything about that decision. You have to talk to Vernell."

Nahla asked, "What about this Alejandro and Jasmine? Who are they?"

"I have no idea who they are. You have to believe me," Femi pleaded.

"Anything else I need to know?" Nahla asked.

Femi cried, "I have nothing else, Nahla. Please can I speak to my family?"

"I have a question." Chopp asked, "Vernell is at which hospital in Palmer?"

"Baystate Med...Eh." Femi's head fell to the right and blood seeped from his neck. His body shook for a moment but then he exhaled and stopped.

With two swift swipes, Nahla slit his throat in two places. Femi was gone.

"Let's go!" Nahla wiped the blade on his shirt.

Nahla and Chopp picked up their things and walked out. Baker and Diggy stood waiting behind the door.

Nahla said, "Clean this up for me," and handed Baker an envelope full of money. She patted Diggy on the head and said, "I'll make sure you get something nice next time I see you."

Baker saluted Nahla and walked into the room. Diggy followed. He slammed the door shut behind them.

CHAPTER 12

Nahla and Chopp took the hour-long drive to Palmer. It was windy and a few flurries were visible but nothing was sticking to the ground. Chopp drove. For the first five minutes of the drive he kept his eyes glued to the road, maneuvering past trucks and other vehicles. Nahla stretched and bent her fingers to bring the old bones back to life.

"Don't rush. We have time," Nahla assured him. She turned in her seat to look at him and said, "Thank you."

Chopp smiled. "You've helped me handle my shit. I can help you handle yours." He reached over and put his hand on her thigh, then touched her face. It was as warm and soft as he remembered.

Nahla gently touched his hand and smiled again. He put his hand back on the wheel. She didn't realize until that moment how much she missed his touch— how the size of his hand almost swallowed her face, making her feel small again. She had been so preoccupied with the kids and Marly, she hadn't considered a reignition of feelings for Chopp as a possibility. They'd been suppressed and denied for so long.

Chopp was dying to ask, "So... outside of all this, have you seen Marly?"

"Not you, Chopp, breaking the rules."

Chopp smirked and said, "Eh. Maybe a little bit."

Nahla smiled, turned away and said, "Chopp, Marly and I... We've done a little bit more than see each other."

Chopp understood what she meant.

"Before all this, we hadn't spoken in about two years," Nahla confessed. "I needed a break from everything after the fight with Kay. It was too much. Since all this happened we kind of got close again and... you know. But, it's like a merry-go-round with her. I thought this time would be a little different. I went by the shop yesterday to get the coordinates for Kay. That's when I met her fiancee. She's engaged."

"Really? Hmm. I didn't know that."

"Neither did I. She tried apologizing but... anyway, I can't focus on that right now."

"So, where do you think she is in all of this?" Chopp asked.

"Where do *you* think she is in all of this?" Nahla replied. "Seriously. Tell me how you feel. I trust you."

Chopp looked at Nahla and didn't want to stop looking, but his job at the moment was to focus on the road. He replied, "Marly has always been conflicted about two things, her work and you. She loves you both, but work, business is always her priority. I think she keeps it that way because she can't give you all of her, Nahla. Who can and frankly, why would she? She's prioritizing what she can control. You've never been a sure thing for anyone. So, I think she will always choose business first, but I don't think she would cross you this badly. My advice is, don't let any biases cloud your judgement and don't make excuses for her. Let's get more information and if you find anything that tells you otherwise, act accordingly."

"I will."

There was a momentary pause before Chopp spoke again. "I have to admit, the day I found out about the two of you, I finally understood what I was putting you through. The shame I felt, realizing how I must have made you feel. The other women... they'd just show up to the gym demanding my attention. You never embarrassed me." Chopp paused for a moment then continued. "I shouldn't have allowed that."

Nahla said, "I knew about them, Chopp and made my choice. That wasn't it."

"It was a lot of it," Chopp admitted. "I should have given you more respect than that. Then I knew it was too late. The way you kissed her, I knew. I knew you loved her."

"I loved you too, Chopp."

Chopp was still hurt. "You loved me but not like that, Nahla, it was different. That kiss kicked me in the balls, something serious." He laughed. "You loved me, yes, but you were in love with Marly and I think you still are."

"I wanted it to be you, Chopp, but you left, then the kids came. You were so good with them but you didn't want this with me. We had our chance to do and be more but... Honestly, things happened so unexpectedly and fast with Marly; I kind of got swept off my feet," Nahla admitted.

"I thought choosing my children meant I couldn't choose you. You deserved more than me being indecisive and constantly in and out of your life like that. My kids would have loved you. And you would have been a great mother. I didn't give you a chance. Marly saw what I saw in you, but acted on it. I should have never left a space for someone else to come into your life and show you what you deserved."

Nahla smiled and said, "Things happen I guess. Doesn't mean that I don't love you Chopp. I always will. Endless tie." Nahla reached over and gently rubbed the back of his neck and ran her thumb over his right ear.

Chopp took her hand into his and kissed it. He held her hand for the rest of the drive.

As they got closer, Nahla opened her laptop. She pulled up the town records and searched for the main electrical supply to the hospital then hacked into the mainframe of the grid. "I just need the main power supply off. The backup generators will go on but the cameras will remain off since the system requires too much energy. We will have 15 minutes for the main supply to turn back on and another five minutes for the cameras to reboot and get back online."

"What room is he in?" Chopp asked as he loaded his gun.

Nahla typed on her computer. "Give me a minute. Almost in." Nahla typed a little more and said, "421A." She pulled up a 3D map of the hospital. "Right here."

Chopp added, "He's gonna have protection in the hallway."

"Then we will take the roof. We can get into the vents here." She pointed at the map. "There's a supply closet. We go in here and enter the hospital stairwells to the 4th floor and improvise."

Chopp giggled. "Improvise?"

"Do you have a better idea?" Nahla asked.

An ambulance drove past them heading to the hospital. Chopp cut off the ambulance before it reached the hospital. They hijacked the ambulance and changed into EMTs' clothes. The patient in the ambulance was unconscious. Nahla used her computer to shut off the grid as they arrived. The lights went down just as they pulled up. "15 minutes!"

They opened the back of the ambulance to chaos; the lights had completely blacked out. Moments later, the low emergency lights flickered on. Doctors rushed to meet them, assisting with the patient's removal from the vehicle. Chopp stayed behind the wheel and moved the truck as soon as the body was out. He parked it off to the side, and then both he and Nahla, dressed in EMT gear, walked into the hospital.

"Keep your head down," Chopp warned Nahla. They slipped into the first locker room they found. Quickly, they donned lab coats, face masks, and hats before exiting. "Stairwell," Chopp whispered, pointing the way.

Nahla looked at her watch and said, "10 minutes."

They ran from the first floor to the fourth where they saw three men outside of Vernell's room. Chopp quickly grabbed a clipboard off the wall and pretended to read from it. The guards stood up and Chopp said, "We have to move him. Help us get him to the emergency elevator." The guards complied. "Put these on." Chopp gave them masks to wear. "We want to keep his wounds as germ free as possible."

Without questioning, the men agreed. They followed as Nahla and Chopp pushed Vernell in his hospital bed out of the room to a back hallway to the only elevator that would work using the backup generator. Half of Vernell's face was bandaged. He asked, "Where am I going?"

Nahla responded, "Your unit is compromised. We need more power to run your machines so we need to transfer you right now."

"What about the rest of the people?" Vernell asked.

"We will move them. Nurses are up there assisting now, but the administration said you get priority. We don't ask questions, we just do what we are told, sir," Chopp added.

Vernell felt a sense of superiority. With the swipe of a stolen badge, the doors to the elevator opened. Six went in. The doors closed and opened again. Three came out. Chopp and Nahla were back in their EMT gear. Nahla jammed the elevator door shut with the clipboard after it closed. Vernell tried to scream but they put a breathing mask over his face, strapped him down and covered his head. On their way out they pulled the fire alarm. The alarm went off and the first floor erupted. Mayhem! They pushed Vernell right through the lobby and loaded him into the ambulance.

"Two minutes," Nahla said with a smile.

They drove off.

Nahla and Chopp sat in the back of the ambulance while Vernell gathered himself together. He was coughing and wheezing, so Nahla removed the mask. "What are you doing to me?" Vernell asked.

Chopp pulled out his shears. He opened and closed the blades, allowing the cold metal parts to make a snipping sound as they rubbed past one another. He said, "We met with your friend Femi Odemwingie about an hour ago. Let's say I gave him a trim. He told us to come see you."

"Where is he now?" Vernell looked afraid and asked, "What did you do to him?"

"You don't wanna know," Nahla answered.

She took out her knife and cut the bandages from Vernell's face. "Vile creature. You meant this fate for someone else. However, karma has a way doesn't it?"

Vernell whimpered and asked, "What do you want from me? Please. I can help you get anything you need. I have money and access to things. Name your price."

Nahla looked at Chopp and said, "Everyone offers money."

"It's so pathetic," Chopp added.

"Do we really look like we came for money?" Nahla asked.

Vernell looked down away from Nahla and admitted, "No. You look like you came for vengeance. I don't know what you want."

Nahla smiled and leaned in closer. She said, "I'm going to say some names and you need to tell me everything you know. Do you understand?"

Vernell looked her directly in the eye, scanned her face and squinted whatever muscles were left on the right side of his face. He knew they were serious. Vernell had engaged in so many crooked business dealings that he couldn't narrow down his list of enemies and guess who these people were.

Nahla put her knife against his scorched flesh. She pulled out her phone and showed him pictures of his family. "Do not waste my time." Nahla put her phone away and turned around facing her back to him. She leaned over to whisper something to Chopp as Chopp took a sip from his flask.

"You look like her," Vernell whispered.

"Excuse me!?" Nahla whipped back around and stepped back over to Vernell. She poked him in the neck with her knife. "What did you just say?"

"The girl. Green dress. Marly's girl. You look like her." Vernell said without wincing.

"She's not Marly's anything." Nahla's face was stern.

"So you *do* know Marly. The girl worked for Marly, no? Well, you look like her." Vernell coughed.

"Neither of them know I'm here, but I'm here for the girl. Not Marly," Nahla replied. "Now speak!"

Vernell understood his fate was already written and his name would be forever etched in the book of death. "Flask. Please." He dragged his hand up to point at Chopp's flask. "Allow me one last drink."

Nahla backed off and nodded.

Chopp obliged. He passed the flask to Vernell. With shaky hands Vernell grabbed the flask. After watching him struggle, Chopp reached over and helped him. He took a large gulp and breathed out heavily.

"Thank you." Vernell licked his dry lips that were partially scorched. "Did Marly send you here?"

"I told you. She doesn't know I'm here and I'm asking the questions," Nahla said. "So, don't fucking lie to me. The truth will make things easier for you. We know you tried to kill Patterson. We know you wanted Solemn Oak. So, explain to us the involvement with Cranston, Alejandro and Jasmine and why the girl is being made to hunt the Tank." She shoved her knife through his left hand into the bed.

"ARGH!" he screamed! "I'm fucking talking you, you psycho bitch!!"

Nahla looked back at Chopp and smiled. "He called me the B word. Not good."

"Definitely not good." Chopp asked, "Left. Right. Hand or foot!?"

Vernell said, "Kiss my ass you piece of shit bastard! Fuck you!"

Chopp shrugged his shoulders and snipped off Vernell's index finger down to the knuckle.

Vernell wailed! Blood squirted across the vehicle.

Nahla leaned over and said, "Never call me a bitch. Ever." She took out her phone again and showed him the picture of his family. "Your wife Susanne Bailey, maiden name Knox. Your son, Caleb, sophomore student at Northeastern University. Your eldest son Dale, named after your father. 38, years old with daughters, Talia and June. Your daughter..."

"Okay! Okay!" Vernell's tears ran down the unscorched side of his face. He took a moment to catch his breath. "I knew Patterson and the girl were dating, but I didn't know anything about her. That little fucker! The ACPP wanted to put his rambunctious conceited ass in my position. I built this company. I would have stepped down for an executive position on the board, but they wanted me completely out. Only Cranston was on my side. Cranston came up with the plan and had him watched. That girl, she was around but it wasn't clear what was going on. I didn't want to kill her. I asked that boy Hanzel 1000 times if he was coming alone, he said 'Most likely yes.' What does that even mean? I didn't mean for the girl to be there or get hurt. I don't know who botched the attack, but I assumed it was Marly."

"After the attacks were botched, we did some research on who she was. Cranston investigated and realized Marly knew her. Femi confirmed and he told me she was the one who owned the building. We had been looking at the building for months. He said she worked for Marly at some point. As much as I have done for Marly she didn't want me to know, but he told me anyway. Marly was gonna try and negotiate a side deal with the girl and we didn't want that. To get Marly to back off of the property, we accused her of sabotage and Cranston put a bounty on her head if she didn't cooperate."

"Keep talking," Nahla insisted as she finally slipped the knife out of his left hand. "Tell me about Alejandro and Jasmine."

Vernell grunted as the smooth metal made additional cuts on the way out. He reached over and grabbed his hand. He breathed heavily as the pain rocketed up his arm and said, "Alejandro and Jasmine work for Cranston. They went to her house pretending to be detectives but Patterson was there so they backed off."

"What did they go there for?" Nahla asked.

Vernell coughed. His lips began to bleed. "I assume to see if she knew anything or... probably worse but when that didn't work, Cranston came up with some idea to send the girl into the woods for a wild bear he kept hearing about from his friends on the Wildlife, Fish and Games Regulation Board. He wanted Marly to convince the girl to go but based on the stories, it wasn't going to end well for the girl. He expected Marly to fail so he could have a reason to take her out and assumed the girl would fail the hunt and she'd be out of the picture altogether."

"He was trying to kill her?" Nahla inquired.

"This has gone on long enough. Where is Cranston?" Chopp asked. He was getting impatient and felt as if Nahla was getting emotional.

"There's no touching Cranston. He's constantly surrounded by guards."

Chopp giggled. "Sounds fun!"

"Where is he?" Nahla put the blade to Vernell's neck and pressed into the burnt flesh. "Last time I'm asking."

"Arrgh! At the lake! At the fucking lake in Becket, dammit!" Vernell looked at her and said, 1227 Silver Fox Lane!"

Nahla took her left hand and gently placed it on his head. She turned around and said to Chopp, "I'm done here. Burn it!"

Chopp nodded.

Nahla suddenly turned around, took her knife and scraped into the melted layers of skin on Vernell's face. Vernell screamed. She held his head down as she took off a layer of skin. Then she jammed the knife into his neck behind his esophagus and ripped it through the front of his neck, severing his throat. She closed her eyes as blood squirted over her face, and listened to Vernell gargle and choke on his own blood. Nahla breathed deeply and loudly through her nose. She only exhaled when his squirming and gasping for air had ceased.

Nahla and Chopp took a canister of gasoline from the truck. They poured the gas all over the inside and outside of the ambulance, threw their clothes inside, set it on fire and sped off in their truck. Chopp handed Nahla a wet cleansing cloth to clean her face. After she wiped her face clean she lit it with a lighter. Due to the alcohol content it quickly went up in flames and she threw it out of the window.

12:03 am Kayo woke from a dream. She couldn't remember exactly what happened but her heart was racing a mile a minute. Kayo looked at her watch realizing she still had a few hours left to sleep. The signal on her phone was still shotty. She was hoping she would receive or be able to send a text to Patterson, but to try was useless. She hadn't heard from anyone, including Juno or Nahla. She stretched a bit and wrapped herself into the wool blanket, hoping sleep would take her away again, but the idea was futile. She was anxious about the hunt and she couldn't stop thinking about the last time she encountered this beast.

The night was eerily quiet. She expected to hear more than just rustling leaves and faint howls of coyotes off in the distance. Kayo reached into her backpack, pulled out the book of letters and began to read again, hoping it would make her sleepy.

My Dear Brother Kayron,

Thank you for the last letter and the poem. You used to write them for me all the time. Maybe they were your attempt at writing raps and not poems but I loved them just the same. I miss you. Work is good. Chopp and I are getting along probably a little too well. He's helped me make space between myself and some old friends. I know he has his faults but he takes good care of me. Don't be mad at me but I'm really falling for him even though I probably shouldn't. I also want to cut to the chase and let you know, I'm going to be a mom. Maybe. I know. Scary thought. I haven't told Chopp yet. I don't know how to, but hopefully I will by the time you get this letter. He's got so much going on, I don't know exactly how to tell him, but I will. I'm going to let him decide what we will do about it. I don't want to force him into something he doesn't want to fully support. If this doesn't work out, we must promise to never discuss it again. Just move on. Am I crazy to feel a bit excited about it? Of course I have my fears and my doubts. I wanna get this right. I don't wanna fuck up, but I think I'm ready to do this now.

Anyway, I went to see Eve and the twins last week. She was doing okay. The kids are doing well in school. Ayrah is a trip. LOL. She always has something slick to say. She's like her mother I swear. Oree is such a sweet kid, athletic and handsome! They're getting big. I wish Eve could get it together for them. They're good kids. I think she knows that but her addiction gets in the way of her being able to enjoy them and vice versa.

It's almost the anniversary of mom's death. I may go visit her gravesite. If there's anything you would like me to say on your behalf, let me know. Also, send me some pics of my baby Kay. I haven't seen her in so long. Tell her Auntie Nah is always watching so be good!

Hope to see you soon.
Love always, Nah.

Kayo's mouth dropped. *Nahla was pregnant?* Obviously she didn't have the baby, but Kayo was curious about what happened. *Did she also have a miscarriage or did she decide not to tell Chopp and get rid of it?* Nahla was a mysterious creature. The idea of Nahla being excited about it was even more confusing. She couldn't imagine Nahla settling down and, of her own free will, starting a family. Chopp already had a few children by two different women and Kayo wasn't sure what kind of family man he would be. *Maybe Nahla gave up on the idea of being a family to maintain her lifestyle with multiple lovers.* Nahla always had "friends", Kayo heard as she got older, but Chopp was the main one, or so she thought until recently. He was the only one she brought around them. Recent revelations made Kayo question everything she thought she knew about her aunt's love life.

Kayo considered how difficult it must have been for Nahla to give up total freedom for three children out of nowhere and change her lifestyle all together. One day her quiet cabin on a small farm became a home full of uncoordinated and strange two legged creatures. The mostly empty refrigerator soon had fresh bottles of milk and dozens of eggs. Bare cabinets turned into pantries of nonperishables, peanut butter, crackers and oats. More wood needed chopping and bathrooms desired constant cleaning.

The first few months were frenzied. She needed to regain and maintain order or she was going to end it all for everyone. Structures, schedules and routines became their way of life. Kayo showers at 5, Ayrah at 5:20, and Oree at 5:40. You snooze, you lose. Breakfast will be made by 6:20. She was up at 3:30 am filling her morning with workouts, chores and making breakfast. She had to learn how to make quick meals like spaghetti and taught herself how to cornrow hair— sort of. The children helped her organize her carefree life.

She was strong enough to commit, and even wise enough to know her limits, using the creation of Freedom Day to find solace and independence from the world that had abducted her. Sunday sunrise began the start of her sabbath. A day to worship herself, her personal freedoms and the partake in the sanctity of her practice of love. One day a week she would indulge in her secret affairs, live routine free and unrestrained. By Monday morning, she was back in the gym, back in the kitchen, back working the farm, prepping for the market.

Finding out about Nahla and Marly was a psychological blow. If Kayo survived, she didn't know how she was going to adjust to the thought of Marly being around. The thought of them cuddling on the couch or playfully kissing made her cringe. The thought of Marly even touching Nahla was off putting. The entire concept was strange but Kayo decided to make peace with it. Nahla was happy. *It's about time.*

She realized part of Nahla's sadness was because of her. It wasn't just the fact that Nahla gave up her prime years to take care of her nieces and nephew. Their fight was a turning point. Kayo never considered how disrespectful she was to show up to the house drunk and belligerent making demands. Looking back, she realized how patient Nahla had been. Nahla spoke calmly but firmly. She acknowledged Kayo's anger, but also reminded her there's a limit and some barriers shouldn't be crossed.

The hammock tent rocked back and forth as the wind picked up a bit. Kayo turned her head and listened. *Nothing.* She turned her attention back to the book of letters, curious of her fathers response.

> *Nahla,*
>
> *You being a mother... I didn't see this coming. The idea of the father being Chopp gives me pause. He was like a brother to me in the service, which is why I trusted him to watch over you since I can't. I didn't expect that the introduction would lead to this especially after having a long conversation with him that you were off limits. I have some words for him but now is not the time. However, anything I have to say will be said at*

some point in the future. Ultimately, I think you will be a great mother. Chopp will be a great father, but if you're looking for anything more from him, I can't say he will be the one for that. Frankly, I believe you deserve more. If you're happy, I'm happy. I'm excited to be an uncle and I hope I can be half of what you are for Kay, Oree and Ayrah. Be ready! Parenting is living in a constant state of paranoia. LOL.

Speaking of Kay. She has been diagnosed with hyperacusis which explains her hearing sensitivity. She just received hearing aids. She loves them because she can pretend to be deaf and ignore people. She's a mess. She's doing well in school, but we don't like the school she's been assigned to. She's on the waitlist for a charter school about three blocks from the house. She's been such a good kid— such a gift. We are lucky.

Last thing if you go to see mom, read this poem to her on my behalf:

You are missed
as fleeting time on a Sunday eve,
rushing into Monday's work
I long for a return

that will never come.

Yet, I find you in me,
my child wears your grin,
an old scarf you wore in winter
hugs my neck and keeps me warm
but does not have your scent.

As wind blows west or east,
I listen if you whisper,
wonder if you watch,
if you do, I give permission
and pray I never disappoint.

Hope to see you soon, Nah. Your big
brother misses you. Love you forever.
Kayron
PS. C reluctantly says "Hi." :)

Kayo's eyes grew heavy, with the weight of sleep tugging at her soul, demanding surrender. She was powerless against it. Leaning her head back against her pack, she drifted off, with the book of letters safely nestled against her stomach, her hand resting on top. The night was still as she slept securely in her hammock tent, which swayed gently like a bassinet or the comforting cocoon of a mother's womb, lulling her in the heart of the wilderness.

Snug and serene, she was enveloped by the gentle whistle of wind slipping between the tattered leaves of maples and oaks. This was a place she vowed never to return, yet here, in the forest's honest embrace, she felt safe yet insecure. Here, she could die in peace, amidst what she regarded as God's gift to humanity—a world that gives to those who respect it but takes from those who do not. It demands attention, deference, commitment, and a spiritual connection to understand its ways. It must be nurtured, prioritized, and obeyed, or it will yield unimaginable ruin.

How then, is humanity's relationship with nature different from its relationship with love? Does not love also give, take, require nurturing to avoid ruin? From the same source of thunder, lightning, storms, fires, biting frost, and damaging winds, comes forth comfort, life, beauty, warmth, and nourishment. No wonder lovers are drawn to relationships marked by dramatic emotional swings; it's in our nature to be captivated by this tumult. One cannot truly appreciate the calm of the ocean without ever experiencing the might of its waves.

"I will never return!"—the lies we tell ourselves. "I'm done!"—one falsehood following the next. Yet, here she was, cradled once again in her first love's arms, at peace, without regrets. She belonged here, under the moon, beside a tranquil stream, captivated by the divine authority and enchanting spell of her deciduous love. Like the sun, she would always return, shackled and chained, a prisoner to its seduction, eternally bound to this endless tie.

AFTERWORD

Read The Dragon's Game II for the conclusion.